her
pretty
face

ALSO BY ROBYN HARDING

The Party

her
pretty
face

Robyn Harding

SCOUT PRESS

New York   London   Toronto   Sydney   New Delhi

Scout Press
An Imprint of Simon & Schuster, Inc.
1230 Avenue of the Americas
New York, NY 10020

First Scout Press hardcover edition July 2018

SCOUT PRESS and colophon are registered trademarks of Simon & Schuster, Inc.

For information about special discounts for bulk purchases, please contact Simon & Schuster Special Sales at 1-866-506-1949 or business@simonandschuster.com.

The Simon & Schuster Speakers Bureau can bring authors to your live event. For more information or to book an event contact the Simon & Schuster Speakers Bureau at 1-866-248-3049 or visit our website at www.simonspeakers.com.

Interior design by Jaime Putorti

Manufactured in the United States of America

10 9 8 7 6 5 4 3 2 1

Library of Congress Cataloging-in-Publication Data is available.

ISBN 978-1-5011-7424-7
ISBN 978-1-5011-7426-1 (ebook)

To Tegan

Because she wanted one dedicated to just her.

And because she's awesome.

her
pretty
face

Arizona Globe   Friday, March 1, 1996

STILL NO SIGN OF MISSING TEENAGE GIRL

Parents frantic one week after daughter's disappearance

PILAR HERNANDEZ

Phoenix

Courtney Carey, 15, left her parents' home in the Phoenix suburb of Tolleson on the evening of February 23 to meet friends, and has not been seen since. Carey's friends say she did not show up to meet them as arranged, which is out of character.

Police, family, and friends scoured the area but have found no sign of Carey. She is described as a white female, 5 foot 4, with brown hair and brown eyes. She was last seen wearing jeans, a red flannel shirt, and running shoes.

If you spot her or have any information regarding her whereabouts, please call police.

frances

Frances Metcalfe was not the type of woman who enjoyed large parties, especially large parties where you had to dress up in a costume. Given the choice, she would have stayed home and pierced her own nipples with dull knitting needles, but fund-raisers for Forrester Academy were not optional. Despite the thirty-thousand-dollar tuition fee, the elite private school's coffers needed regular infusions of cash.

The night's theme was *The '80s!*

Like, totally come as your favorite '80s pop star!

Frances had taken the invitation literally and dressed as Cyndi Lauper. She admired the performer's LGBTQ activism, and Lauper's music had been the soundtrack to a more innocent time. But the full skirt and layers of belts, beads, and scarves may not have been the most flattering choice for Fran-

ces's curvaceous body type. With her bright red wig and colorful makeup, Frances felt as if she looked like a cross between a
deranged clown and a heavyset bag lady.

She wandered self-consciously through the school gymnasium, taking in the neon streamers and hand-painted posters.

SO RAD!

GRODY TO THE MAX!

AWESOME!

The childish, handmade decorations, courtesy of Ms. Waddell's sixth-grade class, stood in stark contrast to the high-end
catering: attractive servers in black-and-white circulated with
trays of ceviche on porcelain spoons, seafood-stuffed mushroom
caps, and Wagyu beef sliders. Frances had vowed not to snack
at the party. She had filled up on raw veggies before she left
home as all the fitness magazines recommended. Despite their
plethora of articles devoted to the psychology of overeating
("Feeding Emotional Pain," "Replacing Love with Food"), the
magazines still recommended loading up on crudités to stave
off the assault of caloric party fare. But eating at a party had
nothing to do with hunger; it had everything to do with fear.

Maybe *fear* was too strong a word for the gnawing in Frances's stomach, the slight tremble to her hands, the prick of sweat
at the nape of her neck. It was low- to mid-level social anxiety;
she'd suffered from it for years. When one had secrets, when
one's past was something to be hidden and guarded, mingling
and making idle chitchat became daunting. The extra twenty-

two pounds Frances carried on her five-foot-five frame, and the meager check she'd just deposited in the decorated donation box (it would undoubtedly prompt snickers from the fundraising committee, several of whom were married to Microsoft multimillionaires), did nothing to boost her confidence.

But the apprehension Frances felt tonight could not be blamed on her past, her weight, or her unfortunate ensemble. What she felt tonight was real and present. The parents at Forrester Academy did not accept her, and their hostility was palpable. Meandering through the crowd, watching backs turn on cue, Frances hadn't felt so blatantly ostracized since high school. She plucked a second glass of wine from the tray of a passing waiter and stuffed a truffle arancini into her mouth.

She'd had high hopes when her son, Marcus, was accepted into Forrester, one of greater Seattle's elite private schools. Marcus was entering middle school; he was more mature now, and calmer. The diagnosis he'd received at the beginning of his academic career—ADHD combined with oppositional defiant disorder—was beginning to feel less overwhelming. The behavior-modification therapies Frances had religiously employed over the past few years seemed to be working, and cutting sugar and gluten from her son's diet had made him almost docile. Frances knew Marcus would thrive in the modern glass-and-beam building, would blossom in the more structured, attentive environment of private education. The new school was to be a fresh start for Frances, too.

The Forrester mothers didn't know that Frances lived in a modest, split-level ranch dwarfed by mansions in tony Clyde Hill, a residential area in northwest Bellevue. They didn't know that her husband, Jason, had bought their eighties-designed, cheaply constructed abode from a paternal aunt for roughly a fifth of its current value. They were unaware that the Metcalfes' Subaru Outback and Volkswagen Jetta were leases, that Jason's salary would not have covered their son's tuition if not for the help of a second mortgage on their run-down house, a house full of clutter that Frances seemed powerless to control. They were starting school with a clean slate. It would be a new chapter for their family.

It lasted three weeks.

It was the incident with Abbey Dumas that destroyed them—both Marcus and Frances. Abbey had teased and taunted Marcus until he had lashed out in a repugnant but rather creative way. During recess, Marcus had found his tormentor's water bottle and he had peed in it. It wasn't that big a deal. Abbey was fine, basically. (She'd had no more than a sip before she ran screaming to the teacher.) It was the *disturbing nature* of the incident that the school community couldn't forgive. Disturbing: like the actions of a sixth grader could forecast a future spent torturing cats, peeping under bathroom stalls, keeping a locked basement full of sex slaves. Frances had promptly booked her son a standing appointment with a child psychologist, but Abbey's parents had called for

Marcus's expulsion. Forrester Academy stood by him, though. They didn't just *give up* on their students. The school community was stuck with them.

The chocolate fountain loomed ahead of her, an oasis in the desert full of faux Madonnas and Adam Ants. Frances knew she shouldn't indulge, but dipping fruit in molten chocolate would give her something to *do*, keep her hands busy, and make her look occupied. She'd already exhausted the silent-auction tables, writing down bids for spa packages and food baskets, while desperately hoping that she didn't *win* any of them. Jason had disappeared, swallowed by the crowd of parents, all of them made indistinguishable by their mullet wigs and neon garb. She made a beeline for the glistening brown geyser.

She could have chosen a piece of fruit—minimized the caloric damage—but the platter of sponge cake looked so moist and inviting that she stabbed the largest piece with a long, wood-handled fork and dunked it into the sweet flow. She had just stuffed the sodden confection into her mouth when she sensed a presence at her elbow.

"Hi, Frances." There was a notable lack of warmth in the woman's voice, but at least her tone wasn't overtly antagonistic. Frances turned toward Allison Moss, so taut, toned, and trim in head-to-toe spandex. "Physical"-era Olivia Newton-John. Great.

Frances mumbled through a mouthful of cake, "Hi, Allison."

"You're . . . Boy George?" Allison guessed.

Frances frantically tried to swallow, but the sponge cake and chocolate had formed a thick paste that seemed determined to stick to the back of her throat.

"Cymdi Lumper," she managed.

"The decorations are adorable, aren't they? I love that the kids made them themselves."

"So cute." It came out an unappetizing glug.

Allison forked a strawberry and put it in her mouth, forgoing the chocolate entirely. "How's Marcus?" she asked. "Enjoying school?"

Was there a hint of derision in her voice? A touch of cruel curiosity? Or was Allison genuinely interested in Marcus's well-being? The Abbey Dumas incident had occurred almost a month ago now. Perhaps people were starting to forget? Move on? "He's doing okay," Frances said. "Settling in, I think."

"Starting at a new school can be tough." Allison smiled, and Frances felt warmed. Allison understood. Being the new kid was hard, and that's why Marcus had done what he did. Abbey had picked on him and he'd overreacted. It was stupid. And gross. But he was just a boy. . . .

"How's—?" She couldn't remember Allison's daughter's name. Lila? Lola? Leila? The girl was Marcus's age, but they were in different classes.

"Marcus is so big," Allison continued. Apparently, she didn't want to shift conversation to her own offspring. "He obviously gets his height from his dad."

"Yeah. Jason's side of the family is really tall."

"It's nice to see him here. We don't have the pleasure very often."

Somehow, Frances's husband, Jason, was not the outcast that she and their son were. Jason was tall, dark, and handsome (all but his height inherited from his beautiful Mexican mother). "He could get away with murder with that smile," one of the infatuated Forrester mothers had once noted. Jason had also distanced himself from his difficult offspring and ineffective wife through work. His tech job kept him at the office until eight every night, and until midnight a few times a month. Obviously, the sole breadwinner, working to put food on the table for his family, could not be blamed for his son's behavioral issues. That fell squarely on the shoulders of stay-at-home mom Frances.

Her gaze followed Allison's across the room. It took a moment to recognize her clean-cut spouse in the fedora he'd donned for the fund-raiser, but she knew his confident stance in his pleated trousers, his strong broad back in the cherry satin blazer. (He was dressed as John Taylor from Duran Duran.) Jason was talking intently to a petite Asian woman with a lion's mane of synthetic hair and a very short leather skirt. Tina Turner, obviously. She was laughing at something he had said, her head thrown back, her hand lightly resting on his shiny red forearm. She was attracted to him; it was obvious even from this distance.

"He seems to be enjoying himself," Allison said, and there it was, subtle, but there: that condescending, mocking edge that Frances had come to expect from the Forrester mothers. Allison had veered from the usual narrative, though. Normally, Frances felt judged by these other parents as a poor mother, but Allison had taken a new tack and condemned her as an inadequate wife. It was effective. While Frances had developed something of a protective shell against criticisms of her parenting, she was completely vulnerable to assaults on her marriage. She knew that people, especially women, were surprised to learn she and Jason were a couple. He was gregarious, attractive, and fit. She was quiet, dull, and chubby. "Such a pretty face . . ." No crueler words had ever been uttered.

Allison was still watching the exchange between Frances's husband and his flirtatious admirer. "Isn't May adorable? And those legs! Her husband moved to Hong Kong to run Expedia's Asian office, and she decided to stay. Divorce is hard, but May's handled it so well."

The adorable May was now clinking her wineglass to Jason's. What were they toasting? Their mutual superiority to the people they had chosen to marry? Frances knew she was projecting her insecurities onto Jason. Her husband routinely assured her that he loved her, that he still found her sexy, that he had no regrets. . . . But it was evident—to Allison, to Frances, to everyone—that he could do much better. A bitter-tasting lump was clogging her throat as she watched her husband chuckle at May's comment.

"May will find someone better." Allison turned to Frances and smiled. "But not Jason, obviously. He's married to you." And then, as she reached for another piece of fruit, she murmured, "Too bad."

Had Allison really just said that? Was she that cruel? Frances wasn't sure she could trust her own ears. Her brain was spinning, lucid thought replaced by pure emotion: hurt, jealousy, anger. Time seemed to pause as she looked down at her diminutive companion, so poised and perfect and pleased with herself. In that suspended moment, Frances thought how good it would feel to kill her.

She could beat Allison to death with the chocolate fountain. The contraption probably weighed less than twenty pounds, and, once unplugged from its power socket, could be easily hoisted and swung like a club. It was an incredibly messy choice of weapon, but there would be a delicious irony in murdering toned, svelte Allison Moss with such a caloric and sugary vessel. Frances could almost hear the metal base cracking against Allison's birdlike skull, see the blood spurting, mixing with the melted chocolate to form a savory-sweet noxious puddle. How many blows would it take to ensure Allison was dead? Three? Four at the most? For once, Frances's heft would come in handy.

Alternatively, Frances could choke out the petite PTA mom with her bare hands. She could clutch Allison's sinewy neck between her chubby mitts and squeeze. Frances would enjoy hearing her croak and wheeze and struggle for breath; thrill as the cruel light drained from her eyes, as the boyish body slackened and then crumpled into a heap on the gymnasium floor. This was a definitively less messy option, but it would take a lot longer. There was a high probability that someone from Allison's crowd would tackle Frances before the job was done.

Frances knew she wasn't psychotic. It was a fantasy, a harmless coping mechanism. That was her self-diagnosis, anyway. She could never tell a therapist about these violent thoughts, at least not one who knew what she had done in the past. But given the treatment she'd received at the hands of the Forrester community, was it any wonder her mind went to these dark places? She wouldn't really kill Allison Moss—especially not in her son's school, and definitely not in front of its entire parent population. The scandal would be legendary. She could see the headlines:

MIDDLE-SCHOOL PARENT PARIAH SNAPS, MURDERS COOL
MOM AT SCHOOL FUND-RAISER

With the slightest shake of her head, Frances dislodged the homicidal whimsy. She gave Allison a tight smile and turned away, reaching for another piece of sponge cake.

"Hi, Allison." The voice was forced, frosty, familiar.

Frances halted her fork in midair. She turned to see Kate Randolph's tall, willowy frame looming over Allison Moss, and her heart soared. Her friend—her only friend in the school community—wore a white button-down shirt knotted under her breasts to reveal a flat, tanned stomach; faded men's Levi's; and heavy black boots. Kate's caramel-colored hair had been back-combed and sprayed into a sexy bouffant. The effect was that of an eighties supermodel (and not a homeless clown, like Frances).

"Kate. Hi," Allison said, suddenly deferential. "You look great."

"Thanks." Kate gave Allison's spandex ensemble an obvious once-over. "Wow. . . . You're really confident to wear an outfit like that at our age."

Allison's smile stayed in place, but insecurity flickered in her eyes. "I work out a lot."

"Still . . . gravity."

The tiny woman folded her arms across her breasts and changed the subject. "How's Charles enjoying sixth grade?"

"So far, so good. And Lulu?"

"Lila."

"Right."

"She's great. Really blossoming."

Kate gazed around the gym. "With all the money we're paying, they couldn't have hired a professional decorator?"

Frances saw Allison flinch, like her precious Lila had painted the rad posters herself . . . which she probably had. The wisp of a woman set her strawberry fork on the table. "I should get away from this chocolatey temptation. Nice to see you, Kate."

With a slight wave to Frances, she walked away from the two of them.

"That was awesome," Frances gushed. Kate's biting comments were far more rewarding than actual murder.

"Why, thank you, Cyndi Lauper."

Frances smiled. "I didn't think you'd come. You said you hate these things."

Kate picked up a fondue fork. "I couldn't let you face these stuck-up bitches alone. And besides, Robert said Charles would be expelled if we didn't show up."

"He's probably right." Frances looked over to see Kate's husband, Robert, a fit fifty-something, talking to Jason. Robert Randolph was tall and dignified, almost attractive except for a slight overbite that gave him a mildly cartoonish affect. The older man's costume consisted of a gray blazer with pronounced shoulder pads over a white T-shirt and a pair of black jeans. (David Bowie, maybe? Or David Byrne?) He'd been a lawyer in a past iteration (clearly a successful one to nab a hot, younger wife like Kate); dressing up was obviously not part of his lexicon. Jason and Robert were talking, laughing, the adorable May suddenly neglected. Frances watched as May casually wandered off.

"I'm so glad you're here." Frances turned back to Kate. "I was about to drink this entire chocolate fountain out of sheer boredom."

Kate stabbed some cake and doused it in chocolate. How could she eat like that and still stay so slim? "Daisy agreed to babysit her brother tonight, but only if he was asleep before I left."

"That doesn't sound like such a bad gig. Charles is so sweet."

"Daisy hates him."

"No, she doesn't. She's just fourteen."

"I'm not so sure," Kate said, through a two-hundred-calorie mouthful of cake and chocolate. "He drank all the orange juice this morning. I thought Daisy was going to stab him with her butter knife."

Frances laughed and realized she was enjoying herself. It was all due to Kate's presence. The two women shared a sense of humor and a disdain for Forrester's snobby, cliquey, yummy-mummies. With statuesque, self-assured Kate in her corner, Frances felt more confident, less vulnerable to attack. Their friendship was still in its adolescence, but Kate had already earned Frances's devotion.

Kate set her fondue fork down. "Where do I get some wine? Daisy's charging me twelve bucks an hour. I've got to make the most of this night."

"I'll show you to the bar," Frances said. Together, they picked their way through the crowd.

daisy

Daisy was high. About twenty minutes ago, she and Liam had perched on her mom's Pottery Barn patio sectional and sucked marijuana smoke from Liam's intricate glass bong. They had exhaled into the crisp autumn night, the pungent fumes mixing with the steam from their warm breath, and giggled about getting a passing squirrel stoned—like it wasn't paranoid enough already. Now they were inside, on the cream-colored sofa, Daisy's legs thrown over Liam's lap as they kissed.

Daisy was undeniably lit. Her brain was dumb and foggy, but all her senses were heightened. She could feel *everything*: Liam's hot tongue darting between her teeth like a pleasant electric current; his taut, muscular thighs beneath hers; the growing tingling in her belly and groin. Every molecule in her body was alive, vibrating with sexual energy. She wanted to get closer to Liam, to meld into him and disappear. She was ready for something more meaningful, more intimate. . . .

Abruptly, Liam pulled his lips from hers. "What was that?" He cocked his head, listening.

"I didn't hear anything." Her mouth searched for his again, but he turned his face away.

"I think it's your parents." He unceremoniously dumped her legs from his lap and jumped to his feet.

"You're paranoid," Daisy said, watching him stuff his bong into his backpack, his eyes darting to the front door. "You're like that squirrel."

Liam allowed a small smirk and Daisy reached for his hand. "They won't be home for hours," she said, pulling him back down to the pale sofa. "I promise."

Her words seemed to assuage him, because he let her kiss him again. She could feel his body responding to her, hear his breath getting faster and heavier. Daisy threw a leg over both of his and straddled him. She lowered herself onto him and felt how much he wanted this, too. Shifting slightly, she reached for his zipper.

"Stop." He grabbed her hips and tossed her off him.

"No one's here, Liam."

He looked at her then; his face—adorable in its adolescent transition from cute to handsome—was red . . . very, very red. "I don't think . . . I mean, it's just . . . *I* just . . ."

Unbidden, an image of Liam's face on a squirrel's body— nervous, worried, racing around the backyard in a fit of paranoia—appeared in Daisy's drug-addled mind. A bubble of uncontrolled laughter burst through her lips. Fuck. She was so stoned.

But the junior quarterback wasn't laughing. He was leaving. Liam snatched up his backpack and marched toward the door. Daisy's laughter stopped abruptly. "Where are you going?"

"Home," he muttered, already stepping into his shoes.

Daisy hurried over to the entryway. "I'm sorry. . . . I wasn't laughing at you. I'm just high."

"Whatever."

She grabbed his forearm with both her hands. "What's wrong, Liam?"

His cheeks blushed a deeper red as he struggled to get the words out. "This is just . . . moving too fast."

His words stunned her. Weren't teenage boys supposed to be obsessed with sex? Desperate to get laid? Trust Daisy to find the one guy who was too uptight, or too immature . . . or too gay, maybe?

"I'm sorry," she said, gently. "I thought you wanted me to touch you. I thought you liked it."

"I didn't. And I don't."

"It felt like you liked it to me."

"We're fourteen."

"Uh . . . yeah?"

"Your parents could come home any second! Your brother is asleep upstairs!"

"So . . . ?"

Liam's eyes, glassy but intense, bored into hers. "What is wrong with you, Daisy?" His words weren't angry or cruel, they were merely . . . curious.

Suddenly, Daisy felt completely lucid, the pleasant fog of her high dissipating, leaving her painfully clearheaded. She opened her mouth, but no words came out, because there were no words. Liam had pegged her: there was something very wrong with her.

Without another sound, her would-be lover yanked open the door and left. Daisy followed him onto the front steps, watched him sprint down the drive, onto the quiet street, and into the night. He was running away from her, like she was a teenage praying mantis who would devour him once sexually satisfied. Her breath visible in the cool dark air, she stayed there, watching his diminishing form. Liam was still running, fast, his football conditioning serving him well. Finally, when the boy was no more than a bouncing speck, Daisy closed the door and went back inside.

The house suddenly felt emptier. Well, it *was* emptier. But it felt large and vacuous, the pale color palette her mom had chosen for their new home cold and sterile. The rooms were pristine as always: her mother was a clean freak. She vacuumed and dusted daily, cleaned blinds and scrubbed floors on Wednesdays and Saturdays, bathrooms on Tuesdays, Thursdays, and Sundays. "I just like things tidy," her mom would say, but it was textbook OCD. The woman had *issues*, as evidenced by the numerous prescription pill bottles she kept *hidden* in her bathroom vanity. They were all for anxiety. Daisy dipped into them on occasion, when she wanted to numb herself, but they made her lazy and sleepy.

Daisy stood at the large picture window that looked out onto the backyard, and stared into the thick darkness. The home was situated on a quiet street, the backyard bordered by a copse of evergreens. Through the heavy branches, she could just make out the twinkling lights of the homes perched on the hillside surrounding the still, dark waters of Lake Washington. It was a stunning view, but the beauty was lost on Daisy in her current state. The rejection stung. She had wanted to be with Liam tonight, had wanted to get close to him, to take things further—maybe, possibly, even all the way. She'd offered him her virginity, and he'd thrown it back in her face like . . . tickets to a Nickelback concert. It wasn't because she wasn't pretty: her reflection in the blackened glass confirmed that. She'd inherited her mom's lithe frame, her lustrous hair and light gray eyes, and her dad's olive complexion. The combination was striking; she was used to double takes when she walked past, from boys, men, even women. Unlike her peers, Daisy wasn't obsessed with her looks. She didn't even have Instagram, which made her a ninth-grade anomaly. Her appearance was a genetic gift from her parents—but the strong resemblance to her mother muddied her gratitude.

Pulling herself away from the window, she wandered through the frigid rooms. Her parents rarely went out. Kate and Robert were "homebodies," they said. More like recluses. Her mom was a housewife and her dad was a consultant, something to do with law. He'd been an attorney, years ago, but now he worked from home, his office tucked between the master bedroom and her brother's room. (Daisy's room was across the hall—way too close to the rest of her family.) Because they moved so often, her mom and dad barely had a social life, so when Daisy got a bit of space, some privacy, she wanted to make the most of it. She'd had big plans for tonight, but Liam had ruined them.

She found her phone on the sofa and checked the time: 10:25 p.m. Perhaps the night could still be salvaged? She had friends, of course she did. Girls who looked like Daisy were instantly popular, no matter the defects in their personality. But Daisy knew none of her pals would be "allowed" out at this hour of the night. The sheer terror in which her cohort held its parents confounded her. They were always afraid of being "caught," like they were defenseless fish and their parents were going to bonk them on the head and fry them up for dinner. Daisy didn't crave her elders' approval, didn't live in fear of disappointing them. In fact, her parents' opinion of her was largely irrelevant. Maybe this was because her mother had stopped loving her?

It wasn't abrupt, angry, or violent; it was a gradual detachment that started when Daisy was about twelve. Her mother had loved her when she was little, or at least she'd played the part of a loving mom. There had been hugs, cuddles, bedtime stories, and lullabies. But once Daisy reached double digits, she felt her mom cooling toward her. Kate hadn't abandoned her maternal role entirely: she still cooked Daisy's dinner, did her laundry if she put it in the basket, and gave her money for new running shoes or a raincoat, but her indifference was undeniable. Her dad's apathy was less noticeable, perhaps because he'd been less hands-on to begin with. Robert loved both his children, in his reserved, distracted way. But Kate only loved Charles.

At first, Daisy had thought it was a normal part of growing up, this growing apart. But when she saw her friends interacting with their maternal figures, she realized that what was going on between her and her mom was far from typical. When she observed her mom cuddling her brother, sharing a joke with him, helping him with his homework, she knew the distance between her and Kate wasn't natural. She had felt twinges of envy initially, but she pushed them away, calcified herself to the jealousy. And eventually, the benign neglect ceased to bother her. In fact, she felt freed by it. It gave her more room to explore life, to find her path, to become her own person. The only effect was a deep resentment toward her annoying eleven-year-old brother. At least she was normal in that respect.

A surge of claustrophobia suddenly gripped her; she needed to get out of the house, she needed air. She didn't feel stoned anymore, she felt itchy and agitated: *confined*. Silently, she pad-

ded across the gleaming hardwood floors to the carpeted staircase and crept up it. When she reached her brother's door, she
opened it a crack and peered inside. As predicted, the boy was
sleeping soundly—the sleep of the innocent, the carefree, the
protected. His room was spotless (their mom still cleaned it for
him like he was four, not eleven), and a bastion of adolescent
masculinity: baseball gear, soccer cleats, a hockey stick and hel-
met. . . . Charles was destined to grow up to be a douchey jock,
Daisy knew it.

Closing the door, she scampered back down the stairs to
the front entryway. She stepped into her shoes, grabbed the
house keys, and slipped into the cold night. She locked the door
behind her—just in case. But nothing bad happened around
here. Nothing dangerous, or dramatic, or even remotely excit-
ing. She'd only be gone for fifteen, twenty minutes tops. Charles
would be fine.

The autumn air was cool and crisp, and yet, somehow, still
damp and cloying. Everything in Bellevue, the upscale suburb
just northeast of Seattle, felt clammy to Daisy after the dry, brittle atmosphere of Billings, Montana. Toast was not as crunchy.
Crackers had a slightly stale, leaden texture. When Daisy showered in the mornings, her towel remained moist, even twenty-
four hours later, musty and smelly. Her hair was wavy now,
bouncy and difficult to manage. Daisy had been happy in Billings; she'd thought they were *all* happy in Billings. And then,
abruptly, her parents had announced the move.

Daisy didn't know what had precipitated their relocation this time, but every two to five years, her parents felt the need to uproot their children and resettle in another pocket of the country. Daisy had been born in New Hampshire. They'd stayed until she was two, and then they'd moved to Topeka, Kansas, where Charles was born. Since then, they'd lived in the Florida Keys (a cottagey house in Islamorada infested with enormous cockroaches); Moorhead, Minnesota (snow, lots of snow); and Billings (crisp toast and stick-straight hair). "It's for my work," her dad said vaguely, like he'd never heard of conference calls or telecommuting. Were her parents really that restless? That rootless?

In Minnesota, Daisy had let herself become attached to a girl named Beatrice. When the Randolphs inevitably left, the division was torturous. She wouldn't go through that again. Her walls were up now, her relationships arm's-length. And she'd discovered a certain liberty in her transient lifestyle. With an out on the horizon, she was free to focus on her short game. Unlike her peers, Daisy didn't have to worry about long-term consequences, didn't have to protect her reputation at all costs. She could fool around with Liam if she wanted to. . . . Well, if *he* had wanted to.

It was still early for a Friday night, but most of the houses lining the paved street were silent and dark, evidence of the sleepiness of the neighborhood her parents had chosen. All their communities, while geographically diverse, had this in common. They were quiet, suburban, *boring*. Clyde Hill was a blend of the super-rich (tech workers with high salaries and stock options) and the semi-rich (tech contractors with decent salaries and no stock options). The homes were a mixture of neo-Mediterranean, neocolonial, and modern mansions interspersed with more modest homes, ranches and split-levels, a handful of bungalows. (Daisy didn't know the architectural terms; she labeled them mansions, big houses, and shacks.) Even the small homes had luxury cars nestled in their attached garages (sports cars for commuting to Amazon or Expedia or the Microsoft campus; massive SUVs for shuttling the kids to school and soccer practice). Virtually every residence had an aggressively green, professionally landscaped yard.

A car was rumbling toward her—an older model, something big and muscular and American. Daisy didn't know much about cars, but she knew this gangster model was out of place in their conservative suburb. As the vehicle approached, it slowed to a crawl, its headlights shining directly into Daisy's face. She stepped onto the grassy shoulder to let it pass, but, with a squeak of its brakes, the car stopped, about twenty feet from her.

Daisy raised a hand to her brow to block the glare. The headlights were blinding, the beams making her eyes sting. She stood, waiting for the car to move along, but it didn't. It idled there, the big engine purring like a mountain lion. Squinting into the light, she tried to make out the car's occupants, but it was too far away, like the driver had known precisely where to pause to conceal his identity. Daisy strained her neck forward, focused her eyes in the glare, but all she could make out were two hands on the steering wheel . . . large, blunt, masculine hands.

Her heart was beating fast—a normal fight-or-flight response—but she wasn't afraid, not really. Objectively, she knew she was vulnerable. Those hands could belong to a serial killer, a gang rapist, the head of a sex slavery ring. Alternatively, the driver could be a nosy neighbor who would call her mom and dad, alert them that their fourteen-year-old daughter was roaming the streets at night, mildly stoned, leaving her adolescent brother home alone. But it was more likely that the vehicle contained a suburban nobody, driving home from a boring dinner party or a dumb movie. A mild sense of curiosity had caused him to pull over, nothing more.

"What?" she snapped at the humming machine, dropping her hand from her eyes and glaring at the impervious windshield. "What do you want?"

The car just sat there, idling, its occupant watching her. The hands remained motionless—at ten and two—their grip solid but relaxed. For just a moment, Daisy's teen invincibility faltered, her signature brand of indifference wavered. The hair on her arms stood up and a tiny frisson ran through her—not fear, exactly, but *the creeps*.

"What the fuck?" she yelled, raising her arms in what she hoped was a menacing manner. "What's your fuckin' problem?"

The windows remained sealed; the engine continued to grumble. The car stared her down, a metallic lion, an automated grizzly.

Daisy bent down and plucked a rock from the shoulder of the road. It was about the size of an egg, but rough and jagged. "Fuck off!" she screamed, arm cocked, ready to fire. "Quit staring at me, you pervert!"

Nothing.

She ran forward, about five feet, and threw the rock—not as hard as she could (she didn't want to shatter the windshield, though she may have been overestimating her own strength), but hard enough. It hit the hood of the car with a thud, then rolled off the sloping surface, back to the pavement. It was too dark to see if the assault had done any damage, but the sound was indicative of some decent scratches.

As the rock landed on the road, the car's gears audibly shifted and its engine roared to life. The car took off, speeding past her with a gust of heat and exhaust.

Daisy watched the red taillights receding. "Fucking weirdo," she muttered in its wake. When the car had disappeared, she prepared to continue her stroll, but found herself stuck, motionless, on the shoulder. She still had time to spare before her parents would arrive home, but she didn't want to venture farther. To her surprise, the encounter had unnerved her. It had been benign, really, but there had been something ominous and thrilling about the standoff. As she walked back toward home, Daisy felt strangely clear and alert.

For the first time since they'd arrived in Bellevue, Washington, she felt alive.

dj

THEN

DJ's sister had been missing for eleven days. Courtney had taken off after a fight with their parents, and hadn't been seen since. "She just needs to cool off," his dad had said, when she didn't return the first night. "She's playing with us" he said, the second night, "she wants us to worry." On the third night, his mom called the police.

They were looking for her now: the police, their dogs, their helicopters. The community had organized search parties, had plastered the town with MISSING posters. Still, nothing. His parents were frightened and frantic and blaming each other. It was late, and DJ should have been asleep, but instead he was lying in his bed, the acrylic comforter pulled up to his chin, listening to them fight.

"Of course, she acts like a slut!" His dad's angry voice bellowed from down the hall. "Like mother like daughter."

"She hates you!" his mother screamed back. "That's why she ran off in the first place. That's why she fell in with a bad crowd!"

DJ stuck his fingers in his ears, but he could still hear them. His eyes fell on his Power Rangers poster, the glossy image reflecting the light that sneaked through his curtains and slipped under his door. His sister had given it to him for his eleventh birthday last month. "The red one is the best one," Courtney had said. DJ used to like the blue one best, but now he realized his sister was right, the red one was better. He wished he could turn into a Power Ranger—red or blue. He could go downstairs and stop the fighting. He could go out and find Courtney and bring her home. If he was stronger, if he had superpowers, he could fix his family.

Courtney had been a happy little girl. DJ remembered her giggle, how she had skipped when she walked. She'd played outside with her friends then: jump rope or hopscotch or elaborate games of make-believe with princesses and evil queens and knights who rode snorting horses. And then, almost overnight, his sister changed. She got rounder and prettier. She spent hours in front of the mirror, curling her shiny dark hair and applying heavy makeup that made her look older and sleepy. She wore tight shorts and tiny shirts that showed off her breasts and her belly. His friend Carlos couldn't stop staring at her when he came over to play Legos. This made DJ uncomfortable, so he stopped inviting Carlos around.

Courtney had gotten angrier, too. She was always yelling at her parents, slamming doors, and storming out of the house. Her father called her names: a little tart, a whore-in-the-making. Her mother cried and cajoled and pleaded with her daughter to stay home, to talk about her problems, to respect their rules. But his sister never did. She had friends who "got her," she said. When he was fifteen, DJ wanted to find friends like that, not pervs like Carlos who only came around to ogle his sister's boobs.

The doorbell rang then, and the house fell silent. He realized what his parents would be thinking: a neighbor had heard them fighting and called the police. But DJ knew different. He knew it was the police at the door, but their presence had nothing to do with the yelling and screaming. Courtney was dead. He knew it with a certainty that made his bones ache, made his stomach fill with acid and his teeth gnash together. He heard his father open the door and muffled male voices. Then his mother screamed. Without hearing a single word, DJ knew that his sister had been murdered.

Maybe he did have superpowers.

frances

NOW

Marcus was melting down in the backseat of the Subaru. Frances had let him play a game on his iPad as they drove to school (negotiations should not be seen as "giving in" when parenting a child with his issues), and now he was refusing to go into the school until he reached the next level.

"I understand that the game is important to you," she'd said, her voice calm but firm, "but you know that school starts at nine, and that being late is inconvenient for the teacher and the other students."

"I don't care!" he'd screamed. "I hate the teacher! I hate the other kids!"

"It's perfectly fine for you to feel that way, but—"

"I hate YOU!"

He hadn't meant it, she knew that, but it still hurt. No matter how many times Marcus hurled this assault at her, she never stopped feeling the sting. Her son must have known it, must have seen her smart and cringe each and every time, and yet still he said it. Regularly. She reminded herself that Marcus was a child with problems: his synapses fired differently, empathy was a difficult concept for him to grasp. Frances had not borne a child who was simply heartless and cruel.

She stared blindly out the front window as her son yelled and screamed and cried in the backseat. He was eleven now; most children Marcus's age sat in the front seat, and most had outgrown such tantrums. To make matters worse, the boy was so large that a stranger would think it was a young teenager blubbering and wailing behind her.

"Breathe," she said, as much to herself as to Marcus. Frances could feel her composure slipping. If Marcus had been having this outburst at home instead of in the parking lot of Forrester Academy, she would have been fine. She was used to this behavior and she knew he would eventually settle. It was the fear that one of those judgmental supermoms would happen by and witness her child's explosion, observe her inability to calm him, that was sending her anxiety through the roof. She felt perilously close to cracking.

At times like these, her son was not easy to love, but she did, madly. She loved his large, awkward body; his soft, brown hair; his meaty, rosy cheeks. She loved his deep brown eyes, the tinkling of his laughter, the way his tongue poked out of his mouth when he was concentrating. When he was born, she'd wanted the world for him: academic success, sporting prowess, popularity. . . . Now, she just focused on day-to-day survival.

He was about five when they noticed something wasn't quite right. Marcus fought with other children, fidgeted in class, cried constantly. His kindergarten teacher had called Frances and Jason into a meeting. "We'd like to do some tests," she'd said, an ominous tinge to her voice.

"Maybe he's gifted?" Frances had suggested hopefully as Jason drove them home in the Hyundai they owned at the time. "Maybe that's why he's acting up? He's bored. He's understimulated."

"Maybe . . ." Jason said.

"He's always been bright," Frances continued. "Remember when your mom sent him that puzzle game for his third birthday? He solved it faster than I could."

Jason either didn't remember his son's master puzzle-solving skills or was unimpressed by them. He patted her hand. "Whatever it is, we'll deal with it," he said, ever stoic, ever calm and accepting.

How Frances had craved that designation. If Marcus was extremely intelligent, then his other issues were just par for the course. Being *gifted* often meant that children were a little weird. But being average (or, God forbid, below average) and weird was another story altogether. When Frances revisited that time, she hated herself. What kind of mother based her love for her weird son on his IQ? She was horrible. But when the results came back—average intelligence, signs of ADHD and oppositional defiant disorder—Frances found that her love for him had not diminished at all.

She blamed herself for her child's issues. Jason had been a good boy, a good student, and was now a good man. It was Frances who'd had problems. While she'd excelled academically, she had exhibited a lack of impulse control, incredibly poor judgment, and an inability to understand consequences. Had she been *normal*, she would never have committed the heinous act that she had. She had put her own parents through hell; she didn't deserve an easy child.

"I hate school!" Marcus screamed, kicking the back of the passenger seat. "I want to burn it down!"

"I understand your feelings, Marcus."

"No, you don't! You're stupid!"

Frances's homicidal fantasies were never directed at her son. Even in their darkest moments, she couldn't imagine harming a hair on his inordinately large round head. What she did dream about, in times like these, was running away. She could get out of the car, close the door on her son's rage, and just walk off. She could stride across the Forrester Academy parking lot and down the hill to the Bellevue Transit Center, where she could catch a bus into Seattle. There, she could go to a hotel and sneak onto an airport shuttle that would deliver her to Sea-Tac. She could fly to South Africa or Scandinavia or New Zealand and start over. Frances had done it before: closed the door on a dark chapter and become a new person. But she was a mother now. It changed everything.

Suddenly, there was a light tap-tap-tap on her side window. Frances didn't want to look, but, instinctively, she did. Instead of the angry, judgmental, Botoxed face she was expecting, she met the sympathetic gaze of her friend Kate. Relief flooded through Frances. She turned the key in the ignition and lowered the window.

"Rough morning?" the blond woman asked with genuine concern.

"You could say that." She noticed Kate's son, Charles, hovering behind his mother. He was watching Marcus impassively, like he was monitoring a science experiment, a chimpanzee in a glass box with an abacus. Frances gave a weak smile. "Marcus doesn't want to go to school."

"We know the feeling." Kate looked at her son. "Don't we, buddy?"

"Yeah."

Kate leaned down, rested her hands on her knees, and peered in at Marcus. Distracted by their presence, his tantrum had dwindled to an incessant whimper. Kate said, "Maybe he'd go in with Charles?"

"I don't know. . . ."

"You'd like that, wouldn't you, Charles?" she said, loud enough for Marcus to hear.

"Sure." Charles was surely the most compliant child ever created.

"It's okay," Frances said, knowing Marcus was not that easily defused. "We don't want to make you late." But Charles was already rapping on the back window and waving at her son. To Frances's surprise, Marcus undid his seat belt and scooched from the back passenger seat across to the driver's side.

"Want to come in with me?" Charles asked through the glass.

In the rearview mirror, Frances saw her son wipe his tear-streaked face with his fleshy paws. "Okay." Without a word to his mother, he opened the back door and exited the car.

Frances climbed out of the driver's seat and stood with Kate, watching their boys cross the front courtyard toward the school doors. The adolescents walked in companionable silence until Charles leaned his head slightly toward Marcus and said something indiscernible. Marcus glanced at his friend, and a smile—light, carefree, happy—danced on her son's lips. Frances suddenly felt she might cry.

"They're so cute," Kate said.

"They are." Frances pushed through the tremor in her voice. "Thank you."

"Charles likes Marcus. He doesn't have a lot of friends, either."

Really? Charles seemed so exceedingly normal: athletic, articulate, engaged. . . . Was it possible the boy had hidden challenges? That Marcus wasn't the only one battling his way through childhood? A lump formed in Frances's throat at the prospect that her son was not alone.

"Do you have time for a coffee?" Kate asked.

Frances looked up at the tall woman, so elegant, so put-together. She couldn't help but wonder why such a perfect specimen would covet her friendship. Kate could have anyone, could be part of the mommy in-crowd, on the maternal A-list. What could she possibly see in damaged Frances?

They were both new to the elite private school, having arrived on the same warm August morning: Frances, so desperate, so obsequious, so ingratiating; Kate, cool, aloof, distant. . . . The attractive blond had barely hit Frances's radar then (all instruments had been focused on the alpha moms, like Allison Moss and Jeanette Dumas). And Frances had made some progress with them. There had been a moderately successful playdate, a mid-morning coffee klatch, a power walk. . . . And then, Marcus had urinated in Abbey's water bottle and it all blew up.

Frances would never forget that day. She had stood on the edge of the playground while her son, comfortable with his recent ostracizing, tossed a basketball in the general direction of a hoop mounted on a tall post. To her right, a gaggle of Forrester mothers audibly gossiped about them.

"Something's wrong with him. He should be in a school for kids with behavior issues."

"He's sick. He's perverted. He needs help."

The next voice was even louder. "It's selfish to send him to a school like Forrester. He's putting all the *normal* kids at risk."

Frances turned toward them, her face burning with anger and shame. It was the first time, in years, that her mind had gone to that murderous place. A machine gun factored into this particular fantasy, bitchy moms splattered all over the playground. It was a brief illusion and sanity quickly prevailed. She obviously couldn't shoot them, but she needed to speak up—for herself and for her son. But what could she possibly say?

Before she could craft a retort, a tall, fair-haired woman had materialized. She walked right up to the nattering group.

"He's just a kid, you toxic bitches."

It was crass, rude . . . and fantastic! The moms' jaws dropped open and no one spoke. What could they say? A lot, as Frances knew all too well, but this woman didn't seem to care. She walked past them, casually, and joined Frances on the side of the playground.

"I'm Kate," she said, pointing toward the basketball hoop. "Is that your son?"

"Uh . . . yeah."

"Mine's over there." Kate indicated Charles: cute, sporty, normal. The refrain of criticism renewed behind them, louder now, and directed at Kate, the interloper. But the willowy woman remained unperturbed. She wasn't afraid of the other mothers like Frances was; their judgments and criticisms didn't faze her. Frances was slightly in awe of her.

"Coffee sounds great," Frances said now, and then, "Shit!" Her hands flew to her chest and gripped her large, unfettered breasts. "I didn't even put on a bra this morning."

Kate burst into laughter and Frances had to giggle, too. "I was hoping I could drop Marcus at the kiss-and-drive," she explained, crossing her arms. "I wasn't planning to get out of the car."

"I have an idea," Kate said, eyes dancing. "Go home and get dressed. Wear something hot. I'll pick you up at eleven-thirty."

Frances was supposed to go to Curves this morning. Her goal was three workouts a week, but she rarely (okay, never) attained her objective. And Kate's animated offer was impossible to turn down.

"Where are we going?"

"You'll see."

Frances didn't own anything "hot," but her long, silky top was flattering at least. It covered her hips and her butt, and the low neckline flattered her ample cleavage (now propped up by a sturdy bra). She wore a pair of slim dark jeans, boots with a medium heel, and a black blazer. She'd taken time with her makeup, too, applying a becoming daytime look. Frances felt almost pretty . . . until she looked across to the driver's seat and Kate. Her companion was effortlessly stylish in expensive, faded jeans, a suede jacket, and enormous hoop earrings. Watching Kate masterfully pilot the Lincoln Navigator down I-90 toward Seattle, Frances's confidence plummeted.

"Thanks for agreeing to this," Kate said, glancing over with a smile. "It's a real treat to spend a day with a friend."

"My pleasure," Frances replied, her self-esteem rising a couple of notches. "I don't usually do things like this."

"Things like what?" Kate teased. "You don't know what we're doing yet. I could be taking you to some depraved underground sex club."

"Of course." Frances shrugged. "That's where I spend all my Tuesday mornings."

Kate's laughter tinkled, and Frances felt warm and happy. She was having a girls' day out. Like other women did. Like women whose children didn't require special diets and structured routines and constant research into treatments and behavioral modification therapies. Like women who didn't eschew close relationships because their past was full of terrible secrets they'd protect at all costs. As the SUV exited the freeway, Frances felt a shiver of anticipation. Today felt like the start of something.

daisy

NOW

Daisy was seated cross-legged in the school hallway eating her lunch (a bag of Doritos) with Mia Wilson and Emma Menendez. Mia and Emma were the kind of girls who attached themselves to prettier, cooler girls in the hopes that some pretty and cool might rub off on them. In actual fact, hanging around with someone like Daisy made them look less pretty and cool by comparison. Lucky for Daisy, they hadn't thought of it that way.

"What did you do this weekend?" Mia asked, offering Daisy her Ziploc bag of carrot sticks. Mia, a vegan, ate raw vegetables all day and little else. She was very thin and her skin was pale, almost translucent, under its coating of foundation. Daisy wondered if peer-pressuring Mia into eating a cheeseburger would improve her pallor.

Daisy grabbed a wet carrot stick from the bag and took a bite. "I had to babysit my gross brother."

"That sucks," Emma said. In contrast to Mia's cruelty-free sustenance, Emma was eating a ciabatta bun full of some nitrate-laden sausage that had ended the life of at least one pig and possibly a cow. Emma was cute and curvy and rosy-cheeked. "Was it *so* boring?"

Daisy's mind drifted back to her make-out session with Liam, how high they'd been, how sure she had been that they were going to explore each other intimately. Then she thought about that big, muscular car purring in front of her, about the large hands gripping the steering wheel, the eyes, obscured by the darkness, watching her. Goose bumps pimpled her arms.

"Totally boring." She snapped off a piece of carrot in her teeth. "What did you guys do?"

"I binge-watched *Gilmore Girls* on Netflix. Again!" It was ghostly Mia, who had moved on to cucumber slices.

"Oh my god," Emma gushed. "I love that show. I want to erase my brain so I can rewatch it."

"It's actually better the second time."

"This would be the fourth time for me." Emma turned to Daisy. "Have you watched it?"

Daisy didn't watch much TV, and if she did, it certainly wouldn't be a trite dramedy about a mother-daughter relationship. "I haven't," she said, "but I hear it's good."

"So good," Mia said.

"You *have* to watch it," Emma echoed.

Daisy was about to change the subject by asking Emma what brainless TV show had taken up her entire weekend, when Tori Marra joined them.

"Hey guys," she said, crossing her feet and lowering her tiny body to the floor next to Emma. Tori was petite, a dancer, with a shock of short, platinum hair that contrasted with her Mediterranean coloring. She was the alpha female of their social set: loud, mean, in charge. Daisy was cool with that. She'd never considered herself a leader, despite the omnipresence of a sycophantic group of wannabes at every school she attended. Daisy couldn't help but enjoy the admiration, but she preferred to do so quietly, passively.

"How was everyone's weekend?" Tori asked, and the girls responded with various iterations of tedium.

"Really?" Tori said, cocking an eyebrow at Daisy. "*You* had a boring weekend?"

"Yeah."

"Even Friday night?"

"Uh . . . yes."

"That's not what Liam Kenneway said."

Emma and Mia gasped, scandalized, but Daisy maintained her composure. "Really? What did Liam say?"

"I don't know if I should repeat it here. It's kinda . . . *personal*."

Daisy caught Emma and Mia exchanging a panicked glance. They couldn't be dismissed for this! Daisy also clocked the smug, almost triumphant glint in Tori's dark eyes. A hint of jealousy had always emanated off the compact girl, a subtle resentment toward Daisy's effortless popularity. Her glee in this moment confirmed it.

"Go ahead," Daisy said coolly. "We're all friends here."

"Liam said you guys . . . *did it*."

Emma and Mia gasped again, but Daisy remained nonchalant. "Did he?"

"Yep," Tori said, with a cruel smirk. "And that's not all he said."

Daisy's heart was thudding in her chest—anger, betrayal, fear—but she would not give this little blond bird the satisfaction. "Tell me."

"He said you did some weird stuff to him."

"*Weird stuff?*"

"Kinky stuff. Porny stuff." An ominous smile. "*Butt* stuff."

"Oh my god," Mia muttered over Emma's simultaneous "Ewww!"

"He said," Tori continued, clearly delighting in her narrative role, "that you . . . *licked* his butt."

"Gross!" Emma shrieked, and Mia visibly cringed.

Blood was rushing to Daisy's cheeks, betraying her blasé affect. Liam was trying to destroy her socially. But why? Had her laughter damaged his ego so badly that he felt he had to disparage her? To hurt and humiliate her? It was the only possibility.

"He said you seemed really *experienced*," Tori said, biting her lip to hold back a blatant smile. "Like you must have done a *ton* of guys at your last school."

"That's not true!" Emma said, with unearned confidence. Her voice was less assured when she added, "Is it, Daisy?"

It wasn't. Of course, it wasn't. But Daisy didn't respond. She rose to her full height, looming over the girls on the floor. "Where's Liam?"

The tiny diamond stud in Tori's nose caught the fluorescent light and sparkled, rivaling the cruel twinkle in her eyes. "He's by the vending machines with his friends. But I'm not sure you want to go over there." She feigned sympathy. "It was getting pretty graphic when I left."

Daisy turned on her heel and walked away. "Should we come with?" Mia called after her, halfheartedly, but Daisy didn't respond.

As promised, Liam was ensconced in a group of his peers, regaling them with tales of Daisy's sexual expertise.

"She's a total freak," he was saying. "I would never have guessed it."

"Maybe she's a nymphomaniac," Dylan Larabee suggested.

"Probably. She couldn't get enough!"

"Hi, Liam."

All eyes turned toward her: the freak, the nympho, had been conjured by their words. Liam paled and she saw the terror in his eyes. He had been caught in the act: lying about her, vilifying her, slut-shaming her. Daisy could destroy this little twerp and he knew it. She could tell his posse that he couldn't get it up, that he had a tiny penis, that he had prematurely ejaculated. Or she could just tell them the truth: that he had run away from her because he was too *scared*, too *childish*, *not ready*.

She opened her lips, prepared to ruin him, but then she looked at his face. It was white, trembling, almost tearful. Liam was a soft little boy—a *child*—trying, desperately, to maintain his rank in the social order of Centennial High School. Daisy wasn't like him. She was strong and resilient. She would recover from his slander, and if she didn't, so what? Her family would move again, she'd go to a new school, and make new friends. If she took Liam down now, he might never recover.

She pasted on a smile. "I had so much fun on Friday night."

"Umm, okay . . ."

"Thank you for that."

"N-no problem."

"And, I just wanted to say . . . ," she leaned in, and lowered her voice a tad, ". . . your butt tastes *great*."

She sauntered away, savoring the stunned silence she left in her wake. The character assassination would resume when the boys recovered from their shock, she knew that, but for a moment, she felt satisfied. She was stronger, braver, tougher than these kids.

She was invincible.

frances

The rustically hip Edgewater Hotel was perched (as per its name) on the edge of Elliott Bay, offering stunning views of the Pacific and silhouettes of the distant Olympic Mountains. The restaurant, Six Seven, served seafood in an upscale yet funky environment: tree-trunk pillars, ornate light fixtures, a massive river-rock fireplace. . . . Frances had been here before—for an anniversary dinner with Jason—a couple of years ago. It must have been their tenth, so it would have been three years ago in June. (For all other anniversaries, they celebrated with takeout Thai food and a movie. Marcus didn't react well to babysitters, so they were reserved for milestone occasions only.)

A distinguished host ushered Kate and Frances directly to a window seat (a table for four, though they were only two), and a handsome young waiter arrived promptly with a wine list and menus. Excellent service was to be expected at such a popular restaurant, but Frances knew that Kate's looks were a contributing factor. There had been a short period when Frances had experienced a similar attentiveness. She had been beautiful, for a moment, like a peony that blooms spectacularly before quickly losing its petals. Then she started putting on weight, and gradually became invisible.

Kate was perusing the wine list. "White or red?"

"We're *drinking*?"

Her friend looked at her like she'd suggested they were about to drop acid. "Just wine . . . Unless you want something stronger? They make a great martini."

"No, no . . . I have to pick up Marcus after school."

"I'll pick him up when I get Charles." Kate smiled. "I'm the designated driver. Feel free to get tipsy."

Frances did not get tipsy in the daytime. She had responsibilities, she had obligations, she had secrets to keep. She couldn't afford to drop her guard. But then the waiter was pouring them glasses of a crisp California Sauvignon Blanc, and Kate was offering up a toast. "To friends," she said, her smile warm and sincere, and Frances clinked her glass to Kate's and drank. The moment felt almost celebratory. Maybe Frances *could* get tipsy in the day . . . just this once.

When they had ordered (mussels to share, followed by smoked-salmon tacos for Kate and an arugula salad for Frances), she took a sip of wine. The late-October sun was shining over the ocean, a last glimpse of blue sky before the long dreariness of a Pacific Northwest November set in. Well-fed seagulls swooped and dove over the navy water, and, above a layer of thick forest, the Olympic Mountains rose. A gleaming white ferry trudged across the blue vista. Frances had lived here since her early twenties, but the natural beauty never failed to impress.

"It's stunning, isn't it?"

"Mmm . . ." Kate murmured her agreement.

"Do you like living here?"

"It's okay," Kate said. "Better since I met you."

There was something almost flirtatious in Kate's tone that made Frances's cheeks pink.

Kate clarified. "We move so often that I usually don't bother making friends. But when I met you . . . I don't know . . . I just felt a sort of *connection*."

Before Frances could respond, Kate said, "Oh god. That sounded weird." She took a drink of wine. "I'm not hitting on you."

Frances laughed, remembering the day Kate had come to her defense on the school playground. "I feel the same way."

"I'm glad."

"Do you miss Montana?" Frances asked.

"Not really. We were only there a couple of years before we had to move for Robert's work."

"He's a legal consultant, right?"

"Yeah. He only deals with very specific cases."

"What type of cases?"

"Environmental. Boring." Kate unfolded her linen napkin and placed it on her lap. "What does Jason do again?"

"He works in procurement at a tech company, so boring-*er* . . . which I know is not a word."

Kate chuckled. "But it should be."

"Jason seems to like it. He works a lot. And I think he's underpaid. But he's not one to complain."

"What about you?" Kate asked. "Did you work?"

"I did. In human resources. But then Marcus . . ." Frances didn't quite know how to phrase it without sounding disloyal. She picked up her wineglass and swirled the platinum liquid. "He's a full-time job."

"Kids are a lot," Kate said, with an understanding smile.

"Yeah . . . but I always wanted to be a mom. It sounds old-fashioned to say it, but I never really dreamed about a career." For some reason, a lump of emotion clogged her throat. "I dreamed about having a family."

"That's what feminism means to me," Kate said. "Allowing women to pursue their dreams, whatever they are, without stigma or judgment." She toyed with her fork. "I never really thought about having kids. Not seriously, anyway. Until Robert. He was desperate to have a family, and I wanted to give him that."

"You must really love him."

"He saved me," she said. And then, noticing Frances's concerned expression, she elucidated. "From myself. I was headed down a bad path and Robert got me back on track."

"And now, you have your beautiful family."

"Yep," Kate said, flippantly. "And I can't work anyway. For one, I've got a useless art history degree. And for two, we never stay in one place long enough."

"How long will you stay here?"

"I don't know . . . ," she lowered her chin slightly and looked up at Frances, ". . . I'd like to stay for a while."

Their eyes met, and Frances felt an odd sensation stirring in her, something akin to arousal. If she hadn't known better, she'd have thought Kate was flirting with her. It was rather effective. Frances had never considered herself sexually adventurous, and certainly not bi-curious, but as she looked across the table at her friend—so elegant, so pretty—she briefly wondered what it would be like to kiss her. She really shouldn't drink during the day.

"Food's here," Kate said, as the waiter approached. Frances was glad of the distraction and the sustenance.

As they ate, they discussed the Forrester experience. "My kids have been to a lot of schools," Kate said, picking up her second salmon taco (seriously, how did she stay so skinny?), "and the Forrester mothers are the worst I have ever encountered."

"Really?"

"They're pure evil. They have their own level of cuntyness . . . which I know is not a word."

"But it should be," they said, in unison, before dissolving into laughter.

When Frances had composed herself, she forked an arugula leaf. The salad was light, the dressing tangy, and she was glad she hadn't given in and ordered the burger that had tempted her. Combined with the cold glass of wine and the excellent conversation, Frances felt utterly satisfied with her low-calorie lunch.

Kate leaned forward. "Someone's staring at you."

"What?" Frances was bewildered.

"Don't look . . . but the two guys in the booth. They've been watching us."

"They've been watching *you*," Frances retorted. "Men never look at me."

Kate sat back in her chair. "Are you kidding me? You're gorgeous."

Frances snorted.

"Frances, you are absolutely *luscious*," Kate said, bestowing that adoring gaze upon her again. "And the guy in the gray suit thinks so, too."

Frances glanced, subtly, toward the curved booth. Two men, their business attire casual—collars open, jackets undone—were looking their way. Boldly, Frances let her eyes drift over the man in gray. He was in his early forties, with dark hair graying at the temples. His jawline was strong, his lips shapely, and under thick brows, his eyes were warm and brown. He was attractive; not as attractive as Jason, but Frances knew that her husband would never look at her across a restaurant now. She had met him in that (very short) window when she had been slim and pretty. The man in gray smiled at her and, for a moment, she was again. She smiled back.

"Oh my god," Frances whispered, fiddling with her salad in an attempt to maintain composure, "I think I just flirted with that guy."

"Good!"

"It's not good. How is it good? I'm married."

"It's harmless. And everyone deserves a little fun. Especially you."

Frances wasn't sure why she, in particular, deserved a little fun, but it felt odd to ask for clarification.

Kate spoke quietly but directly. "Give me your wedding rings."

"What?"

"Pass them to me under the table. I'll put them in my wallet."

"Why?"

Kate held up her own bare ring finger and smiled. Her eyes danced wickedly. "Let's play a little."

Frances was about to object, but the wine had made her feel daring, even reckless. A quick glance to her right confirmed that the two businessmen were standing, picking up their drinks, preparing to join them. Frances realized how much she wanted them to. She wanted to meet someone new, to chat and flirt . . . to *play a little.* She would never cross the line into adultery—she loved Jason, she knew how lucky she was to have him—but she wanted to feel mysterious and attractive and desired. Kate was right; it was harmless. Twisting the two gold bands off her finger, she reached under the table and placed them in Kate's open palm.

"Mind if we join you?" It was the other man, in a navy sport coat, his eyes resting on Kate. He was the more classically hand-some of the two, but he was too slick for Frances's liking. Her guy was more interesting looking, had more character. *Her guy?* Was she really thinking of this stranger in proprietary terms already? Claiming him after one brief moment of eye contact? It was sophomoric . . . but titillating.

"Of course," Kate said, gesturing to the seat next to her. The man sat. His companion slid in next to Frances.

Their names were Pete (her guy, in gray) and Tom (Kate's navy-blue friend). They were from Nebraska, in Seattle for a trade show. "We're in commercial refrigeration," Pete said. (*Boring-er-er,* Frances thought, but didn't say.) Tom and Pete's conference didn't start until tomorrow. They'd come in early to enjoy the city.

"And the scenery," Pete said, eyes devouring Frances instead of the spectacular view their prime table afforded. She blushed at the overt flirtation. The comment was cliché, cheesy, she knew that, but she ate it up anyway.

They bantered about life in the Midwest versus the Pacific Northwest (a thick juicy steak versus fresh seafood, old-fashioned drip versus designer coffee, tornado season or the omnipresent threat of an earthquake), and laughingly agreed to steer away from politics. The men weren't particularly witty or charming, but Pete's eyes on her, the way he attentively refilled her glass (at some point, another bottle of wine had been ordered), made Frances giddy. She had now had three (or was it four?) glasses of wine, and was teetering on the precipice between tipsy and drunk. But she was having a ball.

Finally, Pete asked, "What do you ladies do?"

Nothing. It was Frances's inner voice, that little gremlin that taunted her. Parenting her son, looking after her husband, managing the household, was not a real job. Her efforts were not enough.

"We're location scouts for the film industry," Kate said, lying with aplomb. "We're looking for a seaside restaurant to film a pivotal scene in a movie."

"Oh yeah?" Tom said. "Who's in it? Anyone big?"

"Not really. . . . Just this little actress. Her name's Angelina."

"Get out!" Tom was clearly impressed. "Have you met her?"

"Briefly. In a preproduction meeting." Kate's fabricating skills were impressive.

As Tom peppered Kate with questions about celebrity encounters, Pete turned to Frances. "I'm not impressed by Hollywood."

Frances shrugged. "It's a job."

"Everyone's so plastic. And the women are so scrawny. I like a little something to hold on to, if you know what I mean." The look in Pete's eyes had turned lascivious, and Frances shifted uncomfortably. She focused on the remnants of her salad as Pete leaned in and spoke directly into her ear.

"And you know what they say about fat girls . . ."

She did, of course she did.

"They try harder."

The acidic white wine in Frances's stomach churned and she truly feared she might vomit. Her cheeks burned with shame and humiliation, her eyes threatened to fill with angry tears. Pete's words were vulgar, his tone full of loathing, of contempt. He didn't find her interesting or beautiful or sexy. He was a chubby chaser. He was a misogynist. He was a pig.

"We should go." Frances tossed the linen napkin from her lap onto her plate. She stood abruptly, her thighs hitting the table, jostling the wineglasses.

Kate looked up at her, momentarily confused, but she read the distress on Frances's face.

"Yep. Back to the old grind." She rose.

"Wait," Tom said, distressed. "Can we meet up later?"

"We've got a lot of work to do," Kate replied, fishing her wallet from her bag and placing several bills on the table.

"And," Frances glowered at Pete, "we're happily married." She held up her left hand, defiantly.

Pete let out a small, derisive snort, and Frances realized her ring finger was bare. Humiliation made her face hot, and she felt a flash of that blind, murderous rage that was occurring far too frequently of late. She could not lose it in front of this bastard.

Frances felt Kate's hand slip into the crook of her elbow. Kate's voice, when she spoke, dripped venom.

"Why don't you two *hicks* go upstairs and fuck each other?"

Kate led Frances out of the restaurant.

dj

THEN

*The man who murdered his sister was named Shane Nelson—
allegedly murdered his sister. But DJ knew Shane Nelson had
done it, just like he had known that his sister had been killed, that
night as he lay in his bed, wishing for superpowers. His parents had
talked to the police and the district attorney, but they refused to give
their son any details.*

*"I don't want you to know what happened to her," his mom
said, tearfully. "You're too young to take this in."*

*But DJ wasn't too young. He had grown up fast, he'd had to,
and he deserved to know the truth about what had happened to
his sister. He had loved her, too. Luckily, the local newspapers were
more than happy to oblige. Crimes like this, the murder of a pretty
young white girl, sold papers, and no gory details would be spared.
His parents didn't subscribe to any of the dailies, but DJ had been*

stealing copies off various neighbors' front steps. The May 6 issue
had the specifics he sought.

> Shane William Nelson, a 28-year-old man from
> Phoenix, has been arrested for the murder of
> Courtney Carey, 15. The teen went missing last
> February from the suburb of Tolleson. Carey's
> badly beaten body was discovered in South
> Mountain Park nine days after her parents,
> Declan and Susan Carey, reported her missing.
> She had been sexually assaulted, tortured, and
> strangled. The coroner's report states that blunt
> force trauma to the head was the cause of death.
>   Neighbors said Nelson "kept to himself" but
> seemed to have a lot of friends, both male and
> female, coming and going at all hours. Nelson,
> who is single, has a young son with an estranged
> girlfriend. Nelson has no prior convictions, but
> police questioned him in 1994 in relation to two
> rapes in the Avondale area. Nelson, currently
> unemployed, is in custody pending charges.
>   The police are also speaking to a person of
> interest who, they say, does not pose a threat to
> the public.

DJ's bowels loosened as he read, and he had to run to the toilet.
Maybe his mom was right. Maybe he was too young to know. He
brought the paper with him and he inspected the mug shot of Shane
Nelson as he shit: dark eyes; unruly brown hair; a narrow, chis-
eled face. In another context, he would have looked normal, even
handsome. But DJ could see the cruelty in Shane Nelson's eyes, the
evil in the slight curl of his lips. Why hadn't his sister seen it? How

could she have gotten into a car with this man? Why didn't she run away? Why didn't she scream?

There was a grainy picture of Courtney, smiling coyly, wearing too much makeup, looking like trouble. He knew what people would think. His sister got what was coming to her. If she had listened to her parents, obeyed their rules, she'd be alive today. They'd tell their daughters: See? See what happens when you disobey your parents? When you ignore your curfew? When you rebel? *They would all think it could never happen to their girls.*

There was no photograph of the "person of interest."

frances

NOW

The clock radio on the bedside table glowed in the predawn light: 6:22 a.m. Jason was on top of Frances, pumping away, as was their Friday morning ritual. "Successful marriages make sex a priority," all the magazines and self-help books said, so Frances had suggested they add it to their agendas. Between Jason's work and cycling schedule, Marcus's school routine, his swim classes, soccer, tae kwon do, physical and psychological therapist appointments, and Frances's attempts to hit the gym, Friday, predawn, was the only available slot.

"Take your shirt off," Jason growled into her ear as he bounced on top of her. "I want to see your big, beautiful breasts."

Frances's breasts were currently hiding out under her armpits like they were ashamed of themselves. Jason had always loved Frances's boobs, for good reason. Once, they had been rather spectacular. But weight gain, breast-feeding, and gravity had taken their toll, and the breasts were now a shadow of their former selves. If Frances took her pajama top off, Jason was sure to find the reality, in stark contrast to his fond memories, repulsive, and this session would take even longer. She wanted to make gluten-free waffles for Marcus's breakfast.

"No . . . ," she whispered, "I'm so close. . . ."

Her lie had the intended effect and Jason upped his tempo. "Oh yeah," Frances gasped, "Yes, yes, yes . . . !"

"Oh God," Jason grunted, turned on by Frances's theatrics. "I'm coming! I'm coming! I'm . . ." He trailed off, his handsome face contorting with the effort of his climax. After a few moments, he collapsed onto Frances's pillowy body.

Jason lifted his head. "Did you get there?"

"Of course. Couldn't you tell?"

"I thought so, but I wasn't sure." He kissed her cheek, a loud, affectionate smack, then climbed off her. He grabbed his robe and put it on. "What have you got on today?"

Nothing, the little voice said. *Nothing that matters, anyway.*

"I'm going to the gym this morning." She called Curves "the gym" as much as possible. "Curves" conjured images of overweight ladies sweating on antiquated exercise bikes, whereas "the gym" connoted hard bodies deadlifting barbells; much more impressive. "Marcus has a martial arts class after school. And I have to go shopping. I said I'd make a dessert for tonight. I was thinking tiramisu."

"Tonight?"

"Kate and Robert invited us for dinner, remember?"

"Right." Jason belted his robe. "You and Kate have gotten pretty tight."

Frances smiled, warmed by the thought of the friendship. "Kate's great. She's sweet and thoughtful. And she's really funny even though she's so ridiculously pretty."

Jason pecked her lips. "You're prettier than Kate is."

It was kind, but insincere. While Frances appreciated her husband's compliment, she knew she could not compare to Kate Randolph. Not anymore, anyway.

After their lunch date at the waterfront restaurant, Kate had blamed herself for the toxic encounter with the two salesmen.

"I thought they seemed so friendly, so benign," she said, as she shuttled them back to Bellevue. "I should never have invited them over."

Frances slipped her wedding rings back onto her finger. "You didn't *invite* them."

"I *encouraged* them. . . . I thought it would be fun," Kate said. "And harmless."

"It was fun. Until it wasn't."

"You know what would be *really* fun?" Kate bit her lip as she glanced over at Frances. "We could go back. Pretend we had a change of heart. We'd play along, take things up to their rooms, get them naked . . . and then we'd light their beds on fire and leave."

Frances smirked. "And they'd have to run out into the hall naked."

"Or . . . we could lock the door behind us and let them burn."

Frances, briefly, let herself visualize Pete engulfed in flames, screaming and writhing in agony. *I'm not trying so hard now, am I?* she'd quip, as she watched him blister and char and succumb. She shook off the image and met the wicked glint in Kate's eyes.

"It's a great idea, but we don't have time." Frances looked at the dashboard clock. "The boys have to be picked up at three."

Kate snapped her fingers. "Damn."

The moment was couched in humor, but that look, where they recognized the darkness in each other, forged a kind of bond. A new level of comfort was born, an inherent understanding of each other. Kate and Frances didn't connect with the other Forrester mothers because they were a different breed. They had found each other, and it felt fated.

In the weeks following, the women had grown even closer, enjoying coffee dates, power walks, and a lot of playful texting. On Halloween night, they'd filled their insulated coffee mugs with gin and tonic, and taken the boys trick-or-treating. (Charles had been a Jedi. Marcus had insisted on a *Minecraft* costume constructed of numerous shoeboxes that made it nearly impossible to walk. Thankfully, Charles was extraordinarily patient.) It had only been a couple of months, but Frances couldn't remember the last time she'd felt such a sense of comfort and camaraderie. She knew she didn't deserve the friendship, fun, and frivolity that other women enjoyed. Not after what she'd done. But Kate, somehow, made her feel worthy.

As Jason showered, Frances woke Marcus (gently) and headed downstairs to the tiny, cluttered kitchen. When they'd saved up enough money, they would renovate, knock out a wall and put in a center island. The house had seemed perfectly adequate when they'd moved in as a young couple, but as Marcus got bigger, the environment felt smaller. The boy was already so large, and seemed to grow by the minute. And he needed so much *stuff*, the paraphernalia of adolescence gradually encroaching on their living space. Frances should have been able to keep the house tidy (she had nothing else to do), but she found it hard to muster the energy required for housework.

Grabbing a plastic mixing bowl from an overloaded cupboard and plucking a wooden spoon from the pottery jar on the stove, she mixed the waffle batter. Syrup was not permitted in her son's diet, so she cut up strawberries, hoping to compensate for the lack of glucose. Her husband entered, dashing in his dark trousers and button-down shirt, sifting through the mail that had been slipped through the slot in the door.

"There's a letter from your mom."

The mixing bowl nearly escaped Frances's grip. "Just put it on the table," she said, forcing a casual tone. But her voice sounded tense and tight.

Jason obeyed, examining the other envelopes. Bills probably, always bills. "You haven't talked to your folks in a while."

"We e-mail," Frances said, busying herself at the waffle
maker. It wasn't an outright lie. She did correspond with her
parents, on occasion. But she'd deliberately chosen words to
indicate that their communications were regular, casual, not
awkward, tense, and fraught.

"They should come visit," her husband said, sliding his
thumb under the seal of a missive from the phone company.
"They haven't been here since Marcus was little."

Remembrance of that last visit twisted her gut. Their time
together had been companionable on the surface, but strained
beneath. Frances had chosen to keep the dark aspects of her past
from Jason and Marcus, and her parents respected that. But the
pressure of avoiding subjects, of keeping secrets, of being around
people who knew her—the *real* her—was exhausting. And pretending they were happy, functional, *normal*, wore on all of them.
When Frances looked at her parents, prematurely old and frail,
guilt would gnaw at her insides. The sadness and disappointment
she had caused had eaten away at them, devoured their vitality.
Eventually, the visits had petered out, replaced by birthday cards,
monthly e-mails, and packages at Christmas.

"I'll suggest it," she said, brightly. "Gluten-free waffle?"

After dropping Marcus at school, Frances drove to Curves.
The Bellevue location had closed when the yummy-mummies

jumped on the SoulCycle bandwagon, but Curves suited Frances just fine. And today, she tackled her usual circuit with increased energy, pushing herself harder than she ever had. She wasn't sure why, but she felt strong this morning, positive and powerful. When she left the strip-mall location, she was sweaty and disheveled, but exhilarated. This must be what they called an endorphin rush. Frances rarely put in the effort required to achieve one.

Rather than going home to shower and change, she stopped at a grocery store on the way. She knew she looked a mess, but a rather healthy, active mess. There was a certain pride in being one of those workout people, vital and disciplined. And purchasing the tiramisu ingredients didn't take long. Frances whipped through the aisles, gathering eggs, cream, ladyfingers, and mascarpone cheese. Next, she drove to a specialty liquor store to pick up a bottle of Frangelico. The Italian liqueur was the secret to Frances's acclaimed dessert. Many people used Tia Maria or Kahlúa, which Frances considered pointless, given the strong taste of the espresso. The hazelnut flavor of the Frangelico added depth and complexity.

The store was high-end, with warm lighting, wide aisles, and a staff so knowledgeable they bordered on condescending. Frances politely turned down the owner's offer to help, the proffered taste of a Pinot Noir from an Oregon winery, and headed directly to the liqueur section. She quickly found the unique bottle (designed to look like a friar in his habit, complete with

belted middle) and plucked it from the shelf. As Frances turned
toward the till, she practically bumped into Jeanette Dumas.

Abbey Dumas's mother, dressed in a smart pantsuit and
holding a bottle of prosecco, looked as surprised and awkward
as Frances felt. Of course, they had encountered each other at
school since the "incident," but Jeanette's job (she was an effec-
tiveness consultant, or a leadership coach . . . something along
those lines) meant Frances was far more likely to see Abbey's
Australian nanny at pickup and drop-off. On the few occasions
when Frances had seen Jeanette, they were bobbing in a sea of
parents, students, and teachers; avoiding direct confrontation
had been easy.

But now they were alone, face-to-face, literally inches apart.
Ignorance was not an option.

"Jeanette . . . ," Frances began.

"Frances." The tall woman with her high cheekbones and
unlined dark skin was attractive in an authoritative, imposing
way. From her cropped hair to her rigid posture, everything
about Jeanette's aura said: *Don't fuck with me.* Or with her
daughter, as it turned out.

"Celebrating something?" Frances nodded at the expensive
prosecco clutched in the woman's hand.

Jeanette looked down at the bottle like she was noticing it
for the first time, then her narrowed gaze met Frances's. For the
briefest of moments, Frances feared the athletic woman was
going to haul back and crack her skull with the heavy glass ves-

sel. (The thought had to have occurred to the businesswoman; Frances couldn't be the only one who entertained such fantasies.) But instead, Jeanette gave a curt "No," before turning and walking away.

It could have been over then, but something (the serotonin surge from her exuberant circuit workout? The confidence gained from knowing that she had a friend and ally in Kate? A delayed psychotic episode from an experimentation with magic mushrooms in her twenties?) made Frances call her back.

"Jeanette . . ."

The woman paused, considering her options for several seconds, before finally turning to face Frances.

"I know that what my son did to your daughter was wrong," Frances said, her voice tremulous. "I know it was upsetting. For Abbey and for you. But Marcus is seeing a therapist now and . . . he's just a kid. I feel like this anger isn't healthy for anyone."

Jeanette's expression remained stony. "Marcus *peed* in my daughter's water bottle, Frances."

"Abbey was mean to him and he overreacted. Marcus understands that now. He's very sorry. We both are."

"Abbey *drank* Marcus's urine."

"It was just a sip. And it's not actually harmful. . . ."

"It was traumatic!" the woman screeched. "Abbey will be forever scarred by that incident! Don't you realize how sick it was?"

"Yes, but . . ."

What could Frances possibly say to assuage the woman's outrage? Should she relay the child psychologist's diagnosis? That Marcus had been hurt and angry, had wanted to lash out physically, but knew he couldn't hit, punch, or kick? That, in a way, urinating in the water bottle was evidence of self-control and strategic thinking? But Jeanette would not be impressed.

Perhaps Frances could mention that castaways drank urine all the time, as did lost hikers and plane crash survivors. Granted, it was usually their own urine, but still, they *purposely* drank it. But would that argument hold water with Jeanette? The pun struck Frances, and suddenly, the whole episode seemed unbelievably comical. She burst into nervous, hysterical, inappropriate laughter.

Jeanette's eyes bulged, and her mouth dropped open. She was rightly horrified by the insensitive reaction, but she quickly regained her composure. (Being a corporate trainer or a leadership mentor or whatever she was demanded significant self-possession.) The woman's eyes narrowed again, a snake, poised to strike.

"No wonder your son is so disturbed," she hissed. "You're a fucking lunatic."

I've really done it now, Frances thought—or at least, the lobe in Frances's brain that controlled logic had that thought. But even as she watched Jeanette march to the till, the fury coming off her in palpable waves, Frances couldn't stop laughing. In fact, she was afraid she might wet herself, right there, in the aisle of the liquor store. That would really top it off! The possibility made the whole scenario even more hilarious. Frances was doubled over, legs awkwardly crossed, when Jeanette Dumas gave her one final glare, then exited the store.

Abbey's mother was right. Frances was a fucking lunatic.

daisy

NOW

When the doorbell rang to announce their dinner guests, Daisy was setting out the "guest towels." The term was a label only; nary a guest's hands had touched the plush fabric. But she hung them on the towel rack, as ordered, and set the small, egg-shaped "guest soaps" in the soap dish.

As soon as she'd arrived home after school, Daisy had felt the taut energy pervading her home. She could hear the vacuum humming in another room, not an uncommon sound given her mom's obsession with cleanliness and order. But the way the nozzle was bumping into furniture, crashing into benches and colliding with end tables, was agitated, almost manic. Despite the emotional distance between them, Daisy was extremely sensitive to her mother's moods. She could feel the ululating ripples of stress emanating from Kate's person, hear them in each thud of the vacuum into another piece of furniture. A knot had formed at the base of Daisy's throat.

Dropping her school backpack near the front door, she had walked toward the kitchen. The vacuum was getting louder, its mosquito whine almost painful as she drew near. Kate didn't notice her daughter, so engaged was she in her harried cleaning. Daisy hovered in the entryway, watching her mom push the appliance aggressively through the kitchen. Their physical similarities were striking—practically everyone who met them commented on it—but mentally, emotionally, spiritually, they were so different.

Her mom must have sensed her presence (or read her mind), because she looked up then. "Good. You're here." She turned off the vacuum cleaner with her foot.

"What's going on?"

"We're having dinner guests."

"We are?" Daisy hadn't intended to sound so flabbergasted, but she was surprised. Kate and Robert didn't socialize, they didn't entertain. Her parents kept to themselves, not bothering to invest in friendships and connections that would eventually wither and die when they moved on, following her dad's legal work. Her family's sense of isolation had become the norm.

"Yeah, we are," Kate retorted. "I'd appreciate some help cleaning up this pigsty."

Daisy had stifled a smirk. The house was pristine, as always, orderly and sterile. "What do you want me to do?"

"Organize the front coat closet. And clean the guest bathroom."

The *guest bathroom*. Yeah, right.

"Okay," she agreed. Daisy took a step toward her room to change, but her mom's voice stopped her.

"Maybe you want to go out tonight? For dinner with a friend?"

"Why? Are you trying to get rid of me?"

"Of course not." Kate rolled her eyes. "But you'll be bored. Dad and I will be talking with Frances and Jason, and Charles will be playing with Marcus. I thought you'd prefer to spend time with people your own age."

Her mom was completely unaware that, by complimenting the taste of Liam Kenneway's butt, Daisy had effectively decimated all her friendships. Her peer group didn't know what to make of her comment. Was it a joke? Sarcasm? An admission? Mia and Emma had tried to stand by her, but Daisy hadn't made it easy for them.

"It was a joke, obviously!" Emma's voice had been shrill as she addressed the gaggle of girls holding a postmortem outside the school's front doors.

"She was being funny," Mia seconded. "She'd never do something that gross."

Daisy could have jumped in, could have stood up for herself. But she had walked by without a word, leaving her friends to deduce that she was a degenerate, a sexual deviant, and a

slut. As the chorus of aghast whispers rose behind her, Daisy
knew she had sealed her fate. It was too much to ask a bunch
of naïve ninth graders to accept that one of their own had done
something so *perverted*. Even the bad girls, the *easy* girls, didn't
do weird shit like that. Not at fourteen. Her group of admirers
would find someone else—someone normal—to idolize. Daisy
had been cast out. She was alone. The thought made her feel
oddly gratified.

"Sure." She addressed her mom. "I'll see if Emma and Mia
want to get sushi."

"Good." Kate turned the vacuum on. "Don't forget to put
out fresh hand towels."

Daisy's final task accomplished, she emerged from the pow-
der room to find her parents and brother milling at the front
door with a man, a woman, and Charles's inordinately large
friend Marcus: the Metcalfes. Her dad was hanging coats in the
recently organized closet, while her mom fluttered about, kissing cheeks and ruffling Marcus's mop of brown hair.

"There she is," her dad said, noticing Daisy's hovering presence. "Come meet our friends, Daisy."

The woman, Frances, smiled as she looked Daisy over. "Wow.
You look so much like your mom."

"I know."

"It's a compliment, by the way," Frances said, and Daisy wondered if she had sounded offended by the comparison. Tracking
Frances's gaze, she saw that the plump woman was looking over

at her mom. Daisy realized the clarifier was meant to flatter Kate, and it appeared to have worked. Her mom looked pleased, girlish, delighted. . . . She was practically blushing. Daisy couldn't remember the last time her mother had looked so pretty.

"Thanks," Daisy said, breaking the spell between the two women. "I get told that a lot."

"No one wants to look like their mom," Kate said, bestowing a warm smile on her daughter. To the uninitiated, Kate's affection appeared genuine; but Daisy knew better.

"Do you go to Forrester Academy?" the husband, Jason, asked.

"No, I go to Centennial. The public school."

"It's a good school," Frances observed.

"Daisy insisted," Kate jumped in. "We offered to send her to a private school, but her *principles*"—she did air quotes—"wouldn't allow it."

Robert put his arm around Daisy. "Our daughter believes education should be free for all. She's a *socialist*."

"As you should be at fourteen," Jason said.

"Until real life gets in the way," her dad added, and the adults laughed. Daisy felt excluded, subtly mocked. She pulled away from her father's arm.

"Mom, can Marcus and I go play in my room?" Charles asked. The kid asked permission for *everything*, like some obsequious, adolescent butler. No wonder Kate adored him.

"Of course," her mom said, keeping up the June Cleaver act. "I'll call you when dinner's ready."

Charles skittered out of the room with Marcus lumbering after him. Daisy had met the boy before—there had been a few playdates at their house—but she couldn't help but marvel at the child's enormity. He was an odd kid. She'd heard her parents discuss his issues: tantrums, meltdowns, lack of focus. . . . "But he *worships* Charles," her mom had said. "That kind of devotion is good for Charles's self-esteem."

"I've got to go," Daisy said.

Robert asked, "Where are you off to?"

"She's going for sushi with her friends," Kate answered quickly. Then, to her daughter, "Have fun." She couldn't wait to get rid of her.

"Nice to meet you both," Daisy said to Frances and Jason. The couple did seem pretty decent, even if they had bad taste in friends.

"Nice to finally meet you," Frances said. "Your mom talks a lot about you."

Daisy knew that wasn't true, but she smiled politely. "See you later." She opened the door and walked into the crisp November night.

No one asked when she'd be home.

She decided to ride her bike. It was cool and dark, but it wasn't raining. The bike had a light clipped to the front fender but only a reflector on the back. A small pool of light ushered her forward, but left her virtually invisible from the rear. It was unsafe and illegal, but that didn't bother Daisy as she rode down the narrow shoulder. There was almost no traffic in her subdivision, and there were definitely no cops around. Clyde Hill was too wealthy, too dull, too *dead* to require any law enforcement.

Daisy had no destination in mind as she pedaled, but with only fifteen dollars in her pocket, her options were limited. Just down the hill was the massive Bellevue Collection, a retail paradise of upscale shops, chain restaurants, department stores, and juice bars. But the place would be crawling with her peers. And Daisy hated shopping. She always felt claustrophobic in malls, like she was choking on the recycled air. Again, not a normal teenage girl.

She coasted down 92nd Avenue, the steeply sloping street that led to the commercial strip, but she continued on, bypassing the bustling shopping mecca. A plan had formed in her mind. She would buy a six-pack and find herself a secluded, solitary spot to have a few drinks. There was a Korean church in her neighborhood that had a covered alcove in its courtyard. It wouldn't be cozy, exactly, but it would be sheltered from the wind and any rain that decided to fall. And the booze would keep her warm. Tonight, she wanted to get messy, stupid, fucked-up. Why not? No one cared what she did anyway.

There was a strip mall on Bellevue Way: a 7-Eleven, a dry cleaner, a nail salon, and a furniture store. Daisy pedaled into the parking lot and stashed her bike behind the 7-Eleven. All the businesses were closed at this hour except the convenience store. Still, the parking lot was busy, customers stocking up on Friday night supplies: beer, chips, cigarettes. . . . An older man exited, giving Daisy a quick once-over as he held the door for her (ewww . . . he was practically her dad's age). She slipped inside.

The fluorescent lighting was almost painful after the dimness of the suburban night, the glare rendering the primary colors of the junk food packaging neon. With a quick glance toward the stoned-looking twenty-something at the counter, Daisy walked directly to the bank of fridges. She kept her gait confident, her gaze forward. Daisy didn't look twenty-one, she knew that, but she didn't look fourteen either. And in her experience, shop clerks (make that *male* shop clerks), given the right smile and a few flirtatious words, didn't care. She surveyed the beers, the cold white wines, the alcoholic ciders, until she found what she sought: vodka coolers. Grabbing a six-pack of something fruity, tropical, *girly*, she marched toward the till.

When she reached the counter, the stoner had been replaced by a man with brown skin, a heavy black mustache, and intense, dark eyes. Daisy didn't have the geographical knowledge or worldliness to identify his origins, but she would have guessed somewhere in Southeast Asia. (He was, in fact, a former attorney from Sri Lanka.) As soon as their eyes connected, she knew this guy would be immune to her charms. Shit.

"Can I help you?"

Daisy hesitated, for only a moment, before confidently plunking the six-pack on the counter. "And this," she said, grabbing a pack of strong mint gum and setting it next to the liquor.

"I.D." It was a command, not a question.

"Sure." She pulled out a small wallet from her jacket pocket and fished through it. "Darn. I think I left it in my other purse."

"No I.D., no alcohol."

"I'm twenty-one," she said. "Give me a break."

"No breaks."

"Come on," she pleaded. "Just this one time . . ."

The man slid the pink beverages toward her. "Put them back."

A deep male voice behind her said, "I'll get them."

Daisy glanced over her shoulder, right into the broad chest of a man. The guy was big, six-foot-two or three. He was standing very close to her, mere inches away. She felt too shy to look up at his face.

The clerk glowered up at him. "It is illegal to buy alcohol for minors."

"They're for me."

He was lying. Daisy knew it. The Asian man knew it, too, but he wasn't getting paid enough to take on a customer, especially one so large and authoritative. The clerk shook his head, muttering something about morals as he rang the six-pack through.

As the tall man paid cash for her drinks and gum and bought a pack of cigarettes for himself, Daisy sneaked a look at him.

He was in his mid-twenties, with messy dark hair, light brown eyes, and warm skin. He needed a shave and a haircut, but his unkempt appearance worked for him, made him seem rugged and manly. Observing the transaction, Daisy tried to suppress a smile, but it was working its way through her sophisticated façade. She felt precariously close to giggles, girlish and fluttery and very fourteen, standing so close to this large, adult stranger. Finally, the man grabbed his white plastic bag and left. Daisy hurried out after him.

He stopped as soon as they were outside the door, not bothering to make a show for the underage-drinking police at the till. "Here," he said, extracting his cigarettes and handing her the bag.

"Thanks," Daisy said, struggling to regain her mature affect despite her broad smile. "That was really cool of you."

"No problem." The man didn't return her grin.

Her heart thudded audibly in her chest as she mustered her courage. "Maybe you'd like to join me for a drink?" She held up the bag, and the pink wine coolers showed through the plastic. Shit. She should have bought beers.

The man looked at her intently for a moment. His eyes weren't really brown; they were more hazel, golden. They were cold, aloof, but somehow searing. Daisy felt afraid of him and drawn to him at the same time. "I—I'm twenty-one," she lied, hoping and dreading that he'd agree to join her.

He said nothing, just walked away from her.

Disappointment and relief mingled in her chest as she watched him cross the asphalt to the parking area. His gait was slow and deliberate, like he was in pain but was used to it. He was so strong, so masculine, so adult. Daisy's mind flitted to her make-out session with Liam, his narrow hips, his hairless chest, the soft fuzz on his upper lip. How could she ever have considered gifting that *boy* her virginity?

The man had reached his car, and Daisy fought the urge to run after him. For one thing, it would have been childish and uncool. For another, the guy could be dangerous. Daisy knew nothing about him except that he smoked and was willing to provide alcohol to a minor. Hardly a ringing character endorsement. She watched as he opened the door of a large, dark car and disappeared inside.

She was about to head to her bike when the car's engine rumbled to life. The sound stopped her cold. The taillights gleamed red as the big car backed out of its spot, turned, and then drove toward her. It was an old Buick or something—heavy, boxy, domestic. As it approached, Daisy inspected the hood and saw it: a small divot in the metal surrounded by a handful of scratches. Leaning down, she peered inside, but the man kept his eyes forward, like he'd already forgotten their encounter. But he hadn't. She knew he hadn't. As he drove away, she listened to the engine purr.

Like a mountain lion.

dj

*T*he arrest of his sister's killer did not bring the comfort and closure DJ had hoped for. His mom still spent days in bed, only emerging to dump out her overflowing ashtray (she'd resumed a pack-a-day habit when her daughter's body was found). His father still went to work every day at the meatpacking plant, but when he returned home, he sat in his tattered armchair and drank beer in silence. At school, DJ had become a pariah. The kids avoided him as if tragedy were contagious.

I invited him over one day, and then *my* sister was murdered!

DJ didn't mind; he had no interest in Power Rangers or Legos anymore. His dad had bought him a PlayStation shortly after Shane Nelson's arrest. His mom said a boy his age should be playing outside, breathing fresh air, experiencing nature. But his dad said it would "keep him out of our hair." And besides, there was no nature in their scorched Arizona suburb.

He was playing Tomb Raider that afternoon when a tall, distinguished black man arrived at their house. His name was Neil Givens, and he was the state prosecutor. His parents already knew this man, knew that his presence on their doorstep meant something crucial had happened with the case. There was a woman with him. She looked about the same age as DJ's mom, but, unlike his pale, wispy mother, this lady was strong and healthy and chewed gum aggressively. She was introduced as Detective Margot Williams. His parents quickly ushered the pair inside, inviting them to sit in the living room.

"Go to your room," his dad said absently, but DJ didn't. He'd gained weight when he'd stopped playing with his friends, choosing video games over socializing and physical activity. But, despite his girth, he had a knack for invisibility. He hovered, like a ghost, just outside the seating area, listening.

"What's going on, Neil?" his mother asked.

The prosecutor cleared his throat before he spoke. "An eyewitness has come forward in your daughter's murder."

DJ heard his mother's sharp intake of breath, heard her grab for her cigarettes and light one.

"Nelson's girlfriend was there," the female detective explained. "She saw everything he did to Courtney."

"She was there?" His father's voice was hoarse.

"Why didn't she do something?" his mom asked. "Why didn't she stop him?"

"She couldn't," Neil Givens said. "She was terrified of Nelson. He'd been physically and psychologically abusing her for over a year."

"When she came forward, she was black and blue," Detective Williams elaborated. "She had to do what Nelson told her, or she'd be beaten and raped. She was petrified. She was broken."

They pitied her, felt protective of her. DJ could hear it in their voices.

The attorney continued. "We've had the girlfriend examined by a team of psychiatrists. She shows signs of post-traumatic stress and battered-woman syndrome."

The detective picked up the slack. "Nelson tortured her. He beat her up. He kept her isolated, drunk, high, sleep-deprived. . . . He threatened to kill her family and friends."

"She's what we call a compliant victim," Givens said.

"What does that mean," DJ's dad grumbled, "a compliant victim?"

Detective Williams answered. "It means that she didn't want to hurt your daughter; in fact, she wanted to help her. But she couldn't. She was too afraid."

"My daughter was afraid!" DJ's mom cried. "My daughter was tortured and raped and murdered! And this . . . this girl watched it happen. Now she gets to walk away scot-free?"

"No," the prosecutor said, his voice calm, almost patronizing. "She'll be charged for her role in the crime. But with your approval, the state would like to agree to a plea bargain."

DJ's dad growled, "What kind of plea bargain?"

"She's willing to testify, to tell the jury everything Shane Nelson did to Courtney."

"He assaulted other girls, too," Detective Williams added. "He raped and beat them."

"This girl's testimony will ensure Nelson's put away for good." The lawyer paused here, and DJ could hear his own heart beating in the silence. "In exchange, her lawyer has convinced her to plead guilty to a charge of manslaughter."

"Her lawyer?" DJ's dad snapped. "If she's innocent, why does she have a lawyer?"

His mother's voice overlapped his dad's. "What does that mean? Manslaughter?"

The cop laid it out in quantitative terms. "It means max ten years. Minimum four."

"Four years?" DJ's mom shrieked. "Four years for watching my baby get tortured and raped and murdered? Four years for standing by and letting her die?"

"We'll push for the maximum sentence," the prosecutor offered. "She may serve the full term."

"My daughter will be dead forever!"

The female detective's voice was gentle. "This girl just turned twenty. She's a kid herself. I don't believe she could have stopped Shane Nelson. She wasn't strong enough, mentally or physically. . . . But she can stop him now."

"We have a lot of circumstantial evidence against Nelson," Neil

Givens added, "but it might not be enough. The girlfriend's testimony is crucial if we want to put him away for life."

"Which we do." Margot Williams stated the obvious.

No one spoke for a moment. The smack of the detective's gum and the puff of DJ's mom's cigarette filled the void.

"You're sure she wasn't in on it?" His dad's voice was quiet but angry. DJ felt angry, too, but he stayed silent, loitering unseen.

"She wasn't in on it." The female detective was adamant.

"Definitely not," Neil Givens affirmed.

"What's this girl's name?" His mother's voice was soft.

"Amber Kunik," the prosecutor replied.

Amber Kunik. *The girl who had watched his sister die.*

His father gave a heavy sigh. "Can we think about it?"

"Of course." DJ could hear them getting to their feet. He stepped farther back into the shadows as his parents walked their guests to the door.

Neil Givens spoke. "We'll need your answer within a couple of days."

The next day, his parents agreed to the deal.

frances

Sometime after dinner, it was suggested that Marcus should sleep over. Though he was eleven, Frances's son had never spent a night away from his mother, for obvious reasons. What if he had one of his tantrums? What if he needed Frances in the night? He still wet the bed on rare occasions. It would be humiliating for him if it happened on Charles's air mattress.

But Marcus had begged. "Pleeeeeease, Mom," he whined, plucking at her shirtsleeve as she sat at the dining table.

"You don't have your pajamas."

"He can borrow a pair from Charles," Kate said, like she hadn't noticed that Marcus was roughly double her son's size.

"They won't fit," Frances said.

"I'll sleep in my boxers," Marcus offered. "I do it all the time."

"You don't have your toothbrush."

Jason took his son's side. "His teeth won't fall out if he misses one night of brushing, Frances."

"He has an appointment with his physical therapist in the morning."

"Charles and I are early risers," Robert said. "I'll get the boys some breakfast and have Marcus home by eight-thirty."

"We'll take good care of him," Kate promised. "And you're not far away if he needs you."

Frances had run out of objections. Pushing her anxiety aside, she acquiesced. Her son's quick but warm hug of gratitude almost compensated for her sense of unease . . . almost. She and Kate had followed their sons upstairs to get them settled into bed.

When the comforting sounds of the boys' whispers and giggles had ceased, and their slumber could be safely assumed, Kate asked, "Dessert anyone?"

"Just a tiny sliver," Frances said, automatically. She'd been working so hard at her circuit training, and had been watching her carbs and sugar for almost two weeks. When she'd weighed herself (naked, before breakfast, coffee, or even water), she was down three pounds.

Kate disappeared into the kitchen, returning shortly with a mischievous grin and a small plastic bag containing two oatmeal cookies. Where was Frances's signature tiramisu?

Jason chuckled. "Are those what I think they are?"

"Yep," Robert said, a twinkle in his eye. "One of the benefits of moving to Washington State."

"Legal weed," Kate said, giving the bag of cookies a gentle shake.

"Thanks, but we don't smoke pot," Frances said. Even to her own ears, she sounded judgmental and uptight; a giant buzzkill.

Jason obviously thought so, too. "We used to," he said gamely.

Kate addressed Frances. "We don't either. Not really . . . But the kids are older now. It's legal. We thought it might be fun."

"I never really liked it," Frances said, which wasn't exactly true. She had quite enjoyed being stoned . . . but the associated munchies had put her up a dress size.

"This is a nice mellow indica," Robert said. "It's more of a body stone."

"In-da-couch," Jason said, affecting a weird, semi-Jamaican accent. He seemed quite keen to jump back on the cannabis wagon.

"It makes me feel relaxed and giggly," Kate said.

Relaxed and giggly sounded pretty great. "Okay . . . ," Frances said, smiling at her friend. "I'll try some."

Robert broke a cookie in half and handed a piece to Frances. "Start slow," he advised.

For almost an hour, Frances felt completely unaffected. Robert made tea, and as they sipped it, they chatted about the boys, about municipal politics, about a great foreign movie Robert and Kate had watched. Gradually, the pot took effect. For Frances, it felt like slipping into a warm jacuzzi. Her body felt heavy and relaxed, and the corners of her mouth twitched with amusement.

"The tiramisu!" Kate said, jumping up.

Jason stood, too. "Who needs water?"

"Yes, please." Frances was suddenly aware of a serious case of dry mouth. Her husband followed her friend into the kitchen, leaving Frances and Robert alone at the table.

"So . . . ," she said, scrambling to make conversation. Her brain wasn't firing on all cylinders, and her mouth felt like it was coated in fur. And what did a housewife and a big-shot legal consultant a decade older have to talk about, even when they weren't stoned? "What kind of consulting work do you do again?"

"Labor law," Robert said. "Kate thinks it's boring."

Frances smirked, remembering Kate's comment to that effect. She'd been almost sure that Kate had said her husband's field was environmental law, but she must have misheard.

"Kate said you used to work in human resources."

"For a few years."

"You must have some pretty funny stories."

"Yeah . . . ," she chuckled, "I sure do." But she didn't. Or if she did, she couldn't recollect any right now. Even if she could have summoned a humorous anecdote, her cottony mouth wouldn't have let her articulate it. Where was Jason with her water?

Leaning slightly to her left, she peered into the Randolphs' spacious kitchen. Everything was white and gleaming: cupboards, counters, the stack of plates set out for the forthcoming dessert. How did Kate keep everything so clean? Her model-thin friend was slicing up the tiramisu, her back to the dining area. Maybe it was the lighting, maybe it was the weed, but the scene looked almost surreal, like a picture from a magazine: a beautiful woman in an immaculate kitchen plating a decadent cake. And then Jason stepped into the frame.

He had the plastic container of dark chocolate curls that Frances had lovingly prepared with a vegetable peeler. Standing shoulder to shoulder with Kate, Jason sprinkled chocolate onto the dessert, his water-fetching errand abandoned. He turned slightly and said something—something witty, charming, funny—that made Kate giggle. Their hostess leaned in and whispered into Jason's ear. Frances felt her stomach churn. Kate and Jason looked good together, they looked right; an attractive couple sharing a private laugh as they prepped dessert for their older and overweight guests, abandoned in the dining room.

Suddenly, she couldn't swallow. She needed water, but Jason had forgotten all about his parched wife. He was too busy *garnishing* Kate's cake to worry about Frances choking to death in the other room. Her heart was beating erratically now. She stood, prompting Robert to ask, "Are you okay, Frances?"

She wasn't okay. Jealousy and insecurity were feelings that Frances knew all too well, but this was different. This was another level. She was freaking out! That's when she remembered the real reason she had stopped smoking dope all those years ago. It wasn't because the drug rendered her sluggish and lazy, depositing her on the sofa for hours, watching TV and eating bags of Doritos and ice cream straight from the tub. It wasn't the weight gain, the soft flab created by the lethargy, or the junk food–induced acne. It was the *paranoia*. Frances was already dealing with so many negative thoughts, so many twisted fantasies, so much self-doubt. . . . Why on earth had she agreed to eat that fucking cookie?!

Jason entered with two plates of Instagram-worthy tira-misu. "Dessert is served."

"Where's my water?" Frances snapped.

"Right here, hon." It was Kate, holding two tall glasses of ice water. She handed one to Frances, who drank it in audible gulps.

"You okay?" Jason asked. His eyes were glassy, but his expression was concerned.

"No," Frances said, "I'm not. We should go."

"Make some coffee," Robert said to Kate. "She's too high."

"Coffee doesn't bring you down," Kate responded. "I think you're supposed to drink orange juice."

Jason set the plates on the table. "In college, we used to chew peppercorns."

"Really?" Robert asked. "Did it work?"

"I don't remember."

"Frances, would you like some peppercorns?" Kate asked.

"No, thanks."

"We could sprinkle them on the tiramisu," Robert offered.

A loud snort of laughter erupted from Jason, and soon, he was doubled over. Kate and Robert quickly joined in, and Frances observed as her companions fell about in hysterics. Peppercorns on tiramisu . . . She supposed it was mildly amusing, but she was a little distracted by the fact that she was *dying*—from a heart attack, possibly, or a stroke—to join in the revelry. She was struggling to breathe now. She sipped some more water and waited for her spouse and hosts to compose themselves.

Finally, Jason wiped the tears of mirth from his eyes. Frances addressed him coolly. "I need to go home."

"Okay," he acquiesced, with a sigh.

"With Marcus."

The three adults exchanged a look. Uh-oh. . . .

"He's asleep," Jason said gently, like he was talking down a jumper. "And I'm too stoned to drive."

"I don't care," Frances said. The thought of leaving her son here, in this house full of drug-takers, made her heart palpitate. She loved Kate, and Robert was great, but they had just let their fourteen-year-old daughter walk out into the night without asking: *When will you be home? Where is the restaurant? Who are you going with?* Girls like Daisy were vulnerable, easy targets for rapists, drug dealers, human traffickers. . . .

"You can carry him home."

Jason had the audacity to laugh. "Sorry, babe," he said, noticing her umbrage, "but have you noticed the size of him lately?"

"I've got a wheelbarrow in the shed," Robert offered, indicating the backyard with his thumb. He remained straight-faced for a beat, before dissolving into giggles at the mental image of Marcus's bulky, sleeping body being wheelbarrowed down the street.

Jason seemed to find the notion equally hilarious. He was nearly breathless with laughter when he quipped, "Maybe we could rent a crane?"

"You guys . . ." Kate admonished them, pressing her lips together to maintain composure, as the two males lost it. Again.

Frances's voice was soft. "I need to be with my son," she said, feeling fretful and pathetic, but also determined. She would not, could not, leave Marcus here tonight. The THC was amplifying her anxiety, she knew that, but she had also known that she wasn't ready. She had been pressured and cajoled into agreeing to the sleepover, and now, she realized . . . she couldn't do it.

No one, not even Jason, knew what was at the root of Frances's discomfort. She'd always been a protective (perhaps overprotective) mother, but it was seen as par for the course. A child like Marcus required intense parenting. But the boy, despite his myriad issues, seemed confident and ready to spend a night away from his mom. It was Frances who was not ready. She knew the terrible things that could happen to children when they weren't protected. She would not, could not, let anything happen to her son. This was about her issues alone.

"I have an idea," Kate said, taking Frances's hand and leading her away from the two men, still tittering like schoolgirls.

"Where are we going?"

Kate said nothing as she led her friend through the living room and up the stairs. When they reached the silent second floor, Kate pushed open a door directly opposite Charles's bedroom. "You'll sleep here," she said, "in Daisy's room."

"What about Daisy?"

"I'll make a bed for her on the couch. She watches TV half the night anyway."

"Are you sure?"

"Of course," Kate said, gently pushing her into the room.

Daisy's enclave was feminine, adolescent, messier than the rest of the house, but not by much. Kate directed Frances toward the bed, tidily made with a lilac duvet and numerous complementary throw pillows, and helped her lie down on it. As soon as Frances's body sank into the comfort of the bedding, she realized how tired she was. The paranoia had been successfully diverted, and now she wanted to sleep.

Kate perched on the bed beside her. "I'll set an alarm," she said, laying an afghan over her friend. "You can get up early and Marcus will never know you were here."

It was the perfect solution. Marcus would have his taste of independence, but Frances would be right across the hall if he needed her. Only one thing still bothered her. . . .

"In the kitchen . . . What did you whisper to Jason?"

Kate's brow furrowed, as she struggled to remember. "I think I just said how lucky he is to have a wife who can make tiramisu. I've never been able to bake."

Relief and gratitude welled up inside Frances. She should have known that Kate would never betray her. "Thank you," she said, her words slurring together as the sedative effect of the marijuana took over. "You are such a good friend."

Kate stroked Frances's hair and smiled down at her, loving and maternal. "*You're* the good friend, Frances. I'm so lucky to have you."

Frances had heard about this kind of friendship: intense, powerful, life-altering. Such friendships were unique to women, a bond as profound and meaningful as sisterhood. It wasn't sexual, but it felt like falling in love, like she and Kate were soulmates who had finally found each other. God, she would have considered the notion so corny, inappropriate even, prior to Kate. But now, it felt beautiful. And right. She hadn't even realized how lonely and isolated she had been. Frances let her heavy lids close. Warm and content, she drifted off to sleep.

dj

The trial of Shane Nelson for the murder of Courtney Carey began on August 5, 1997. DJ had begged to be allowed to attend, and, eventually, he had worn his parents down. It was school holidays, so he didn't have to miss any classes. And he would be thirteen soon. He was old enough to look into the face of his sister's killer.

Shane Nelson sat in the prisoner's box, appearing strangely complacent, almost amused, as a parade of witnesses testified against him. For weeks, his friends and colleagues had affirmed that he was violent, a sexual deviant, that they had seen him do cruel and inhuman things. The prosecution called the hiker who had found Courtney's broken and battered body, the coroner who had performed the autopsy, a psychiatrist, and a string of detectives and inspectors who had found Courtney's hair in Nelson's car, his DNA under her fingernails. (DJ learned that his sister had been douched with a bleach solution. No semen was found.) Through it all, Nelson remained unperturbed. Why wasn't he worried? Why wasn't he afraid?

It wasn't until Neil Givens called Amber Kunik to the stand that DJ saw Nelson's composure falter. The defendant's face darkened with repressed rage. Or maybe it was fear? As Amber entered the courtroom, Nelson turned toward her, revealing his profile. DJ watched the prisoner, analyzing his expression. It was pure, unadulterated hatred.

The courtroom was packed that day, everyone desperate to get a glimpse of the prosecution's star witness. Spectators had lined up for hours to obtain one of the 119 seats in the gallery. At least a hundred people had been turned away. The media had latched onto Amber Kunik ever since her identity had been revealed, and they had created a narrative: a pretty but damaged girl fallen under the spell of a sadistic Svengali.

She was calm and composed as she made her way to the witness box, demure in a skirt and blouse, her shiny dark hair pulled back from her face. When she was sworn in, her voice was soft, girlish, innocent. . . . As Amber Kunik took her seat, a hush fell over the proceedings. DJ had glimpsed her on TV, seen photos in the newspaper, but they hadn't prepared him to see her in the flesh. In this drab setting, surrounded by these grim, middle-aged faces, she looked delicate and beautiful.

Before Prosecutor Givens could present his case, the judge addressed the four women and eight men who comprised the jury.

He was an older man with a long, rectangular face that made DJ think of Frankenstein's monster.

"This witness has entered into a plea bargain with the prosecution in exchange for her testimony against Mr. Nelson," Justice Calder said, in a sonorous voice appropriate to his visage. "Under circumstances like these, witnesses often minimize their own role in the execution of the crimes."

The jury nodded that they understood, but they couldn't keep their eyes off Amber Kunik. No one could, not for long anyway.

Neil Givens began by establishing the witness's relationship to the man on trial. Shane and Amber had dated for almost two years, had lived together for fourteen months. The lawyer's tone was gentle, coaxing. Amber seemed so young, so fragile, like she might shatter under any kind of overt pressure. The prosecutor nudged Amber to tell her story.

"Shane wanted a girl," Amber said, in her childlike voice. "I had to help him find one."

"Did Shane tell you why he wanted a girl?"

"He wanted to have sex with her," Amber said. "And he wanted me to have sex with her while he watched."

A low murmur emanated from the spectators. The judge silenced them with a look.

"And where did you find Courtney Carey?" the prosecutor continued.

"She was at the Dairy Queen. She was alone, and she seemed kind of upset."

DJ felt his father tense, on his left. On his right, his mother vibrated with repressed emotion.

"I think she was having a Blizzard," Amber said. "That's how I started talking to her. She was having an Oreo Blizzard and that's my favorite kind, too."

"And mine," the prosecutor said. The gallery chuckled and Amber smiled. DJ wanted to punch Neil Givens for joking with this girl, to scream at the audience for laughing. His sister's murder was not fucking funny.

"I invited her to come smoke a joint with Shane and me," Amber recounted. "She seemed really excited to get stoned. And she liked me, I could tell. She trusted me."

His mom covered her mouth to muffle her sobs. DJ rubbed her back ineffectually. His dad remained still, but a muscle in his jaw twitched.

"How did you and Mr. Nelson get Courtney back to your house?" Neil Givens asked.

"Well, we all smoked up together in Shane's truck, and then Shane said we should have some drinks. Courtney said she liked wine coolers, and that's also what I like to drink. We had that in common . . . like the Oreo Blizzards."

She sounded like a kid, even though she was twenty.

"So, we bought some peach-flavored coolers, and a bottle of Jack for Shane, and then he drove us back to our house."

"And what happened when you got there?"

Amber's eyes flitted toward DJ and his family. They may have connected, briefly, with his mother's, but they promptly returned to the prosecutor. "Shane gave me some pills. I think they were Valium. I crushed them up and put them in Courtney's drink."

"And then?"

"Courtney got really tired and she puked a bit. I told her she could lie down on the sofa. I put a blanket on her and she fell asleep."

"And what did you and Shane do while she slept?"

"I performed oral sex on her while Shane watched."

DJ and his parents were too stunned to react, but the gallery erupted in a chorus of gasps and whispers. It was less the content than the blasé tone of voice that had set them off. Amber didn't sound like a kid anymore, she sounded clinical and detached. She sounded heartless. Judge Calder banged his gavel, trying to quell the whispers of outrage, the murmurs of disgust.

"Order!" he boomed. "Any spectators who can't remain quiet will be removed!"

This got the crowd to settle. No one wanted to miss what came next. When calm had been restored, Neil Givens continued his questioning.

"Why did you perform that sex act on Courtney Carey?"

"I had to. Shane would beat me if I didn't do what he wanted."

"Did Mr. Nelson abuse you in other ways?"

Amber Kunik's eyes filled with tears and her voice trembled. She had become that vulnerable little girl again. "He would yell at me and call me horrible names. He said I was worthless, that I came from trash. He enjoyed hurting me. He enjoyed humiliating me. I was living in hell."

DJ watched Shane Nelson scribble a note and slide it along the table to his lawyer. The defense counsel, Martin Bannerman, was thick and beefy, with the flat-faced look of a former boxer. Bannerman's expression was aggressive, his posture tense, like at any moment he was going to spring out of his chair and object. But he didn't. He remained seated, mute, glancing at the scribbles his client presented to him, listening to Nelson's murmured comments.

The prosecutor continued, in the same gentle, coaxing manner. "And what did you witness Mr. Nelson doing to Miss Carey?"

That matter-of-factness returned to Amber's tone as she described Nelson's vile and repugnant actions. DJ could feel his mother trembling beside him; his dad reached across him to squeeze her hand. DJ wanted to take his mom's free hand and drag her out of the courtroom. He wanted to stand up and yell at this pretty girl to stop saying these violent, obscene things in her nonchalant, almost bored voice. But if he disrupted the courtroom, he wouldn't be allowed back in. And he had to be there.

"And then, I guess Shane got bored of her." Amber looked down, and her voice softened. "He said we had to get rid of her."

"Bullshit!" Nelson blurted.

The gallery dared to whisper after this outburst. A strangled noise escaped from DJ's father's throat, while his mother shivered in silence.

Judge Calder looked down on the witness. "Would you like to take a break?"

"I'm fine," the girl said, bestowing on him a grateful smile. And she was fine. Amber Kunik was completely comfortable relaying the horrifying details of DJ's sister's torture, rape, and murder. She only sounded small and broken when she talked about her own abuse.

But the judge looked at DJ, at his mother and father. They were not fine. They were not fine at all. He banged his gavel.

"We'll recess for today."

frances

NOW

When Frances awoke in the darkened room, she was momentarily discombobulated, but it took only a few seconds to recognize her girlish surroundings. The digital clock glowed 5:42 a.m., and the events of last night flooded back to her. She was in Daisy's room. Marcus was sleeping peacefully across the hall. At least, he should be. Frances's cannabis intake could have rendered her comatose last night. If her son had called out for her, would she have awoken?

She scrambled out of Daisy's bed and scurried across the hall. Cracking the door to Charles's room, she peered inside. In the predawn light, she could just make out the large lump on the floor that was her son's sleeping form. Frances could hear his heavy, nasal breathing as he slept deeply, soundly. With a quick glance at Charles, curled up in a fetal position on his single bed, she closed the door behind her.

On silent feet, she crept down the stairs to the main floor. She would find her purse and her tiramisu pan and be gone before anyone awoke. Marcus would rise with a newfound confidence and independence, never knowing his mother had spent the night just fifteen feet away. A small light over the stove glowed. The spacious kitchen was pristine: Kate and Robert must have cleaned before retiring. Her pan, washed and dried, sat on the bare counter. Now where was her purse?

She recalled setting it down when she entered the home last night, perhaps next to the couch in the living room? Padding to the front of the house, she found the blinds closed and the room pitch-dark. Pausing in the entryway, she waited for her eyes to become accustomed to the lack of light.

"Hey." The voice—young, female, sleepy—came from the sofa. It was Daisy, displaced by Frances, lying on her makeshift bed in the living room.

"I'm sorry to wake you," Frances apologized. "I'm looking for my purse."

"I think it's by the chair." The girl pointed.

Frances followed her direction and retrieved her bag from its spot on the floor. "Thanks, Daisy," she whispered. Her vision having adjusted, she noticed the girl was still fully clothed, her jacket draped over her in lieu of a blanket. Kate must have forgotten to prepare her daughter's camp. "I'm sorry I took your bed last night."

"It's okay."

"I wasn't feeling well, so your mom suggested I lie down for a bit," Frances fibbed. "And then I fell asleep."

"My mom said you were sleeping here because you weren't comfortable being away from Marcus."

Frances felt a stab of betrayal. She had thought Kate understood her insecurities, had expected her to cover for her. She felt embarrassed at being caught in a lie.

"Yeah," she admitted. "I guess I'm too overprotective."

"Not really," Daisy said. "I think parents *should* care where their kids are." There was an edge to her voice, and Frances thought about last night. Kate and Robert had let their fourteen-year-old wander off into the dark, without even asking where she was going, how she was getting there, when she'd be home. Frances moved closer.

"Did you have a nice dinner with your friends?"

"I didn't go for dinner." It must have been the darkness between them that created a confessional aura, because the girl continued. "And I don't have friends."

Frances perched on the arm of the sofa, near Daisy's feet. "Where did you go?" she prodded gently.

"I just rode around on my bike."

"That's not very safe, Daisy."

"Maybe not," she said, with an indifferent shrug, "but it turned out fine."

"There are predators out there, men who look for girls on their own, girls who are lost and alone."

"I can take care of myself," the girl retorted. Frances backed off, took a different tack.

"Why do you feel like you don't have any friends?"

"Because I don't," Daisy said flatly. "There was this thing with a boy. . . . Nothing happened, but he told everyone that it did, that I was a crazy nympho or something. And I just let everyone believe it."

"Why?" Frances was flummoxed. "Why didn't you defend yourself?"

"I don't know. . . . I wanted to push everyone away. I wanted to be alone." The girl's voice trembled. "I think there's something wrong with me."

Frances slipped off the arm of the sofa and sat near Daisy's knees. She could see the girl's eyes, shining with unshed tears, in the dark. "There's nothing wrong with you, Daisy. High school is hard. Life is hard. But you have a family that loves you, and in the end, that's all that really matters."

Daisy's voice was quiet. "You don't really know us."

"I know your mom," Frances said, with a hint of indignation. Though it had only been a couple of months, she knew her friendship with Kate was deep and genuine.

"You might think you do."

Frances didn't respond. Daisy was angry with her mom and trying to disparage her. The girl probably resented her parents for making her move, for fostering new friendships while Daisy was being ostracized. Mother-daughter issues were common, especially in the teen years. Frances's relationship with her own mother was still tense, having never fully recovered from the horrific crisis they'd endured. Frances had needed her mom then, but the woman had emotionally abandoned her. Frances didn't blame her, after what Frances had done, but the desertion still stung. She understood Daisy's angst.

"I know your mom loves you," Frances finally said, not based on anything Kate had said or demonstrated, but because all parents loved their children. It was the most basic human instinct.

Daisy said nothing, and Frances was suddenly unsure how to fill the awkward silence. "I should go," she said, patting the girl's denim-clad knee. "If you ever need someone to talk to, I'm always here."

The girl sat up a little. "Do you mean that?"

There was something so needy, so intense, in the child's voice that Frances hesitated, for half a second, before she said, "Of course I do. I remember what it's like to be your age. Here . . ." She reached down and picked up the girl's phone from the floor next to the sofa. "Put my number in your phone."

Daisy tapped the digits into her contacts. "Thank you," she said, setting the device next to her. "That means a lot."

Frances gave Daisy's leg a squeeze and stood. "Go back to sleep," she whispered, making her way toward the door. As she was stepping into her shoes, Daisy's voice came through the darkness.

"Please don't tell my mom that we talked."

"I won't," Frances said automatically. She knew how to keep secrets.

The predawn walk home was silent, peaceful; even the constant hum of the freeway was muted at this hour. Frances's house was a fifteen-minute stroll from the Randolphs' neocolonial home. It wasn't until she reached it that she realized she didn't have a house key. Jason had driven them there and must have driven himself home once the effects of the marijuana had worn off. There was a spare key hidden in the backyard, under a metal watering can, but picking her way down the overgrown path beside the house in the dark, and rummaging through the yard in search of it, was a recipe for a twisted ankle at least. She rang the doorbell; she had no choice.

After several minutes, a light flicked on inside, and she could see her husband's mussed hair in the glass panes at the top of the door. It swung open to reveal Jason, in his dark blue robe, rumpled from sleep. He looked groggy and mildly perturbed.

"I'm sorry to wake you," Frances said, hurrying in out of the chilly morning. "I didn't have a key."

"It's okay," he grumbled.

"Go back to bed," she said, kissing his cheek. "It's still early."

Jason stretched his arms overhead. "I'm up now. I'll make coffee."

Her husband shuffled to the kitchen as Frances removed her shoes and draped her coat over the banister near the door.

She took a moment to survey her abode. In contrast to the Randolphs' spacious, tasteful, and orderly home, the Metcalfe residence was small, cluttered, and chaotic. Their neutral sofa, sagging in the middle, the cushions fraying around the seams, housed two of Marcus's hoodies and a blanket yanked from Frances and Jason's bed. A dark wood coffee table was almost invisible under its toupee of remotes, mugs, video game cartridges, and spare change. The television sprouted a plethora of tangled cords attached to an Xbox and a number of other consoles, including a DVD player. (When was the last time they had watched a DVD? 2005?) On the floor, near her feet, an immersion blender, in its box, sat waiting to be returned to the store. Scrutinizing the mess, Frances suddenly felt motivated to get things in order, to de-clutter and pare down.

But first . . . coffee.

The late-autumn sun would not rise for another half hour, and with it, their boy would return home. Frances and her husband sat at their small kitchen table (one end relegated to unread newspapers, fitness magazines, school forms, and bills) and sipped their caffeine. They were both quiet and bleary, Jason in his robe, Frances in her slept-in clothing, drinking in silence. Finally, Jason spoke.

"What was that about last night?"

"What?"

"Marcus is eleven, Frances. He's old enough to spend the night at a friend's. Especially when we know the parents."

Frances nodded. She knew he was right, rationally. But feelings weren't rational, they were *feelings*. That didn't make them wrong.

"Our son has a few issues, but what kid doesn't?"

"*Issues?* He tried to get a classmate to drink his pee."

"When I was in seventh grade, Andrew Turnmill took a dump in a Girl Guide cookie box and planted it in our teacher's desk."

"Ewww."

"I know. . . . But he turned out okay, in the end. I think he manages a Whole Foods in Denver."

"Remind me not to shop there."

"Marcus made a mistake and he understands that now. We don't have to treat him like a toddler or a . . . breakable china doll." Jason touched her fingers. "Why won't you let him grow up?"

Her partner was staring at her, and she met his slightly bloodshot gaze. Looking into his sleepy, handsome face, she was tempted to tell him the truth. It would all make sense once he knew what she had been through, the pain and the ugliness and the guilt. It would be a relief to stop pretending, to stop hiding what she'd done. But she couldn't risk it. Jason was too kind, too good, too moral. If he knew who she really was, he would leave her. He could never find out.

"I was just stoned and paranoid," she said. "I'm not going near pot again."

"Good plan."

"What went on after I went to bed?"

"Not much." Jason sipped his coffee, his dark eyes avoiding hers.

"What?" she pressed.

"Nothing. I just . . . got a weird vibe off Kate."

"What kind of weird vibe?"

"It was like she was flirting with me. Right in front of Robert. It was pretty uncomfortable."

It was not uncommon for women to flirt with Frances's attractive husband, but it *was* uncommon for him to notice. Jason, despite his swarthy good looks, was largely oblivious of his effect on other females.

"Did Kate say something? Do something?"

"Not really. It was just a vibe."

Frances thought about the moment she'd witnessed between Kate and Jason in the kitchen. Her friend had assured her it was innocent. Her mind flitted to that day at the waterfront restaurant. Kate had flirted so effortlessly with those salesmen, had even seemed to be flirting with Frances at one point.

"I think Kate's just the flirty type," she said. "How did Robert react?"

"He didn't seem bothered by it. In fact, he seemed cool with it."

"You probably misread the signals. Because you were stoned."

"I guess." He stood with his empty coffee cup. "Or maybe Robert and Kate are swingers."

"They're not *swingers*," Frances retorted. She considered herself a progressive, open-minded person. What consenting adults did behind closed doors was up to them. But she wasn't entirely comfortable with her BFF being a swinger. Especially if her swinging sights were set on Frances's husband.

Jason placed his mug in the sink. "I'm going to shower."

"Okay. I'm going to tackle some of this mess."

"Really?" Her husband looked mildly amused.

"What?"

"Nothing." He kissed the top of her head then shuffled toward the stairs.

Frances had just started sorting the stack of papers into piles—*file, chuck, action required*—when a text arrived from Kate.

Hey early bird. Just having pancakes. Will bring Marcus home in 10 mins.

Frances texted back:

Thanks for having him. And for letting me stay over.

The response came.

No problem. The boys had a great time and Marcus has no idea you were here.

Frances smiled, gratitude forming a lump in her throat. Jason had to have imagined Kate's flirtation. Kate would never do that to Frances. Her spouse had gotten his signals crossed. They would both stay away from pot in the future. She typed:

You're the best!

When the doorbell rang, twelve minutes later, it was Robert with a bubbly Marcus full of details of pancakes and video games and ghost stories. He was hyped up on gluten and glucose, but Frances didn't mind. It was good to see her son happy, enjoying a normal rite of passage: the sleepover. The boy hurried inside, leaving his distinguished chauffeur and his mom lingering at the door. Frances was painfully aware of the slovenliness of both her appearance and her surroundings, as Robert loitered.

"Thanks so much, Robert. For dinner and for having Marcus."

"Our pleasure. That was a fun night."

"Too bad I was asleep for half of it."

"Yeah."

"We'll have you guys over soon," Frances said, pushing the immersion blender box farther behind the sofa with her foot.

"We'd like that," Robert said, and he sounded genuine. Genuine, but not remotely flirtatious. Of course, the attorney would never be attracted to Frances in her current state. She was still in her rumpled clothes, with bed head and smudged makeup. But even at her best, Robert would not be interested. Why would he ever want Frances when he had Kate?

"Have a nice day, Frances."

"You, too." She watched him jog down the steps to his Audi.

daisy

Daisy sat in math class, staring blankly at the whiteboard. The teacher, Ms. Watson, was taking them through exponents, and Daisy was absorbing exactly none of it. Her thoughts were fixed on the big, intimidating man who had bought her those vodka coolers. She couldn't stop thinking about his penetrating gaze, his strong, masculine body, his slight limp as he walked across the parking lot. She couldn't forget his loud, muscular car with the dent and scratches on the hood from the rock she'd thrown that night when he had sat there, inside it, watching her. Why had he been there? Who was he?

When she had corroborated Liam Kenneway's story, she had sealed her fate. By admitting to something so disgusting (seriously, the thought of licking any part of Liam's anatomy, let alone his *anus*, was extremely distasteful), she had become persona non grata at Centennial High. Some would see it as a death sentence, but Daisy was trying to put a positive spin on it. She had set herself free. Free from the high school popularity treadmill, free from the hamster wheel of social jostling and positioning, free to explore new, more adult relationships. . . . If only she could find him.

But that seemed impossible. She knew nothing about the man except a general description of his car—old, big, loud—and a partial license plate: 820 GK. . . . She'd had the presence of mind to remember it as he drove away, not that it helped any. A fourteen-year-old girl could hardly stroll into the DMV and ask them to "run the plates." Daisy feared she would have to wait for him to find her again. She felt certain that he would—there was an intangible connection between them that went far beyond coincidence—but when? The waiting was torture.

The bell rang, and Ms. Watson barked out some homework assignment that Daisy ignored. Gathering her books, she moved through the crowded hallway, enduring a handful of sniggers and an armload of averted eyes. At her locker, she grabbed her jacket and her backpack and slammed the door closed. She could no longer linger after school, making small talk, joking around. She was the joke now. Though she was reluctant to go home, it had become her refuge.

The November sky was ominous, a capacious gray pillow stuffed with raindrops desperate to fall. A collapsible umbrella was nestled in the bottom of her backpack. Daisy paused outside the main doors, unzipped her bag, and dug for the compact tube. She wouldn't make it home before the skies opened. But she stopped rummaging when she heard it: the familiar rumble of that big car starting up, the sound now seared into her memory. Looking toward the parking lot, she saw the vehicle. And through the windshield, she saw the man.

For a moment, she wondered if it was a coincidence. He might be picking up a niece or nephew; he might be dating a teacher (God, no!). But she knew he was there for her. When she met his gaze, he grinned. It was slight, barely there, but it was enough. He had dimples, adorable but incongruous with his masculine face. As she walked toward him, she realized it was the first time she had seen him smile.

Somehow, she maintained her composure, strolling across the lot. She wanted to run, to skip, a child hurtling toward Santa Claus. But she didn't want to appear puerile. And she didn't want to attract the attention of her schoolmates . . . although, what did she care? She was already *Daisy, the ass-licker*; may as well add *Daisy, the girl who gets in a car with a strange guy who's twice her age* to her title.

She opened the door and climbed in. Without a word, or even a look, the man backed the heavy car out of the parking spot and drove toward the street. Daisy sat, rigid, as the man waited for a break in after-school traffic, doting parents chauffeuring their teenagers to soccer or piano or home to pizza pockets and video games. When the car finally pulled onto the road, Daisy was pressed back in her seat by the surge of power from the massive engine.

They traveled several blocks in silence before the man spoke. "I guess you failed a couple grades."

"What?" She glanced over at him, saw a glimmer of humor.

"You're twenty-one, but you're still in high school."

Daisy felt her cheeks get hot. She stared straight ahead. "I'm eighteen," she lied. "Twelfth grade."

In her periphery, she saw the man nod slowly. She couldn't tell if he believed her.

"Where are we going?" she asked.

"I'm giving you a lift home. It's going to rain."

As if he controlled the skies, fat raindrops escaped their cloud enclosure and plopped down onto the windshield. He turned on the wipers.

"Do you know where I live?" she asked, glancing over at him. She didn't want to go home, not yet. She had waited so long to see him. She wanted him to take her somewhere, anywhere, just not home.

"You live in Clyde Hill. I saw you walking that night."

"Yeah. On Twenty-Sixth Street." She had to ask. "What were you doing there?"

"Visiting a friend."

"Right." *Then how did you find me at the 7-Eleven? How did you know what school I attend? Have you been following me? Watching me? Who are you?* But she wouldn't interrogate him.

She said nothing, just listened to the wiper blades slapping rhythmically against the windshield. Daisy wanted to look over at him, to examine him, imprint him on her brain, but she was too afraid.

As he guided the powerful car up the 92nd Avenue hill, he said, "I'll drop you off a block from home, so your parents don't freak out."

"They don't care."

"Really?" She felt his eyes on her. "Your parents don't mind you getting a ride home with a stranger?"

She looked at him then. "Nope."

"They don't care about you?"

"My mom doesn't. My dad cares a bit."

"Poor little rich girl," he teased.

Daisy hated being mocked, loathed condescension. But she couldn't get angry, couldn't risk scaring him off. Still, she needed to respond, to clarify at least.

"We're not rich," she said. "Like, we have a nice house and nice cars and stuff, but we never take fancy vacations. We don't have a boat or anything. My mom doesn't even work and my dad's a consultant. I don't even know if he makes any money anymore."

The man said nothing. He turned right onto 24th and charged down the wide street before hanging a left on 96th Avenue. When they were precisely a block from her home, he pulled over, but left the engine running.

"Thanks for the ride," Daisy said. She sat still in her seat, didn't reach for the door handle. She wanted him to say something, to ask to see her again, ask her name, her number, anything . . . but he didn't. When the silence became too awkward, too disheartening, she opened the door and got out of the car.

"Want to get a drink sometime?" He had been toying with her.

"I'm eighteen," she retorted. "I can't go to bars."

"We can have a drink at my place."

She had been playing with fire, and now she was about to go up in flames. "Okay," she said.

Pushing through the tremors in her voice, she gave the man her number.

dj

THEN

*A*mber Kunik's testimony went on for four days. The state's attorney kept the pretty brunette on the stand, where, in her relaxed, measured voice, she told the court every vile act that she and Shane Nelson had performed on Courtney. Amber's candid descriptions of the abuses heaped on DJ's sister—the beatings, the sodomy, the degradation—made him want to vomit. His mother wept softly. His father sat silent and stoic, but he was withering, like Amber's words were a cancer, eating him alive.

At regular intervals, Neil Givens would ask Amber, "Why did you do that to her?"

"Shane made me do it."

"I was afraid Shane would beat me."

"I had to make Shane happy."

Occasionally, Martin Bannerman would object to something

the prosecutor said, but mostly he just listened. Shane Nelson continually leaned in to whisper in his attorney's ear and scribbled copious notes for his pained representative. DJ wanted to know what they said. He strained his ears and eyes, but the defendant was too far away.

On the fifth day, DJ and his parents woke at 7 a.m., got dressed, and prepared to go to court as usual. They were eating cereal when the phone rang. His mother answered. After a few moments, she hung up.

"That was Detective Williams," she said, her pale features twisted with concern. "She and Neil are coming over. They've got something to tell us."

"Aren't we going to the trial?" DJ asked.

"Recessed today."

His parents exchanged a look: worry, dread. DJ wasn't sure why. The worst had already happened.

Or had it?

frances

On Sunday, Robert and Jason took the boys to a Seahawks game. At first, Frances had objected—it was too expensive, Marcus would be overstimulated—but both her husband and son were incredibly excited, and Robert had gotten some sort of *deal* on tickets through a colleague. (Frances privately wondered if there really was a connected colleague or if Robert was subsidizing the ticket price himself.) Ultimately, she didn't have the heart to object.

Kate was coming over today. They were going to put on the football game to see if they could spot the boys in the crowd, though Frances knew they'd be so engrossed in conversation that they could easily miss them. Frances had relegated Jason's flirting suppositions to a dusty room in the back of her mind and closed the door on them. She'd seen Kate several times since the dinner party, and her friend had acted perfectly nor-mal. If Kate had really come on to Frances's husband, surely there would be some residual awkwardness? Even Jason agreed: he must have misread Kate's behavior.

Her companion was due any minute. Frances surveyed the state of her living room. She had made a significant dent in the clutter as of late, and had invested in some cheap but colorful throw pillows for the worn, beige sofa. An expensive bouquet (Frances knew a discount florist) perched on a side table, brightening the room with its out-of-season blossoms. The coffee table was laden with their football party snacks: a large bowl of tortilla chips, a seven-layer bean dip (made with low-fat everything—she hoped Kate couldn't tell); a plate of buffalo wings (Frances would allow herself one); and a bowl of cheese-and-caramel popcorn, just for whimsy. It wasn't as good as Kate's pristine house or her magazine-worthy spread of food, but it would do. When the doorbell rang signaling her pal's arrival, Frances hurried to answer it.

"We're making margaritas!" Kate said, as she swept into the room, bottles clinking together in the canvas tote she was car-rying.

"Sounds great," Frances said, taking the bag from her guest. "I've got beer and wine, too."

Kate was removing her coat, but she stopped. "I hand-squeezed twenty limes. There will be no beer or wine." Frances laughed, and led the way to the kitchen.

Earlier that morning, Frances had hidden all her countertop appliances in the oven, leaving a clean, uncluttered space for bartending. Kate dug in the bag and removed a bottle of golden tequila, another of Cointreau, and a glass jar of bright green lime juice.

"What a morning," Kate said, as Frances grabbed ice, rocks glasses, and a box of salt. "I need a drink."

"What happened?"

"I was vacuuming Charles's bedroom and I accidentally sucked up his gerbil."

"Oh, no!"

"I don't know how the little bugger got out of its cage," Kate said, rubbing a lime wedge around the rim of a glass. "I always tell Charles to keep the door latched."

Frances poured salt onto a saucer. "Was it okay?"

"It was alive, but I think its back was broken." Kate turned the glass upside down in the salt. "It was squeaking and wriggling, but it couldn't stand up or walk."

"Oh god, what did you do?"

"I finished him off and went and bought a new one."

Finished him off?

"I put it in a plastic bag and smashed it on the pavement." Kate clocked her friend's horrified expression. "It was suffering, Frances. It was the humane thing to do."

Of course it was. But the thought of crushing that tiny creature on the driveway made Frances cringe. Despite what she had done, despite what she had witnessed, she was not inured to death.

"Charles won't notice," Kate said, pouring a large shot of tequila into the glass. "This gerbil is actually Freddy the third."

With their cocktails in hand, the women moved to the sofa. Frances took a sip of her strong, tart beverage. It was delicious but potent. She flicked on the game (it had already started), and Kate dove into the snacks.

"What are the odds that we'll spot them in that huge crowd?" Frances asked, nibbling her allotted chicken wing.

"Almost zero, since we'll be too busy talking, drinking, and stuffing our faces."

"My thoughts exactly." They clinked their glasses together and drank. "Marcus is still talking about the sleepover last week," Frances said, setting her glass on the coffee table. "I think it's the highlight of his life so far."

"Charles had a great time, too." Kate scooped up some bean dip with a chip. "We should plan a family getaway. Rent a cabin somewhere."

"That would be fun."

"Or better yet, let's leave the kids at home and have a couples-only vacation."

The door to the dusty back room in Frances's mind creaked open. "Do you and Robert go on a lot of couples-only vacations?" She had intended a casual tone, but her question sounded pointed, even to her own ears.

"We don't," Kate responded between crunches. "I just thought the four of us would have fun together."

"We would . . ." Frances said, biting a chip.

"But?"

Kate could read her like a book; their connection was that strong. Frances swallowed. "I wasn't going to say anything but . . . Jason got a *weird vibe* off you the other night at dinner. After I went to sleep in Daisy's room."

"What kind of weird vibe?"

Frances suddenly felt sheepish. "He thought you were flirting with him. That Robert was okay with it. That maybe you guys were . . . swingers."

An incredulous laugh erupted from her friend. "Oh my god!"

"I know," Frances said, her cheeks warm. "I told him he was mistaken. He doesn't usually smoke pot. It messed with his perception."

"I'll say." Kate picked up a chicken wing. "Jason is an attractive guy, but I'd never come on to him."

"I knew you wouldn't."

Kate daintily picked meat from the bone with her fingers. "If Robert and I were into that, I'd talk to you about it first."

"Of course. I knew Jason had misread the situation."

"If we ever *were* going to swap partners, it would definitely be with you guys." Kate nibbled chicken as she talked. "I mean, we're all attractive people. And our friendship is strong enough to endure any awkwardness."

Frances felt both flattered and uncomfortable. "I guess."

"Robert would probably love the idea," Kate said, a twinkle in her eye. "He thinks you're hot."

It was Frances's turn for incredulous laughter. Robert Randolph had never given her any indication that he thought of her as anything more than his wife's friend, or Marcus's mother.

"I'm serious." Kate set her bare chicken bone on the edge of the plate. "He likes the voluptuous type. But he's stuck with tall, gangly me."

"Poor Robert," Frances quipped, "his wife looks like a supermodel."

"You always want what you don't have," Kate said, sipping her margarita. "I'm sure Robert would love to get his hands on those big tits of yours."

Frances choked on a mouthful of tequila and lime. She coughed and sputtered, her face burning, her eyes watering. She was not accustomed to blatantly sexual conversation—especially when it concerned her best friend's husband and her own . . . *tits.*

"Jesus, Frances." Kate thumped her on the back. "I was just teasing."

"I know," Frances croaked, feeling like a Pollyanna. "Went down the wrong tube."

Kate watched her struggle to compose herself. "Do you want some water?"

"I'm fine."

"For the record," Kate said, grabbing a handful of popcorn, "Robert and I are monogamous. I'm not going to let him anywhere near your boobs."

"Okay."

"Unless you want me to . . . ?"

Frances gaped at her friend, chewing her popcorn. Kate's gray eyes were coquettish, challenging. Then a smile curled her lips.

"Gotcha again."

Frances laughed. Kate was just playing with her, teasing her for having such salacious suspicions. And now she knew. Her best friend and her husband were a regular, traditional couple. She and Jason had nothing to worry about.

To celebrate, she reached for another chicken wing.

dj

THEN

*As soon as DJ saw Neil Givens at their front door, he knew some-
thing significant had happened. The attorney was always so dashing, so
impeccably groomed. But as he entered their home that day, he looked
unkempt and exhausted. Detective Williams was with him. She looked
her usual robust self, but the intensity of her gum chewing had increased
to an alarming degree. Her jaw was going to lock up if she didn't relax.*

*His dad led the guests to the living room, where they sat. DJ
perched next to his mother on the arm of the sofa, causing it to
creak under his significant weight. A steady diet of junk food, video
games, and trial observation had made him soft and fat. But the
bigger he got, the more invisible he became. No one bothered sending him to his room anymore.*

*Givens took a deep breath, then began. "We've recently received
some new and damning evidence in the case."*

It should have been good news, but the man's tense demeanor was contradictory.

"Nelson's ex-girlfriend has brought forward some videotapes."

"Of what?" His mom's voice was barely a whisper.

"Nelson videotaped several of the girls he assaulted, including Courtney." The prosecutor swallowed, audibly. "Her actual murder wasn't recorded, but her rape and abuse were."

"Jesus Christ!" his dad roared. His mom's tears slipped down her cheeks in silence. DJ considered running to the bathroom and throwing up.

"The tapes were hidden under the floorboards in Nelson's young son's bedroom," Detective Williams explained. "The boy's mother just discovered them. She brought them forward right away."

"I understand this must be unsettling for you," Neil Givens said, "but they're good news for our case against Nelson."

DJ's dad nodded his comprehension. His mom blew her nose into a tissue. DJ waited. He knew there was more to come.

"There's something else," Detective Williams said. "It's about Amber Kunik."

"What about her?" His mother's voice was hoarse with dread and tobacco.

The prosecutor coughed into his fist before speaking. "The video-tapes show Amber Kunik to be a more . . . enthusiastic participant in your daughter's abuse than she previously led us to believe."

"What?" his dad snapped.

The police officer spoke, her jaw clenched on that wad of gum.

"Amber's actions on the tapes are not those of a battered, trauma-tized victim."

"Amber is clearly enjoying herself," Givens elaborated, "as much, if not more, than Shane Nelson is."

"Oh my god!"

"Fuck!"

The prosecutor looked down, his face ashen. "We would never have offered her the plea deal if we had seen this video."

"Cancel the deal!" his mother shrieked.

"You can't let her get away with this!" his dad boomed.

"I wish I could. But it's too late."

"The bitch played us," Detective Williams griped, gum smacking. "The lawyers, the psychiatrists, all of us. She's a master manipulator. A psychopath. She enjoys playing with people, she gets off on it."

"We underestimated her," the lawyer muttered. "We're sorry."

"You're sorry? You're fucking sorry?" His mom sobbed into her cupped hands. His dad placed a comforting arm around her, and DJ patted her back. Their guests sat awkwardly, waiting for his mother's wails to subside. When they finally did, the detective and the lawyer got to their feet.

Detective Williams broke the uneasy silence. "The good news is, Shane Nelson will go away for a very, very long time."

"But Amber Kunik?" His mother's eyes were fiery.

Neil Givens reluctantly met her gaze. "She'll get away with murder."

"Jesus fucking Christ."

It was DJ's own voice. He hadn't even realized he had spoken.

daisy

NOW

The alarm on her phone sounded at 6:45 a.m. Daisy rolled over and turned it off, then checked her text messages: nothing. Still. After the ride home, the offer of a drink, the intense yet undefinable energy between them, the man had not been in touch for almost four days. *The man.* She didn't even know his name; he didn't know hers. But here she was, pining for him like some silly little schoolgirl. Well, she *was* a schoolgirl, but she wasn't silly. She was harder, tougher, stronger. She'd had to be.

Throwing the duvet off her, she reached for her fuzzy pink robe. She kept it at the end of her bed for quick access on these cold, damp November mornings. Wrapping herself in its artificial softness, she scurried to the bathroom. Ennui clung to her as she performed her morning routine: shower, apply makeup, blow-dry and straighten hair. Her efforts were not for her peers.

Now that she was the school pervert, they were all too busy gossiping about her proclivities to care about her appearance. But, if he—*the man*—showed up at Centennial, she wanted to look mature, sophisticated, confident. With wavy hair and no makeup, Daisy almost looked her age.

When she was dressed and ready, she descended the stairs to the quiet main floor. Her brother would still be asleep. Classes at Forrester Academy didn't start until nine, and her mom always chauffeured her golden child directly to the door. Daisy's classes began at eight-thirty, and she had a ten-minute walk followed by a twenty-minute bus ride to school. Her parents would be eating breakfast—invariably toast and coffee—while perusing various news aggregators on their iPads. Their companionable silence would be broken only by her dad offering her mom coffee refills or another slice of toast. Robert doted on his wife nearly as much as Kate doted on Charles. Daisy was left out of the loop of affection.

As she reached the main floor, she heard her father's voice, tense and strained. When no response came from her mom, Daisy realized he was talking on his phone. She paused at the base of the stairs, around the corner from the kitchen, and listened.

"Of course I'll come, Marnie. I'll book a flight as soon as I hang up." There was a pause, then Robert continued, his voice hardened. "I know she's not welcome. I wouldn't do that to Mom. Not right now . . ." Silence as her dad listened to this Marnie person. "You've made your position perfectly clear," he snapped. "I'll text you my flight details." He hung up.

"Where are you going?" It was her mom's voice, stressed, concerned. "You know I don't like being left on my own."

"My dad died." Robert's voice was choked with emotion. "Heart attack."

"Oh, hon . . ."

Daisy's cheeks burned with outrage, betrayal. She rounded the corner, saw her father in her mother's arms. "What the hell is going on?"

"Daisy." Her father stepped back. He looked caught, guilty.

"You said your parents died years ago," Daisy cried. "In a car accident."

"I know. I—I'm sorry."

"I've had grandparents this whole time? Why would you lie to me?"

Her father, always so confident and poised, was flustered. "I haven't spoken to them in years, since before you were born. My sister just called. . . ."

"I have an aunt, too? Why have you kept them from me?"

"We fell out years ago. It was messy. It's hard to explain."

"Try."

Robert opened his mouth, but nothing came out. He looked overwhelmed, shaken. Daisy had never seen him at a loss for words. Her mom took over.

"Your dad's family hates me," she said, tersely. "Surely you don't find that so hard to believe."

Daisy didn't. But enough to disown their own son, their

own brother? To never meet his children? Daisy's eyes narrowed at her mother. "What did you do?"

She witnessed her father's panicked glance at his wife before he addressed his daughter. "When you're older, we'll explain everything." The sentence was barely out of his mouth when her mother spoke.

"She's old enough to know."

"Kate . . ."

"I'm old enough to know what?"

"I had an affair," her mom said. "When you were a baby. I hurt your father terribly and his family has never forgiven me."

Daisy looked at her dad. He didn't look hurt. He looked . . . relieved. "It was a long time ago." He exhaled. "I've forgiven your mom. But my family couldn't. They're . . . very religious."

Okay . . . Daisy addressed her mom. "And *your* family? Were you honest about them?"

"You've met my mother, Daisy."

Daisy had, a handful of times. Her grandmother was obese, parked perpetually on a sofa in a double-wide trailer stuffed with knickknacks and yappy little dogs. She was not far away from Bellevue—in Portland, Oregon—but they had yet to visit since their relocation. Grandma Marlene loved her daughter, and seemed fond of, if disinterested in, her grandchildren. But she emanated an odor of greasy hair and decay.

Her dad stepped forward, gave Daisy's upper arm a squeeze. "I'm sorry you found out this way. We were trying to protect you, but perhaps we should have been more forth-coming."

Daisy said, "Can I come with you? To the funeral?"

"That's not a good idea."

"My grandpa just died and I never got to know him. I've got a grandmother and an aunt in . . . ?"

"Berkeley."

"I want to meet them. Before it's too late."

"It's not the right time," Kate said. "They're grieving. You can't just show up on their doorstep."

Her dad spoke more gently. "I'll talk to them, Daisy. I'll tell them about you, that you'd like to get to know them. I'll let you know if they're receptive."

Daisy bit her lip and nodded. *If* they're receptive. She already felt rejected by these strangers. These people she hadn't known existed until moments ago already had the power to hurt her. For some reason, it made her want to cry.

"I'll get Charles up." Her mom moved past her without a word of comfort. Her dad headed to the coffeepot.

"Coffee?"

"I'm late." She hurried toward the door.

It was raining, as usual, as Daisy trudged to school. Her back-pack was heavy, the homework she had ignored weighing her down. The hood of her raincoat was pulled low over her eyes, creating a tunnel effect as she walked through the puddles. Her feet, in her Nikes, were getting damp, but she barely noticed. The revelation that she had relatives was shocking, the fact that her parents had lied about them, disturbing. She had always felt so isolated, like her family was an island—or, more accurately, an iceberg—drifting from place to place with no ties and no connections. But she did have people—she had an extended family. If they didn't want to know her, it was all her mom's fault.

Her phone, deep in her pocket, vibrated. She extracted the device and looked at the screen. Raindrops splattered the tiny words:

How about that drink?

It was him. She'd allowed herself to be distracted for a moment, and, like a watched pot that won't boil, he had contacted her. She texted back:

Sure.

His response came:

Wednesday. 10:00 PM. I'll pick you up at the 7-Eleven
where we met.

k
See you soon Daisy

The man knew her name.

frances

Frances walked through the quiet, gleaming halls of Forrester Academy. It was two-forty-five, and classes were still in session behind heavy oak doors, leaving Frances alone with the trophy cases, the tastefully displayed student artwork, the framed photos of successful alumni. She always felt nostalgic when she walked through a school, even one so different from the run-down public institution she'd attended. It was the innocence of childhood that she missed, that carefree era before responsibilities and regrets. Frances's childhood had not been idyllic, but she had been happy enough . . . until the act that had destroyed everything.

Marcus's teacher, Ms. Patterson, had called Frances in this afternoon. The sixth graders were doing a special art project in Ms. Waddell's class, leaving Ms. Patterson free for administrative duties. The teacher wanted to discuss Marcus's behavior. Jason couldn't come, of course, but Frances had promptly agreed to the meeting. A thick lump of dread was lodged in her chest, heavy and sticky, like the mucus that had tried to suffocate her when she'd had pneumonia as a child. What had her son done now? She prayed he had not peed in someone's soup.

A door opened just ahead of her and Allison Moss emerged. Fuck. Compact Allison was wearing a white smock over her designer casual outfit (before Frances's brief inclusion in the power-mommy circle, she had not known that four-hundred-dollar sweatpants were a *thing*). Allison's garment was splattered with white goop—paste or glue of some sort, indicating that she had been volunteering for the special sixth-grade art project. Of course she had.

"Frances," the petite woman said, looking positively stunned to encounter her in the deserted corridor, "what are you doing here?"

"Uh . . . my son is a student here." It was a smart-ass response, but it was out before she could censor herself. And Frances no longer feared Allison Moss and her power clique. With Kate in her corner, she was indestructible.

Surprisingly, Allison's response was pleasant. "I've been making papier-mâché"—she pronounced it with a flawless French accent—"with the sixth graders. Marcus is making a blowfish."

"Ah. . . ." Frances was at a loss. While she knew how to deal with a bitchy, judgmental, condescending Allison Moss, she was ill-prepared to deal with a friendly one.

"Your son's quite artistic, isn't he?"

"I guess." This had to be a setup.

But Allison's smile looked sincere. "I've been doing art with the kids all week. It's a pleasure to work with such a creative child."

"Thanks. I'm here to see his teacher."

"Of course. I'll let you go." The pasty woman took a step and then paused. "A few of us are forming a grounds committee. We want to plant a community garden here at the school, to teach the kids about agriculture, and growing their own food, and the environment. Maybe you'd like to help? You and Kate?"

Suddenly, it all made sense. Frances's friendship with cool, confident, beautiful Kate had validated her, made her worthy. But did she still crave this über-mom's acceptance? Did she still want to be a part of the cool clique? Thanks to Kate's friendship, she was rather indifferent.

"Maybe. I'll talk to Kate."

"We'd love to have you both on board. Have a nice day, Frances."

Ms. Patterson was alone in the classroom, seated at a heavy blond desk, her head bent over a pile of student papers. Frances rapped on the open door to announce her presence.

"Frances." The teacher stood and smiled a greeting. She was about thirty, pretty in a wholesome, schoolteacherish way. "Come in and take a seat." She indicated a chair opposite her desk.

Frances obeyed, her heart fluttering with dread.

"Thanks for coming in." Ms. Patterson gave her a smile intended to comfort. "It's wonderful to see parents engaged in their child's education."

Frances cut to the chase. "What did Marcus do?"

Ms. Patterson chuckled. "He hasn't done anything wrong. In fact, he's become a real pleasure to have in my classroom."

Frances's shoulders sagged with relief. "I thought . . ."

"I'm sorry. I should have told you there was nothing to worry about in my e-mail."

That would have been nice. But she was too pleased to be annoyed.

"I know Marcus got off to a bumpy start," the teacher continued, "but he's really settled in. He's engaged in lessons and contributing to class discussions."

"That's wonderful," Frances said.

"He's come a long way socially, too. I think his friendship with Charles has done wonders for his self-esteem."

"I agree."

"The other kids are more accepting of Marcus now. They seem to have left the water bottle incident behind them." She gave Frances a warm smile. "With Charles in his corner, Marcus feels a new sense of belonging."

Charles had done for Marcus what Kate had done for Frances. She and her son had been saved from the solitary life of the social pariah by the Randolphs. Frances may not have deserved such a pure friendship, but Marcus did. He was innocent and good. Gratitude welled up inside of her, threatening to manifest in tears. "I'm just . . . so happy to hear that," she said, trying to compose herself.

Ms. Patterson recognized the emotion on Frances's face. "It's wonderful to see your son excelling," she said. "I think he's going to have a great year."

As she strolled back to her car in the parking lot, Frances felt light and buoyant. Marcus's newfound sense of independence had relegated her to the pickup line or the lot—under no circumstances was she to wait outside his classroom or in the foyer. She didn't mind. The boy's autonomy was more evidence that he was maturing, moving in the right direction. Despite the financial sacrifices she and Jason had to make, Forrester was the right place for their son.

As she approached her Outback, Kate's black Navigator pulled into the parking lot. Her friend exited the car and headed toward the school (of course, the always amenable Charles had no issues with his mom coming inside to retrieve him). As usual, Kate was effortlessly stylish, polished, and put together, but when Kate glimpsed her face, her expression was grim, somber.

"Kate!" she called. The woman turned around, and her countenance brightened slightly. They moved toward each other.

"Robert's dad died."

"Oh, Kate. I'm so sorry." She hugged her. Kate accepted the embrace, but she didn't soften into it, she didn't fall apart. Frances released her.

"We weren't close," Kate explained. "In fact, Robert's been estranged from his parents for years."

"Sometimes it's harder when there are unresolved issues," Frances offered.

Kate pressed her lips together and nodded. "He's going to the funeral. In Berkeley."

"Will you and the kids go?"

Kate shook her head. "Robert's parents never liked me. It's a long story."

"When does Robert leave?"

"Tomorrow."

"Come for dinner tomorrow," Frances said. "You and the kids."

"I don't want to impose."

"You won't be. Marcus will be thrilled. And you and I can cook and have some wine. You shouldn't be alone at a time like this."

"What about Jason?" Kate asked. "Will it be awkward after the whole *swinger* thing?"

Embarrassment pinkened Frances's cheeks. "No. It was a misunderstanding. It's all forgotten."

"Okay. . . ." Kate gave her a grateful smile. "That sounds nice."

Frances squeezed her friend's arm. It was the least she could do after all Kate had given her. And all Charles had given Marcus. "Daisy might be bored by the boys and the adults, but she can watch a movie. Or she can bring her homework."

"She'll probably have plans."

"She's welcome to join us," Frances said.

"I'll mention it to her," Kate said breezily. "Thanks, Frances. I don't know what I'd do without you."

The school bell rang then. Both women turned their attention to the stream of children pouring out the front doors.

dj

THEN

*T*he day the tapes were played for the judge and jury, DJ wasn't allowed to go to court. In fact, he wasn't allowed to go at all anymore. It was September, and school was back in session. His mother insisted his education had to come first.

"One of us has to try to lead a normal life," she said.

But that day, as he sat outside in the baking Arizona heat, eating his packed lunch (a deli-ham-and-mustard sandwich, a bag of chips, and eight Oreo cookies), he wondered if it would have been less upsetting to be in the courtroom. He was alone, as usual (no one wanted to sit with the fat kid, the kid with the murdered sister, the kid who did nothing but play video games), and his mind was running wild.

He could hear his sister's screams in his imagination, hear her cries of terror and pain. Had she called out for her mother?

Screamed for her daddy to save her? Courtney would have begged for her life, pleaded with Shane and Amber not to do those disgusting things to her, not to make her perform those debasing acts. What had they made her do? What DJ was envisioning was probably worse than the reality. It had to be. . . .

But when his parents came home that evening, DJ knew he had gotten it wrong. What his mom and dad had seen in court that day was worse than anything he could have conjured. They walked into the house like zombies: pale, lifeless, destroyed. His mom didn't look at him; she went straight to her room. She didn't even take her cigarettes with her. His dad went to a cupboard and took down a bottle of scotch. He never went back to beer.

The next morning, when DJ got out of bed, his mother was gone.

daisy

NOW

The final bell had rung, prompting Centennial High's students to pour into the main arteries like carpenter ants in a colony. Daisy moved through the masses like a spirit. No one noticed her anymore. She was thankful the snickering had diminished; the cruel comments and scandalized whispers about what she had done to Liam Kenneway had nearly stopped. But her peers' opinion of her had ceased to matter. Her mind swirled with thoughts of estranged relatives, her mother's infidelity, her upcoming *date* with the enigmatic stranger. . . . School politics was low on her list of things to stress out about.

Her recent anonymity was comforting, in a way. There was a downside to her striking looks: salacious leers, envious glares, idolizing gawks. Now she was virtually invisible, and she kind of liked it. With her head down, she reached her locker and fiddled with the lock.

As soon as she opened the door, something fell out. The object must have been balanced on the top shelf, tipped by the physics of the opening door. It was small but heavy as it thumped on Daisy's chest, then bounced down her body. When it hit the floor, it rolled a couple of feet before stopping. Daisy looked at the small black object. It was shaped like a spade, but it had a flat base. What the hell was it?

"Oh my god!" a male voice shrieked. "It's a butt plug!"

Fuck.

"It fell out of Daisy's locker!"

They hadn't forgotten her. She was not invisible. Ninth graders could not be expected to forgive such depraved, deviant sexual behavior so quickly. Someone was seeing to her continued humiliation. But who? Who, in her fourteen-year-old cohort, even knew what a butt plug was? And who had the brass balls to buy one? To plant it in Daisy's locker? Her money was on Tori Marra.

Everyone was freaking out now, a chorus of shrill disgust filling the hallway. A nerdy boy kicked the offending object across the hall, and a female student booted it on. It continued that way, a game of butt-plug hot potato, each player crying out in revolted delight.

"Pick it up, Daisy! It's getting ass germs all over the floor!" It was Tori Marra. She was standing next to Dylan Larabee, their attractive faces alight with cruel glee.

Daisy's heart was pounding, her cheeks on fire. If she picked up the sex toy, she'd be admitting ownership. But how else to get this horrible hockey game to stop? Even if she tried, she wasn't sure she'd be able to retrieve it. Daisy would be forced to chase the butt plug as it skittered across the waxed floors, a dog careening after a squirrel. The humiliation would be supreme.

An Adidas running shoe came down on top of the spinning black toy, stopping the action. The trendy footwear belonged to Liam Kenneway, the boy who had rejected her advances, then turned her into a freak, a pariah. He bent down and picked up the plug.

"Who put this in Daisy's locker?" His voice was cold and commanding as he held the anal sex toy aloft. It was a comical milieu, but no one dared giggle, and the squeals had been silenced. Liam was too cool, too popular, too good at football to mock.

As expected, no one stepped up.

Liam strode to the garbage bin at the end of the row of lockers and slammed the sex toy into it. It rattled in the empty barrel, the sound sending relief flooding through Daisy.

"Whoever put that thing in Daisy's locker is an asshole," Liam declared. (No one dared chuckle at the word choice.) "Daisy and I never did anything weird. I was just fucking around, trying to be funny. Leave her alone."

Coats and books were grabbed, locker doors slammed, and students headed home. Only Liam and Daisy remained standing, an awkward face-off in the evacuated hallway. Their eyes met. Daisy felt a confounding mixture of gratitude and contempt. Tentatively, the boy closed the gap between them.

"I'm sorry I said you did those things." His voice was soft, sincere. "I was embarrassed and mad. I wanted to hurt you."

"Well done," she snapped, past resentment winning out over current appreciation.

"I went too far. I know that. But . . . why didn't you deny it?"

Daisy shrugged. "I guess I didn't want everyone to turn on you."

"So you let everyone turn on you."

"I can handle it," she said. "We'll move in the next year or so, anyway; we always do. I don't care what the kids at Centennial think of me. And you do."

Liam looked at her for a long moment, his attractive face perplexed. "You're not like the other kids here."

No kidding.

"You seem older. And wiser. It's like you understand things the rest of us don't."

Daisy shrugged, mildly flattered.

"I don't know who put that thing in your locker, but I'm sorry. Hopefully, now, everything will go back to normal."

"That would be nice."

"But we'll still say we had sex, 'kay?" His expression was

hopeful. "I mean, it would be too much if I said I was joking about that, too."

Her voice was flat. "Sure."

Liam smiled, then sauntered down the hall. Daisy grabbed her coat and shuffled toward home.

frances

NOW

Frances had gone to Pike Place Market to buy fresh prawns and handmade pasta. She'd picked up two bottles of Pinot Grigio and a decadent chocolate mousse cake for dessert. As she set the table with her wedding china, she worried that she was creating too festive a mood. Her dinner with Kate was a somber occasion. Robert's father had died. Charles and Daisy had lost their grandfather. But when Kate arrived with two bottles of sparkling wine in hand, Frances realized her worries were for naught.

They fed the boys first (pasta in a simple tomato sauce), and let them abscond to Marcus's room. Jason was working late, so the two women sat down to their meal alone. As Kate oohed and aahed over the pasta dish, Frances was glad she'd made the effort. Her friend seemed comforted and consoled. In fact, Kate didn't seem at all upset about her father-in-law's demise. Other than the phone perched next to her plate, it could have been a completely normal evening.

"I know it's rude," Kate said, referencing the device beside her, "but I don't want to miss Robert if he calls. He might need to talk."

Frances had expected her to mention Daisy. The fourteen-year-old was not in attendance. "Where's Daisy tonight?" she asked, casually.

"With friends," Kate said, sipping her white wine.

"What are they doing?"

"Who knows." Kate shrugged. "These prawns are perfect. I always overcook them."

Frances smiled her thanks, but her friend's indifference toward her daughter's whereabouts concerned her. Kate seemed to have ultimate confidence that Daisy could take care of herself. Frances did not. That morning, in Kate's living room, the girl had revealed her insecurities and self-doubt to a virtual stranger. She was not the strong, competent kid her mother thought she was. Frances knew, more than most, how vulnerable a troubled teen was, how easily she could be hurt, manipulated, led astray. But how could Frances burden Kate with this knowledge now? She would wait until Robert was home, until they'd dealt with their grief.

Kate's phone on the table vibrated to signal a text. She picked it up and looked at the screen for a moment.

"It's Robert," she muttered, chewing her pasta. "They're having the wake now."

"It must be hard for him, going through this without you."

"It's better this way." Kate put the phone down and picked up her fork. "Robert's sister and his mom can't stand me."

"Why?" Frances was slightly incredulous as she bit into a prawn. How could Robert's family not accept his pretty, sweet, funny wife?

"They thought I was too young for him. They didn't trust my motives." Kate twirled fettuccine onto her fork. "Robert was a big fancy lawyer when we met. I was *beneath* him."

"But surely they can see how happy you've made him? And the beautiful family you've created together?"

"People don't see what they don't want to." Kate reached for the bottle of wine, refilled Frances's glass. "What's Jason's family like?"

"Jason's dad passed before I met him. His mother is *positively regal.*"

Kate giggled as she topped up her own glass.

"She is!" Frances elaborated. "Conchita speaks Spanish and English and French. She owns an art gallery in Denver. And she looks like Sophia Loren. She's always intimidated me, but we get along fine." She sipped the cold wine. "I'm more comfortable with Jason's sister. She has four kids, so her life is utter chaos. We relate to each other."

"*Families* . . ." Kate rolled her eyes as she nibbled a prawn.

"I'm an only child. Dad's gone. Mom lives in a trailer park in Portland with her fur babies. We've had our issues but we get along okay. What about your family?"

Frances chewed a mouthful of pasta, her mind flitting to the letter that had arrived a couple of weeks ago. She had waited until she was alone in the house—Jason at work, Marcus at school—to read her mother's missive. It began casually, with family news: A cousin had had a baby; her older sister had been promoted at work; Dad joined a chess club. But then, as always, the tone shifted.

> *We miss you, Frances. We miss our grandson. We want to be a part of your life. Please let us back in.*

But her mother didn't mean it. It was parental obligation that kept her reaching out to her estranged daughter. Why would her mom and dad want to be reminded of the devastation Frances had caused? The pain and the hurt and the shame she had brought into their lives? Frances wanted to cut them loose, absolve them of their responsibilities, allow them to heal and move on. But every few months, a letter arrived. And every few months, Frances burned it over the sink and washed the ashes down the drain.

Sometimes, Frances could go days without thinking about what she had done. She would focus on her son and her husband and the life they had built in Bellevue. And then something would remind her—a teenage girl, usually, a tragic news story, or one of her mom's letters. Frances would be forever haunted by her actions, and she deserved to be. Her family did not. They were better off without her.

She swallowed. "We're not close."

"How come?" Kate asked, her eyes seeking Frances's.

Frances met her friend's gaze, and again, they shared that moment of recognition. Kate got her. Frances could open up to her and share her dark secret without judgment. If anyone would listen and try to understand what she had done, it was Kate. But it was a fleeting consideration. Even Kate could not forgive the terrible act Frances had committed. And she couldn't risk blowing their friendship apart. Marcus needed Charles. Her son was happier and calmer, his meltdowns decreased by half, at least. Forrester Academy deserved some credit, as did the child psychologist he saw regularly, but she knew it was the boys' camaraderie that had had the biggest impact. Even the teacher, Ms. Patterson, admitted it.

And Frances had grown to need Kate. The friendship had made Frances more confident, less anxious, and slimmer. She couldn't attribute her weight loss *directly* to Kate, but she was down eleven pounds. Eleven! She had more energy, more motivation, more vigor. Her house was cleaner than it had been in years. Her slim, stylish, organized friend was an inspiration. She couldn't lose her.

"Typical rebellious-teenager stuff," Frances fibbed, setting her fork on her plate. "I put my parents through the wringer."

"I was a bad girl, too," Kate said, a mischievous glint in her eye. "Tell me the worst thing you did."

God, if she only knew . . .

There was a rumble on the stairs, then, announcing the boys' arrival. Marcus barreled into the kitchen, trailed by Charles. Frances's son's cheeks were rosy, his eyes bright. Both boys looked happy, content, carefree.

"Is there dessert?" Marcus asked.

Frances jumped to her feet, grateful for the interruption. "Chocolate mousse cake, coming right up."

daisy

Daisy was back at the 7-Eleven, flipping through a copy of *Us Weekly*. The man had told her to meet him there at 10 p.m. It was now 10:08, and she was still waiting. Behind the counter, the same stern cashier who had been intent on foiling her liquor purchase stood sentry. Daisy felt abashed, conspicuous, but the slight man paid her no attention. She was one of dozens of minors who attempted to buy alcohol on any given night, no one special. Still, she kept her distance.

Her nerves were getting the best of her. The longer she stood, waiting, the more she needed to use the bathroom. And the more she feared that the man would enter while she was in the bathroom and then leave, thinking she hadn't shown up. But the longer this went on, with her anticipating the grumble of the big car, head jerking up every time the door sensor made its electronic ding-dong, the more she was certain she was going to have to run to the toilet. She had always been troubled by a nervous stomach, and she had never been this nervous in her life.

Frances Metcalfe's words replayed in her mind, something about predators, men on the lookout for lonely, vulnerable girls. But that wasn't what this was. If the guy had wanted to have sex with her, he would have gone with her when she'd invited him to join her for a pink vodka cooler. There was something deeper at play here. The way he looked at her, like she was a rare treasure he had stumbled upon. It should have been creepy, but it wasn't.

Daisy checked her phone for the millionth time. 10:10. At what point should she consider herself stood up? At 10:25, she told herself. If the man had not arrived by then, he wasn't coming. And if he did come that late, and she was still waiting, butt cheeks clenched tight, she would look desperate and pathetic, like some adoring fan. Any minute now, the brown man at the counter would notice her loitering, spot the backpack slung over her shoulder, perfect for shoplifting, and tell her to leave. She considered purchasing the magazine, but she had already read half of it.

In the parking lot, she heard the big car. It could have been another big car, or a loud motorcycle, but she set the magazine on the shelf and hurried toward the sound. If it wasn't him, she would go home. The cashier looked up from counting lottery tickets as the door ding-donged, letting her out into the rainy night. The car was there, idling in a parking spot, waiting for her. She scurried through the drizzle and climbed into the passenger seat.

They drove in silence, again, and Daisy experienced a déjà vu moment. "Where are we going?" Hadn't she asked that exact question less than a week ago? But this time the man wouldn't be taking her home. That was the difference.

"To my place. Near the university."

"Are you a student?"

He snorted, like it was a ridiculous notion.

As they traveled, her stomach began to settle, her need for the toilet dissipating. Now that she was with him, she felt more at ease, though perhaps, she should have felt less. An older man, a stranger, was taking her to his apartment. But there was something familiar about the man now, something comforting and safe. She glanced over at him.

"How do you know my name?"

"What?"

"When you texted me, you said Daisy. But I never told you."

He smirked and indicated her backpack. "I was referring to that." She looked at her bag, at the daisy key chain dangling from one of its plastic loops. "I thought I was giving you a nickname."

Daisy smiled back. "What's your name?" she asked.

"David."

David was a man's name; not a boy's name, like Liam.

* * *

Fifteen minutes later, David parked the car in a concrete garage underneath a bland, blocky, four-story building. Daisy trotted along beside him as he led her through the dimly lit basement to a small, musty elevator. She was nervous again, but in a good way—jittery with excitement and anticipation, of what exactly she wasn't sure. Her stomach fluttered pleasantly as the door closed on them. David stabbed the third-floor button.

"Lived here long?" Her voice came out high-pitched and girlish.

"Not really."

"Where did you live before?" She felt compelled to fill the silence with flip words. If she didn't, the intensity of the moment might undo her.

The doors slid open, saving him from answering. David led the way down a carpeted hallway to a pressboard door marked 308. He turned his key in the lock and ushered Daisy inside.

It was a furnished apartment—Daisy had lived in enough temporary housing to recognize the standard-issue beige sofa, the matching laminate coffee and end tables, the mass-produced art on the walls. The Randolphs had spent months in such accommodations as they waited for their furniture to be shipped to them. She hadn't expected a guy David's age to be so transient, but it was evident that this was not a real home.

Daisy dropped her bag in the entryway and moved to the sofa. David went into the galley kitchen and she heard him opening the fridge. He joined her, holding out a pink beverage.

"I got your favorite."

She accepted the vodka cooler, the same kind he had bought for her that night. It was so thoughtful that he had remembered. David sat beside her and cracked his beer. He took a drink, his eyes on her.

"Where do your parents think you are right now?"

"My dad's out of town. And my mom doesn't care where I am." He gave her a quizzical look, so she expanded. "We don't really get along."

"I guess you'll be moving out soon," David said. "Once you've finished high school."

Right . . . "Yeah. Probably. I'm not sure what I'll do."

"There are lots of ways a girl like you can make money."

"I guess. . . ." She took a drink of her sweet, fizzy beverage. "What do you do? For work?"

"Sales," he said. "Importing."

"Cool." She wasn't sure if it really was cool, but she had to say something. She could feel his eyes on her. Taking another gulp, she bravely met his gaze.

She had expected to see something there, perhaps longing or lust. The eye contact would be the prelude to a kiss, maybe even something more. But though his stare was weighty, there was nothing romantic or sexual in it. David was observing her, *examining* her, like she was a specimen in a petri dish.

"You're pretty," he finally said. It was a statement of fact, not a flirtation.

"Thanks."

He said nothing, just stared. David seemed entirely comfortable with the long silences between them. They made Daisy feel panicky and sweaty, compelled to fill them with inane banter. "So . . . do you like animals?"

He responded with a question. "Do you get high, Daisy?"

"Yes." It was a bit too enthusiastic, but she wanted to sound mature, worldly.

Without a word, David stood, disappearing down the hallway. He returned moments later with a small plastic bag full of weed. He tossed it on the coffee table, then looked at the empty bottle in Daisy's hand. "Ready for another one?"

She hadn't realized she'd drunk the whole thing. "Sure."

Alone in the living room, Daisy inspected the transparent bag of marijuana. Nestled in the weed was a small, intricately folded paper envelope. What did it contain? Coke? Ecstasy? Heroin? As David returned with her drink, she realized she was in over her head.

"I should go."

He sat beside her. "You're fine, Daisy. I won't let anything happen to you."

It was as if he had read her thoughts—no, more than her thoughts, her entire psyche. He knew exactly what she needed to hear, even before she did. David had articulated her deepest, most base desire. Daisy wanted someone to care for her. She was fourteen years old, with a cold and indifferent mother and a distracted, distant father. Her parents had secrets, dark tales kept only between them, and no one, not even their children, could penetrate their bond. It was emotional neglect—though Daisy didn't have a precise term for it. Living with two people who shared such a pact was incredibly lonely.

David took her hand, gave it a squeeze. It was loving, almost paternal. Through a lump in her throat, she said, "Okay. I'll stay."

He deftly rolled a joint and they passed it back and forth, toking in silence for a while. As the pot and alcohol took effect, Daisy began to relax. Eventually, David stubbed the blunt out in an ashtray, and leaned back on the sofa.

"What do you want to be when you grow up, Daisy?"

Daisy didn't answer—she couldn't answer. It wasn't just that she was high and pretty drunk; she had been so before, more than once. But she knew the expected answer: CEO, nurse, playwright, mom. . . . When Daisy considered her future, she never thought in terms of specifics. She daydreamed, frequently, about her next chapter, but her visualizations didn't include careers, partners, parenthood. She dreamed of one thing only.

"Free," she said.

David smiled, impressed with her clever answer. "I'll get you another drink."

She accepted the bottle, nursing from it as she melted into the sofa. Her lids were getting heavy, and her grip loose. She downed the sweet alcohol and set the empty vessel on the coffee table. Her eyes would not stay open, so she leaned against the arm of the sofa and closed them, just for a moment. Then she felt a blanket being placed over her, David's big hands tucking her in. She felt cared for. She slept.

dj

THEN

His *mother had written him a letter. DJ found it on his dresser, the* *morning after she left, the rectangular envelope propped against a stack* *of video game cartridges. Its presence meant that his mom had been in* *his room while he was sleeping. If only he had woken up, he could have* *stopped her from going, or begged her to take him with her. But despite* *the horrors of the day, he had slept deeply and soundly.*

He read the missive alone in his room, tears sliding down his *cheeks.*

DJ,

I'm sorry to leave you like this, but I am so broken.
Your sister's death has killed me, too. I need to go home
for a while, to be with my family. I need to surround
myself with nature, with trees and rivers and mountains.

When I stop seeing your sister's torture in my head, when I stop hearing her screaming and crying and begging for her life, I can be your mother again. When I find a way to heal, I'll send for you. I promise.

I know you'll be angry, but please try to understand. Stay strong. Stand up to your father.

I love you.

Mom

DJ dried his eyes with the backs of his hands; then he crumpled the letter into a ball and tossed it into his wastebasket. When he walked out to the kitchen, his father was at the table. He had a mug in front of him—alcohol, not coffee, DJ could smell it—and a bowl of cereal.

"Your mom's gone," his father said, crunching the flakes.

"I know."

"She's weak. Always has been."

"I guess." DJ went to the freezer, grabbed a box of frozen waffles.

"She thinks she can go back home to Alaska and pretend she never had a daughter or a son or a husband. She thinks she can forget about us and all the shit that's gone on here."

DJ dropped the frozen disks into the toaster.

"So I'm the one who has to stay here and deal with the fucking trial, and the fucking lawyers, and those fucking monsters that took your sister." He glowered at his son. "I'm the one who has to stay here and look after you."

"Mom said she'll send for me when she's better."

His dad laughed, a humorless snort. "She's not going to send for you, dumbass." His chair scraped across the tiles as he stood. "You're never going to see her again."

DJ wanted to cave the man's skull in with the cast-iron frying pan that sat on a back burner of the stove, or grab a kitchen knife and plunge it into his dad's chest. But he couldn't. He was too soft, too weak, too afraid. And now his dad was all he had left.

His father set his mug and bowl in the sink. When he leaned in close and spoke, DJ could smell the whiskey that made the man so cruel.

"It's just you and me now, tubby."

He slapped his son's belly and it jiggled on impact. As his dad left the room, the toaster popped. The sweet, yeasty scent of the waffles churned DJ's stomach and he leaned over the sink. For a moment, he thought he might be sick, but he forced the feeling down, swallowed the bile, the rage, the sadness.

On autopilot, he put the waffles on a plate, smothered them in margarine and artificial maple syrup. He sat and shoveled the food into his mouth, trying to mask the taste of hatred and anger, but it lingered. Each bite was bitter, chemically, but he kept eating, waiting for the numbing effect, the almost trancelike state he could achieve when his body was full of sugar. It wasn't working. He put more waffles in the toaster and waited. He couldn't stop eating until the pain was gone, because he knew his dad was right.

He was never going to see his mother again.

daisy

NOW

When she woke up on the tweedy, musty sofa, the apartment was dark, silent. At first, she wasn't sure if it was morning or night, but the hum of activity outside the heavy curtains—commuters, buses, delivery trucks—informed her it was early a.m. The November sun liked to sleep late. She couldn't blame it.

She lifted her head, painfully, from the cushioned arm of the sofa. Her neck was stiff and there was a dull ache between her eyebrows. A hangover. How many drinks had she had? She remembered having a couple, but there must have been more, if the pounding in her head was any indication. The events of the previous night were foggy and unfocused. She recalled arriving, sitting next to David on the couch. He had bought her the coolers she liked—make that *used to like*. The very thought of them made her stomach roil.

Throwing the blanket off her, she sat up, her brain sloshing painfully in her skull. When she tried to stand, the room spun around her. She sat back down, dropping her head into her hands. Oh, god. Everything was moving and swirling and tilting. She was going to be sick. She couldn't throw up on David's carpet. She had to get to the bathroom.

With her mouth watering menacingly, she staggered to the hallway. There were two closed doors: one would be the bedroom, the other the bathroom. If she made the wrong choice, she would burst into David's room and puke on the floor, right in front of him. And then she would die of embarrassment. She chose the door on her right. Luck was on her side.

She fell to her knees in front of the toilet just as a stream of hot, pink liquid shot out of her. She coughed and retched, her stomach forcing out more of the bitter fluid. Tears poured from her eyes as she heaved again and again. She felt poisoned, her body trying to detox itself from last night's indulgences. Her nerves had precluded her eating dinner yesterday . . . possibly even lunch, come to think of it. There was nothing left in her stomach, but still it convulsed, over and over. Daisy worried she was doing some serious damage to her esophagus.

David would hear her and he would be disgusted, but she was too sick to be ashamed. She needed to go to the hospital. She needed an ambulance. Something was very wrong with her.

"David," she called, lifting her head out of the bowl. "Help me."

That slight movement of her head made the room sway again and she puked some more. Soon David would come, bring her a cool facecloth, and maybe a pillow so she could lie down on the floor between bouts of vomiting. Through the fog in her brain, she remembered his strong hands placing the blanket on her, how safe she had felt.

But he didn't come. Even when she called him again, louder this time . . . nothing. His room was directly across the hall. There was no way he couldn't hear her. On hands and knees, Daisy crept out of the bathroom and across the carpeted hallway. With her head down, eyes on the floor, the nausea was less overwhelming. She pushed open the bedroom door and crawled across the threshold. If David was there, sitting in bed, she would look like a lunatic . . . a repulsive, puking lunatic. But even before she lifted her head, she knew. The double bed was unmade but empty.

She lay down on the floor for a moment, regaining her equilibrium. Where was he? When had he left? Was he coming back? She suddenly realized how vulnerable she was—sick, lost, and alone. She could die here, in a stranger's apartment. David might not return for hours, and by then it would be too late. What would he do when he found her lifeless body? Who would he call? Her heart raced and her chest tightened. She struggled to breathe. She didn't want it all to end this way.

With serious effort, she half crawled, half dragged herself into the living room. Her phone was on a side table, resting next to a generically ugly lamp. She climbed onto the sofa, and reached for the device. Resting her head against the cushioned arm (last night's pillow), she scrolled through her contacts with trembling hands.

Her peers were of no use to her. Even if they cared about her—which they didn't—they were too young to drive. Her dad was away. And her mom . . . Daisy couldn't call her mom. No. No way. And then she saw the name, so recently added to her contacts. Frances Metcalfe. The woman had promised to be there for her. Rescuing Daisy from alcohol poisoning in some random guy's apartment was likely not what Frances had in mind, but Daisy was already dialing the number.

"Hello?" Frances's voice was cool and leery. She clearly didn't recognize Daisy's number.

"It's Daisy," she said, her voice hoarse from all the barfing. "I need help."

"What's wrong, Daisy?" The woman's voice was shrill and panicked. "Where are you?"

"I don't know." Daisy was crying now. "I'm in an apartment near the university. I'm really sick and I'm alone and I need help."

"Are you on something? Should I call 9-1-1? Should I call your mom?"

"No!" Daisy cried. "I had some drinks. And some pot . . . Please. Don't. Just . . . come."

"I will." Frances's voice was calmer. "Is there anything around you with an address on it? A bill, maybe, or a magazine subscription."

Daisy's eyes surveyed the sterile space. "I don't see anything."

"Do you have an iPhone?"

"Yes."

"I'll use the Find My Friends app. You'll need to go into the app and allow me to track you."

"Okay." Daisy sniveled.

"It will get me close to you, but you need to find the address and text it to me."

"I'll try." She sniveled again.

"Go outside and check the street name and number if you have to. I'm on my way."

"Thank you."

Daisy hung up and crawled back to the bathroom.

frances

NOW

The bland apartment building squatted on the edge of a busy street. As instructed, Daisy had found the address and texted it to Frances. She parked her car, grabbed her purse and a canvas shopping bag filled with supplies, and hurried toward the four-story structure. The main door of the dated building was propped open; someone was moving in or out, or having furniture delivered. A midsize white moving truck took up two spaces out front. Frances walked past the two men lugging the pieces of a couch or a bed in a massive cardboard box, and hurried inside.

She took the stairs. She didn't have patience to wait for the small, rickety elevator. Her heart pounded as she climbed—exertion and nerves. What would she find when she reached apartment 308? Was Daisy okay? Was she alone? Was Frances putting herself in danger, too? She should have called Kate. Or

Jason, for backup. But she had promised to help the troubled girl and she would. Emerging into the musty hallway, she hustled to the door.

Frances knocked loudly. "Daisy, it's me," she called through the flimsy wood. "Let me in."

It took a few seconds, but the door opened, revealing the teen. The girl was pale—almost green—and smelled of alcohol and sick. Her posture was hunched and pained. She stepped back, allowing Frances into the apartment.

"Are we alone?" Frances asked, surveying the room. It was a furnished apartment: standard-issue hotel furniture and artwork. No personal touches.

"Yes," Daisy answered in a small voice.

"Are we safe?"

The girl nodded. "David's my friend. He's not dangerous." Then her face crumpled. "At least, I don't think he is."

Who the hell is David? How did you meet him? What are you doing, alone and hungover, in his apartment? But now was not the time for an inquisition.

"I brought supplies," Frances said instead, digging in the bag. She extracted a bottle of electrolyte drink and a small container of antinausea pills. "This will rehydrate you and stop the vomiting."

Daisy accepted the drink and removed the lid with shaking hands. She put the bottle to her lips as Frances watched her.

"Oh god," the girl muttered, as her stomach lurched. Pressing the bottle into Frances's grip, she scurried down the hallway.

"Daisy, we should go!" Frances called after her, but the sound of the bathroom door closing drowned out her words.

Frances moved into the galley kitchen, opening cupboards and drawers, searching for a clue to David's identity. The man could be a pervert, a pedophile, a human trafficker. And he could return at any moment. Frances wanted them both gone before he did. The kitchen proved to be fully stocked with cooking supplies and utensils, but devoid of any personal effects. Even the fridge was bare but for two bright pink vodka coolers and a few beers. Wedged between the fridge and the microwave, she found a plastic binder full of takeout menus, the apartment's address written prominently on the front page in blue ink. That was likely where Daisy had found the digits she had texted to Frances.

She moved past the barren living room into the short hallway. Behind the door on her right, Daisy vomited vociferously. Frances hesitated, for a beat, outside the opposite door. Entering David's bedroom was an invasion of privacy. And, frankly, she was afraid of what she might find in there. Camera equipment? Sex toys? Worse? But she pushed past her fears and opened the door.

The bed was unmade, but otherwise, the room was pristine. Didn't this David person have any belongings? She opened the closet and found two shirts hanging, an empty duffel bag on the floor. Moving to the dresser, she pulled open the three drawers: a few pairs of socks, underwear, a couple of T-shirts, and a pair of jeans.

Her heart pounding with adrenaline, she moved to the bedside table. In the top drawer, she found a small plastic bag of marijuana, a bottle of Tylenol, a handful of condoms. Oh, Daisy . . . She opened the bottom drawer: empty. But something compelled her to run her hand around the edges of the vacant compartment. Pressed against the back of the drawer, she felt a smooth, rectangular piece of paper. She extracted a photograph. It was Daisy.

Frances peered at the glossy finish, the washed-out color, the curling edges. It was an older photograph, circa the 1990s. But Daisy wouldn't even have been born. Frances inspected the girl's image. Her hair was darker, her makeup brighter, her face fuller. And then she realized, it wasn't Daisy.

It was Kate.

Her friend was younger, probably about twenty. Her hair was dark and feathered, her makeup colorful and heavy-handed, but there was no denying it was Kate Randolph. Why did David have a photograph of Daisy's mother? What the hell was going on here?

The toilet flushed. Daisy would soon emerge and Frances needed to get her out of here. Something was very wrong with this scenario. She didn't know what, but her every instinct was screaming that they needed to get out. Shoving the photo into the back pocket of her jeans, she hurried into the hall.

The teen appeared, pale, almost ghostly. "Can you take me home?" she asked.

"Yes. Let's go."

daisy

NOW

Daisy sipped the electrolyte drink as Frances chauffeured her back to Clyde Hill. She had swallowed two of the anti-nausea pills and managed to keep them down. They were starting to kick in now, as they flew down the freeway, and she was feeling notably better. It was fortunate. Her improved constitution made the lecture Frances was giving her more tolerable.

"I don't know who David is. I don't know where you met him or what he wants with you. But you can't see him again."

"Okay."

Frances glanced over at her. "I mean it, Daisy. He is not your friend. He's a man who has an apartment. He must be eighteen at least."

Try thirty. . . .

"He gave liquor and drugs to a minor. He shouldn't be spending time alone with a drunk teenage girl."

"Okay."

"It's inappropriate. In fact, it's illegal."

He asked me questions about my life. He didn't even try to kiss me. He put a blanket on me when I fell asleep.

Frances wouldn't want to hear it. She seemed convinced that David was a creep, a pervert, a pedophile. The girl understood how it could look that way, but she wasn't afraid of David. Maybe she should have been, maybe she was a silly, naïve fourteen-year-old, but the man made her feel safe. He made her feel protected.

As they exited the freeway, Frances kept talking. "The internet is filled with predators, Daisy. You can't meet someone online and then agree to meet them in person—especially in private. It's not safe."

She could explain that she hadn't met David online, that he had sat in his big car and watched her in the night, had orchestrated a meeting at the convenience store, had shown up at her school and driven her home. But that would *really* freak Frances out. Daisy was unaccustomed to this type of concern for her well-being. No one ever worried about her. But Frances seemed almost beside herself with worry. Daisy kind of liked it.

"I won't see him again," she mumbled, looking out the passenger window. Frances's Subaru was climbing the 92nd Avenue hill. They were almost home.

"I know you don't want your mom to know."

"Please," Daisy said, turning to face her driver, "don't tell her."

Frances didn't respond. She drove in silence for a few blocks, then pulled the car over on the shoulder. "I won't tell your mom," she said, swiveling to face Daisy. "But you have to promise me that you won't go back to that apartment. Promise me that you won't see David again."

"Okay."

"Say it, Daisy."

"I promise."

Frances accepted her word. Then she drove her home.

The house was empty. Daisy's dad was still away, her brother was at school, and her mom must have been running errands. She went directly to the shower and stood, under near scalding water, reflecting on the night's events. Frances's concerns were not unwarranted. David was older, he was mysterious, he was probably trouble. But she wasn't sure she'd be able to keep her promise to stay away from him. Not because she wanted David to be her *boyfriend*. He was old. *Hot* but old. But for some reason, she liked being around him. She liked how he bought her favorite drinks (her *former* favorite drinks), put a blanket on her when she fell asleep, and looked at her like she was a rare butterfly that he was afraid to touch. But a grown man would want more than that—even at fourteen, she knew it. Frances was right. Daisy had to stay away from David.

When her fingers were starting to turn pruney, she turned off the shower and headed to her room. She felt significantly better, but she'd decided to skip school. Again. Since the butt plug incident, she'd taken a sabbatical. Pulling on her sweatpants and her favorite oversize sweater, she made her way downstairs. She had just reached the main floor when she heard a key in the front door. Her mom breezed into the room, carrying two paper sacks full of groceries.

"Why aren't you at school?"

Not: *Where have you been all night? Who were you with? Are you okay?*

"I'm not feeling well," Daisy said, her hoarse voice backing up her story. Her mom carried the bags into the kitchen. Daisy followed her. "Have you heard from Dad?"

"His flight lands at four." Her mom surveyed the living area. "This place is filthy. Go rest in your room so I can clean up before he gets here."

"Actually, I think I feel better," Daisy said. "I'll go to school."

Kate didn't respond; she was already attacking the imagined grime in the kitchen with a bleach spray and a stiff-bristled brush. As Daisy moved back to the stairwell, her mom's voice halted her.

"I almost forgot"—she kept scouring the sink as she spoke— "your dad had a message for you."

"What?"

"Your aunt Marnie wants to hear from you. He'll text you her e-mail address."

"Really?" Daisy was delighted. "That's great. I'll e-mail her tonight. I don't know what to say. . . ."

"I wouldn't get too excited," her mom said, scrubbing even more aggressively. "Marnie's a judgmental cunt."

frances

Alone in her house, Frances sat at her kitchen table, staring at the photograph of a young Kate. It was a candid shot. Kate wasn't looking at the camera, wasn't smiling, wasn't posing. She was walking—purposeful strides—wearing a dark blazer and a matching skirt. Had David taken the photo? If not, how did he get it? More important, what was he doing with Kate's daughter? Frances sipped the strong cup of tea she'd made for herself, and turned the picture over. For the first time, she noticed the hand lettering on the back. A name.

AMBER KUNIK

Frances's mouth went dry as she stared at the block letters printed in black ink. It was clearly a picture of Kate—younger, with darker hair and heavier makeup, but there was no denying it was her friend. But that name . . . *Amber Kunik.* Wasn't she the woman involved in that sensational murder trial years ago? Amber had testified against her boyfriend, placing all the blame on him, but had ended up in jail herself for torturing that young girl. *Wait. . . .*

Frances grabbed her iPad from where it was resting on the stack of magazines and unopened mail and tapped her password into the device. Opening her browser, she was greeted by a couple of open tabs, recent Google searches:

Artificial colors and ADHD
Which has more calories? Sauvignon Blanc or Pinot Grigio?

With her hands shaking, she typed *Amber Kunik* into the search bar.

A barrage of images and articles, old and new, filled the page.

KILLER KUNIK GETS SWEET DEAL
KUNIK TESTIMONY PUTS NELSON AWAY FOR LIFE
CONVICTED KILLER KUNIK IS A SOCCER MOM IN
MONTANA

A soccer mom? In Montana? Amber Kunik had her own Wikipedia page. Frances clicked, a vein in her temple throbbing as she read. The biography detailed the woman's upbringing, her crime, her trial, prison stay, and subsequent release. Amber

Kunik was a cold-blooded killer. A monster. She had made a plea deal and served only six years for killing a teenage girl. But videotaped evidence had revealed her to be an active, enthusiastic participant in the girl's torture. Amber had, effectively, gotten away with murder.

Kate couldn't be Amber Kunik. Kate was warm and kind and good. She was a wife, a mom, and a devoted friend. The best friend Frances had ever had. Maybe she had an evil twin? But this was not a soap opera. This was Frances's life.

She sifted through the internet images of Amber, a pretty young woman with dark hair, fluffy bangs (stylish in 1997), a genuine smile. There she was laughing with a handsome, dark-haired man, beaming on Christmas morning, then glaring at the camera as she walked toward the courthouse. Frances peered at the face. It was Kate Randolph; there was no denying it. Despite the dark hair, the big bangs, the purple eyeliner . . . there could be no doubt.

Kate was not Kate. Kate was Amber Kunik—a murderer.

Frances felt dizzy and sick. She reached for her tea, but her hand would not close on the handle, didn't have the strength to grip the mug. The iPad fell from her grasp, hitting the table, sloshing tea onto the wood. Frances watched the liquid meander across the surface, heading toward the stack of magazines and school forms to her left. She should grab a cloth and wipe it up, but she couldn't move. She was paralyzed by shock, horror, and confusion.

Because it was not Kate who had the dark past, the shameful secrets, the horrific memories that gnawed at her conscience. That was Frances.

Frances was the killer.

frances

*F*rances Downie was an average teenager in every sense of the word. She was pretty but not beautiful; well liked but not popular; bright but not gifted. She was the middle of Joyce and Bob Downie's three girls. Mary Anne, older than Frances by four years, was the athlete. Tall, strong, and competitive, the eldest sister had won a volleyball scholarship to Rice University. Younger sister Tricia, just eighteen months Frances's junior, was the smart one and the pretty one. School, popularity, beauty—all seemed so effortless for Tricia. With these admirable attributes assigned, Frances was left to be the good one: dutiful, compliant, cooperative. Frances did most of the housework and cooked dinner regularly. Her family appreciated it, even if they forgot to explicitly show their gratitude. The Downie parents loved all their girls, but Mary Anne was her dad's favorite, and Tricia was her mother's. Frances couldn't even blame them.

Their home, in a middle-class suburb of Spokane, Washington, was a modest three-bedroom bungalow. Frances and Tricia shared a room until Mary Anne left for college, when Tricia moved across the hall into the vacated space. When Mary Anne came home for the summer, Tricia moved back in with Frances. Frances would grumble about her privacy, but she was comforted by her sister's presence. She slept better when she could hear the girl's soft breathing across the room. Bob Downie worked for the city, in the permits department. Joyce was a dental hygienist. The Downies had enough, but no extra. Their marriage was companionable, but not overtly affectionate. Frances's entire teenage existence would have been typical, middling, run-of-the-mill . . . had she not walked into the girls' bathroom during third period that day in eleventh grade.

She was in Mrs. Chamberlain's English class when she felt a dampness in her underpants. Her stupid period had arrived early. The elderly teacher was strict about not excusing kids in the middle of class, but when a sixteen-year-old girl grabbed her purse and asked to go to the restroom, the woman knew enough not to refuse. Frances walked through the empty halls, her shoes squeaking on the waxed linoleum. When she reached the swinging door of the main bathroom, she pushed her way inside.

There were six toilet stalls, a bank of sinks, and a wall of mirrors. Perched on the pink Formica counter was April Sutcliffe. The girl was Frances's age, but more mature, more edgy, more rebellious. Teachers branded her trouble. Her peers labeled her badass. She wore thick foundation and black eyeliner, skintight jeans and *low-cut shirts. She was tough and cool and she didn't give a shit. With her was her blond doppelgänger, Rhonda Mullins. Rhonda was holding a plastic bag. April had a can of spray paint.*

"Shit," April said, hiding the aerosol can behind her back. When she recognized Frances, she relaxed. "Oh. Hey."

Rhonda said, "We thought you were Chapman."

The principal, Mrs. Chapman, had been known to pop into the girls' bathroom to look for skippers, smokers, drinkers. And, likely, whatever it was April and Rhonda were doing.

"What are you guys doing?" Frances asked.

"Huffing," April said, casually. Rhonda held out the plastic bag, and April sprayed the paint—an iridescent gold—into it. The blonde bent her head to the opening of the bag and inhaled deeply. She closed her eyes and her whole body relaxed, became buoyant and rubbery.

"Cool," Frances said, like she was familiar with the process, like maybe she'd even done it herself, which, of course, she hadn't. She made her way into a stall.

As she sat on the toilet, affixing her maxi pad, she could hear April taking her turn. The tough girl inhaled deeply, then let out an almost sexual moan. Frances emerged to find the two of them leaning against the countertop, smiling beatifically.

She was washing her hands when April said, "Want to try?"

At sixteen, Frances had attended a handful of parties where alcohol and marijuana were abundant. Her strategy was to hold a room-temperature beer, pressing it to her lips infrequently, then tipping it into a plant or down a sink when an opportune moment arose. When offered weed, she had a mild case of asthma as an excuse. Of course, she would politely refuse April's offer.

"As if," Rhonda snorted, her glassy eyes falling on Frances.

Something, some tiny kernel of teenage rebellion, flared inside of Frances. She hadn't even known she harbored such seditious-ness, but there it was. It occurred to her then that she could redefine herself. She wasn't smart, pretty, or skilled at sports. But she didn't have to be the good sister, the compliant, dutiful, doting sister. She could be the bad one.

"Sure," Frances said, with a casual shrug. The shock on Rhonda's face was satisfying.

April smiled. "Right on." She held the can at the ready as Rhonda passed the plastic bag, now colored gold on the inside, to Frances. She held it open and let April fill it with paint. Putting her face to the mouth, Frances inhaled the fumes, then held her breath like she'd seen Rhonda do.

Stars flashed behind Frances's closed eyelids, and for a moment, she was afraid she might collapse. Then she opened her eyes and exhaled, a flood of euphoria coursing through her.

"Fuck . . . ," she murmured, and April and Rhonda shared a smile, like they were proud of her. Suddenly, Frances was not aver-age, bland, dull. She was strong and confident, pretty and popular, wild and free. It was Frances, not Mary Anne or Tricia, who was the most loved Downie girl. Of course she was. She was spectacu-lar. The high lasted roughly fifteen minutes.

She didn't go back to class—Mrs. Chamberlain would assume cramps, or some embarrassing menstrual mess. Frances followed April and Rhonda to the mall, where they ate fries, looked at shoes, and huffed two more times—once in the bathroom, and once in the loading bay behind a department store. When Frances went home, around four-thirty, she couldn't wait to tell her younger sister about her adventure.

Tricia, despite her looks, brains, and popularity, was sweet and grounded. She was two grades behind Frances, but still, the sisters were best friends. Tricia was the only one who looked up to Frances, who made her feel cool, and smart, and savvy. Today's escapades, with April and Rhonda, would solidify the younger girl's admiration.

"It makes you feel amazing," Frances explained. "Like you're the most perfect person in the world."

Even though Tricia already was the most perfect person in the world (at least in Frances's world), she was enthralled. "It sounds fantastic."

"It was."

"I can't believe you tried it! You're so brave!"

Frances smiled and shrugged, basking in the compliment.

"You don't even drink," Tricia said. "You don't even smoke pot."

"This is different. It only gets you high for a few minutes, so you can't really get into trouble. Like, we could do it right now, before Mom and Dad get home, and they'd never know."

Frances saw the apprehension on her sister's pretty face. Tricia was a good girl, too, but she already had so many other attributes

that Frances had tried to claim the label for herself. Corrupting
her sweet, innocent sibling suddenly felt like a personal challenge.
"There's spray paint in the basement workshop," Frances said, a
dark glimmer in her eye. "Mom won't be home for over an hour."

"I don't know. . . ."

"It's fun. You'll love it."

"I have a lot of homework." Tricia's cheeks were pink. "Are you
sure it won't mess me up?"

"You'll feel totally normal in, like, fifteen minutes. Trust me."

The younger girl did. Frances was her big sister, after all. The
siblings scurried to the kitchen to grab a plastic bag and then rumbled down the stairs.

Their dad's "workshop" was just a storage room for the remnants of household repair jobs. Boxes of nails, screws, tubes of
caulking, tubs of spackle, and a few tools lined the wooden shelves.
The girls found a can of silver metallic spray paint left over from a
school project Tricia had done in sixth grade.

"I made that satellite model for the science fair," Tricia said,
sounding nostalgic for elementary school. Frances realized that was
only three years ago. Tricia was in ninth grade, fourteen years old.
Normally, she seemed older than her years, more mature and composed. But right now, she seemed young, nervous, and intimidated.
Her sister's insecurity made Frances feel older, worldly, wise.

The girls sat on a scrap of carpet covering the concrete floor.
There wasn't a lot of paint left, so Frances mimed a demonstra-
tion. "You just breathe in like this," she said, holding the bag to her

mouth. "Hold it in as long as you can, and then breathe out." She felt like an expert: knowledgeable, experienced, blasé. . . . It was a new feeling for her and she relished it.

"Okay," Tricia said. "I'm ready."

Frances shook the can, the glass pea rattling against the metal of the container. Tricia held open the bag and Frances precisely sprayed, filling the bag with silver. Her younger sister obediently held it to her face and inhaled.

She watched Tricia breathing in the poison, her eyes closed, her face blank, waiting for the chemicals to hit. Then the girl exhaled, her body slackening, face paling. Her sister's eyes opened, but they were blind, unseeing. A small, hesitant smile curved her lips as the feeling hit her.

Upstairs, the front door opened.

"Shit," Frances muttered.

"Girls?" It was their dad, home early from work. Why? Bob Downie was old-school. He'd go nuts if he caught them. There would be slaps and yelling and swearing. The sisters would be grounded for months, the entire summer probably: no TV, no friends, no swimming pool. . . . That was if he caught them.

"Oh my god!" Tricia whispered, and the panic in her eyes was real and visceral.

It's okay, Frances wanted to say. Dad won't know. I'll cover for you. But her sister was already running for the door. Where was she going? What was her plan? But Frances would never find out, because Tricia collapsed.

A fatal ventricular rhythm disturbance. *That was what killed her sister. Frances wouldn't hear the term "sudden sniffing death syndrome" until years later, when enough kids had dropped dead from huffing for it to garner media attention. Inhalants are cardiac depressants, she learned. When that combined with the adrenaline surge Tricia experienced when she heard their dad come home, her heart was thrown into dysrhythmia. And then it stopped.*

Frances admitted it all. She had introduced the fatal act to her younger sibling, had provided detailed instructions on how to inhale the toxic chemicals that stopped Tricia's heart. She was not criminally responsible: the police deemed the death an "accidental overdose." But Tricia would never have tried huffing if Frances hadn't cajoled her into it, hadn't assured her that it was fun and safe and basically harmless. Frances, alone, shouldered the blame. But she never told anyone how she'd felt as she took her sister through the deadly motions: cool, older, superior. It made her hate herself even more.

After Tricia died, Mary Anne stopped coming home for the summers. And then she stopped coming home for midterm breaks and Christmas. She said she was working, training, spending time with friends, but the Downie home had become a dark and dismal place, like grief had sucked all the light from the house. Bob and Joyce kept working, kept breathing, kept living, but their sadness and resentment permeated the air, the furniture, their rapidly aging bodies. They functioned for their remaining dependent daughter, Frances—already their least favorite, now the one who had destroyed their family, destroyed their lives.

Frances endured high school as a pariah, a monster, a murderer. She applied for college, more as an escape than a quest for further education. When she packed up for her move to Bellingham to attend Whatcom Community College, there were no tears. At least her parents had enough guile to hide their overt relief. Her dad helped her carry an overstuffed suitcase to her secondhand Honda hatchback.

"We still love you, Frances," he said, without emotion. Frances nodded, the lump in her throat blocking a response. As she drove away, she let the tears come: tears of loss, grief, and relief.

Her parents could pretend they had forgiven her, but they hadn't. How could they, when Frances could never forgive herself?

daisy

By the time Daisy got to school, it was lunchtime. This was unfortunate, since the hour between noon and one was the worst time for a social leper. She'd spent weeks drifting through the front foyer and the hallways, cliques subtly retracting like sea anemones, their tentacles closing against a predator. Liam's declaration of her virtue may have softened their disgust, but Daisy knew not to get her hopes up. She wasn't interested in reclaiming her former popularity; she just wanted kids to stop planting sex toys in her locker.

Today, she was going to brave the cafeteria. She hadn't eaten since yesterday, and she was weak and light-headed. Now that her stomach had settled, she realized she was famished. Usually, she avoided the packed room with its plethora of odors (grease, fruit peelings, BO), and subsisted on vending machine food. But her hangover required more solid sustenance: a sandwich or even a burger. As she stumbled into the bustling commissary, she tried to lose herself in the mental fog that still clung to her. If she focused hard enough, perhaps she could dissolve into thoughts of David, into the composition of her e-mail to her aunt Marnie.

With a foil-wrapped cheeseburger (emanating a disturbingly armpit-like scent) and a Coke on her tray, she scanned the room for an unobtrusive corner to park in.

"Daisy!" She turned toward the female voice and saw Tori Marra waving her over. Really? Daisy resisted the urge to look behind her to see if the popular girl was gesturing to someone else. Tori waved again and there was no mistaking her intention. Mustering all her confidence, Daisy walked toward the pretty blonde who had recently taken such delight in her humiliation.

"Hey," Tori said, biting into an apple. She was surrounded by a posse of popular girls who had middling grades but excelled at social politics. "Want to sit with us?"

It could be a trap, a setup. Tori, or one of her minions, might stuff a dildo or edible panties into Daisy's backpack. But she was so hungry. "Sure."

Tori nudged Maggie Waters, the cute but vapid girl seated next to her, to slide over, making a space for Daisy. Obediently, Daisy climbed into the vacated spot.

"Dylan Larabee's having a party on Saturday," Tori said. "You have to come."

The host, Liam's sidekick, had branded her a nympho, a slut, who knew what else. . . . "I might have plans Saturday," she said, her mind flitting to David.

"Blow them off!" Tori said. "Dylan really wants you there." She leaned in, lowered her voice. "I think he's into you."

While Dylan Larabee's interest did not excite her, Daisy had to marvel at the magic of Liam Kenneway's endorsement. The quarterback had scolded the other kids, assured them that Daisy liked *normal* sex, not weird butt-play. With a few little words, he had thrown her a lifeline. If she wanted to, she could grab it and drag herself back from high school exile. Did she care enough to reach for it? She had to . . . because Frances Metcalfe was right. She couldn't spend her time in a furnished apartment, drinking vodka coolers with a strange man twice her age, no matter how good he made her feel.

"Okay," she said, biting into her cheeseburger.

Just like that, Daisy was back in.

dj

After his mother left, DJ returned to the trial with his father. Not because his dad needed moral support, but because the boy preferred sitting in court to sitting in school. The process could be slow and laborious, but it was still more interesting than learning fractions or analyzing short stories. And without his mom around, no one cared if DJ passed or failed. He didn't want to repeat seventh grade, but he was sure his teacher would take pity on him. What could they expect, after all he'd been through? First his sister and now his mother . . .

DJ was thrilled when the defense called Amber Kunik to the stand for cross-examination. His fascination with her was undiminished by distance and time, untouched by the things he had learned about her, the acts of which she was accused. He despised her, as was appropriate, but he was drawn to her at the same time.

Not in a sexual way. He was simply in awe of her composure, her placid demeanor, her incredible knack for self-preservation. Watching her charm and manipulate the men and women in the courtroom was mesmerizing. And contemplating the evil that lurked inside such a pretty package was even more so.

Shane Nelson's bulldog of a lawyer was well equipped to take on the attractive witness. Martin Bannerman had the air of a warrior or a gladiator. He looked capable of decimating a biker gang, an army even. He would not coax and cajole, would not treat Amber with kid gloves. That day, he handed the witness, demure in her skirt and cardigan, hair pulled neatly back, a mauve envelope.

"Can you tell the court what that is, Ms. Kunik?" His voice, like his physicality, was distinctly masculine.

Amber kept her eyes on the pale purple rectangle in her grasp. "It's a letter I wrote to Shane. When we were together."

"Would you please read it aloud?"

Something flashed in her eyes—anger? irritation?—but then it was gone. Obediently, she opened the envelope and withdrew the missive. She began to read, her voice sweet and high.

"Dear Shane . . . I'm at work right now, but I can't concentrate. All I can think about is you and how happy you've made me. Every time I think about you, I feel like my heart will explode, and"—she paused, blushing prettily before she continued—"I get so wet."

A murmur rippled through the spectators thrilled by the salacious content. Amber continued.

"You've made me the happiest girl in the world. The day we met is the best day of my life and the only day that will compare is the day we get married. You are so sexy and smart and wonderful in every way. I'm the luckiest girl alive. I will love you always and forever. . . . Amber."

She set the letter in her lap and looked the attorney in the eye. Not once did she glance at the object of her devotion, sitting rigid in his navy suit before her.

"You sound like you were very much in love," Martin Bannerman said.

"I was."

"Those don't sound like the words of a woman who was abused, who was mentally and physically tortured."

DJ leaned forward, eager to watch the witness's unraveling.

"I don't think it's uncommon for victims of abuse to be in love with their abusers," Amber stated, a hard glint in her eye. "Abusive men can be very manipulative . . . very charming."

She sounded educated, authoritative on the subject. She had done her research.

The lawyer now had the envelope in his big hand, and he waved it before the spectators. "How often did you write love letters to Mr. Nelson?"

"Every day."

"Wow . . . You were so in love that you wrote Mr. Nelson a love letter every single day?"

"Shane made me do it. If I didn't give him a letter every day, he'd hit me."

The lawyer didn't respond, didn't react, but a vein in his neck bulged ominously. Martin Bannerman strode across the room to retrieve another envelope, a white one this time. He returned to the witness.

"Do you recognize this missive, Ms. Kunik?"

Amber examined it for a moment. "It's a letter I wrote to my friend Beth. She moved to Tucson after high school."

"Would you read it for the court please."

She complied, repressing her earlier spark of indignation. The letter began with polite inquiries about Beth's new life in the nearby city, but soon segued into Amber and Shane's romantic relationship.

". . . I can't wait until Shane and I get married. My whole life has been leading to this moment. I never liked kids, but I want to have his babies (four at least). I will even try to love his other son. . . ." She trailed off here, her eyes darting to the jury, to the lawyer, to Shane.

The judge stepped in. "Finish reading the letter, Ms. Kunik."

She cleared her throat. "I will even try to love his other son, even though his mom is a drunken whore and he's probably brain damaged or something."

The courtroom erupted in gasps and muttered outrage. Shane Nelson shook his head, disgusted. His lawyer barely suppressed a triumphant smile. DJ knew that people sometimes said harsh, ugly things. Since taking up his steady diet of whiskey, his father said them daily. But in the context of the horrendous crimes she was accused of,

Amber's words, directed at an innocent little boy, seemed exceedingly cruel. Finally, the court would see how evil Amber was.

When the judge had restored order, Bannerman said, "Please continue, Ms. Kunik."

The witness resumed reading her letter to Beth. "I am writing to ask you to be my maid of honor. You're my best friend and Shane likes you. I want you to stand beside me when I become his wife. We can pick out our dresses together. My dad will pay for every-thing. It's the least the pervert could do. . . . Love you lots and lots, Amber."

She looked up, met the lawyer's gaze. She was ready for him.

"Had my client, Mr. Nelson, actually proposed to you?"

"Not officially. But he told me we'd get married. We talked about it all the time."

"Really?" the lawyer asked, strolling around the room, hands clasped behind his back. "Did you talk about it while he was beat-ing you?"

There was that flash of annoyance again. "No. Of course not."

"You said the abuse was frequent, practically constant. And yet, you still found time to talk about a wedding, and children. . . ."

"We talked about it after he beat me." Her eyes pooled with tears, and her voice became small and broken, a victim's. "It was Shane's way of saying sorry, of getting me to forgive him. I thought that once we were actually married, the abuse would stop." She looked directly at the jury then. "I know I was stupid to think that."

The vein in the lawyer's neck bulged. Amber was winning. Bannerman knew it; everyone knew it. And DJ could see through the girl's tears. Amber was enjoying herself. She relished facing off against this powerful attorney. She reveled in the jury's sympathy. The girl had made her deal; she was safe.

Shane Nelson's trial for the murder of Courtney Carey was just a game to her.

frances

NOW

Frances drove to Forrester Academy on autopilot, in a literal state of shock. What she had discovered about her friend made her sick to her stomach. An innocent but troubled young girl had been abducted, abused, tortured, and eventually (not soon enough) murdered. The account had jogged Frances's memory. While no cameras had been allowed in the courtroom, there had been significant media coverage of the case. The country had been transfixed, fascinated by the good-looking young couple capable of such evil. Tabloid news shows like *Hard Copy* and *A Current Affair* featured stills of the comely pair at barbecues and birthday parties, on a motorcycle road trip, posed in front of the Grand Canyon. Frances remembered seeing footage of Shane Nelson, disturbingly attractive even in his prison jumpsuit: tall, rangy, intense. And, despite the horror playing out in her own life at that time, she remembered Amber Kunik.

The image was trapped in the recesses of her brain. Amber, demure in her conservative coat, being led through a phalanx of media to a waiting car. Flashbulbs had popped, reporters had called her name, like the girl was some sort of pop star or movie starlet. Frances recalled the way the burly police officer, or maybe he was a bailiff, had protected Amber's pretty dark head as he helped her into the backseat. And Frances remembered *the look*. When the car door closed, Amber had peered through the window, chin slightly lowered, eyes penetrating the camera lens. The press had had a field day with that moment, playing and replaying it, over the course of the trial. It was that same, slightly flirtatious look Kate had given Frances at the seaside restaurant. Jesus Christ.

But that was twenty years ago, and she wasn't sure her memory could be trusted. And could the media? The press could be biased, sensationalistic, salacious. She knew, firsthand, how tragedies could be twisted and spun for entertainment value. Amber Kunik had accepted a plea deal, and maintained that Nelson had abused and controlled her. But many had doubts, and the media had pounced on that angle.

Pulling into the parking lot, Frances squeezed her car into a vacant spot in the back row, farthest from the school. Kate always parked in the front row. Frances couldn't risk running into her friend right now. The thought made her heart beat erratically and her stomach twist into knots. She'd left her iPad, mid-research, to come pick up her son. Now, as she sat in the school parking lot, she wondered if her brain was playing tricks on her.

Frances knew the toll of living with a terrible secret: the guilt, the self-loathing, the constant, nagging fear of being found out. . . . She knew how it manifested in her marriage, her relationships, and her parenting. Kate couldn't be hiding a murderous past. Unlike Frances, Kate didn't eat compulsively, didn't question why her husband loved her, didn't over-parent her children because she lived in unrelenting terror of them being taken from her. Kate was confident, well adjusted, normal. Unless she was a psychopath?

Marcus was crossing the playground now, his eyes searching for the familiar car. Normally, she would have gotten out and waved to him, but today, she stayed inside, inconspicuous. She couldn't draw attention to herself. If Kate was in the vicinity, she would come over and say hi, she always did. Frances had loved that. It had made her feel special . . . but not anymore.

As her son moved closer, she noticed his small companion walking alongside him: Charles Randolph. Right . . . Frances had agreed to collect the boy because Kate was going to pick Robert up at the airport. (The women had filled out the requisite school forms allowing each access to the other's son.) The distinguished attorney was returning from his father's memorial service. Kate had not been welcome. Did Robert's family know the truth about his wife? Were they horrified? Disgusted? Afraid?

"Hi, Mom." Marcus crawled into the backseat.

"Hi, sweetheart."

Charles climbed in beside him. "Hi, Frances."

She answered through the lump in her throat. "Hi, honey."

The boys chatted amiably about a lunchtime game of man-hunt as she drove them home. They sounded so cheerful, so innocent. Frances's heart ached for Charles. For Daisy, too. They couldn't know their mother's history. They were too young to comprehend her dark, cruel, ugly past. But it was only a matter of time before the truth came out, somehow. This David character knew Kate's identity. Was he going to tell Daisy? Seek some sort of retribution?

If Kate Randolph really was Amber Kunik, if she really had gotten away with murder, why the hell had she had children?

When they arrived home, Frances prepared the boys a tray of nachos (Marcus's mild lactose intolerance suddenly seemed insignificant) and let them occupy themselves. They'd end up on a screen in short order, but, that, too, seemed of less concern. She wanted the boys to enjoy their time together, blissful in their ignorance. Once all this came out, their friendship would be shattered.

Frances retrieved her iPad and resumed her research at the kitchen table. She clicked through the most recent articles:

KILLER KUNIK MARRIED TO HER LAWYER AND LIVING IN

THE FLORIDA KEYS

Robert had been a lawyer. *Amber's* lawyer.

THE SINS OF THE MOTHER: WHY AMBER KUNIK'S
CHILDREN WILL PAY FOR HER CRIMES

Oh god, those poor kids.

Frances sifted through the photos of Kate's past iteration—the shiny dark hair, the youthful face, the same gray eyes. One of the photos didn't fit the melange. A girl with brown hair, the same big bangs, but a rounder face, softer features. Her makeup was too dark, too heavy, an attempt to look older, harder. Frances knew who she was, who she had to be, but she clicked the link anyway.

Courtney Carey. The victim.

The girl was fifteen years old when she was killed. How old was Daisy? Fourteen or fifteen. How could Kate look at her daughter and not see this murdered girl? Not think about what had been done to her? Perhaps that explained Kate's seeming indifference toward her female child. She had emotionally detached herself from Daisy to block her memories of Courtney Carey.

Returning to the search page, Frances sifted through the more recent "sightings" of Amber Kunik. Her hair was now that expensive mix of caramel and honey, her face slimmer, her makeup muted and tasteful. Photographers had caught her hurrying to her car, buying groceries, peeking out from behind a curtained window. Amber had been a predator; now Kate was the prey.

"Excuse me, Frances."

Her head snapped up. It was Charles, Kate's angelic son, standing at the end of the table. Instinctively, Frances pressed the iPad to her chest, shielding the boy from the words and images that would destroy him.

"Yes, Charles?"

"When will my mom and dad be here?"

"Around five-thirty," Frances said, forcing a normal tone. "Are you okay? Do you need anything? Another snack?"

"No, thanks. I need to save room for dinner. It's spaghetti night." The boy smiled. "My mom makes the best spaghetti." He wandered toward the living room, where Marcus, red-faced and sweaty from overstimulation, was playing a video game.

With the iPad clutched to her chest, Frances hurried upstairs to the master bathroom. She deposited the device in the linen cupboard, turned on the shower, and wept. Hot tears poured from her eyes and sobs shuddered through her chest, their sound masked by the pounding water droplets behind her. She was crying for Charles, for Daisy, and, though she was loath to admit it, for herself. Her self-pity was indulgent. The Randolph children, Courtney Carey and her family—they were the real victims. Still, Frances couldn't deny the visceral sense of loss.

The doorbell rang. Shit. How long had she been locked away, weeping? She reached into the shower and turned off the water. Leaning over the sink, she splashed cold water on her face and hurriedly dried it on a towel. She rumbled down the stairs to find Charles opening the door. Kate, looking stylish, pretty, *virtuous*, stood in the entryway.

"Hey, buddy." Kate bent down and hugged her son. As Frances approached, the tall woman righted herself and smiled. "Thanks for picking him up."

"No problem."

"Go get your school bag, Charles." The boy obediently scurried away.

Frances peered past Kate to the SUV parked in the drive. Robert was behind the wheel, his eyes on his phone. Frances should ask how Robert was holding up, should ask how the funeral went. She should call Marcus to come say goodbye to his friend at the door. It was rude to stay glued to his game while a guest was leaving. But she couldn't feign concern, couldn't make idle chitchat, couldn't worry about her son's manners, or lack thereof. She was barely holding herself together.

"Are you okay?" Kate reached out and placed a hand on Frances's cheek. Frances forced herself not to flinch. "You look pale."

"I went to the gym," Frances lied. "I think I overdid it. I'm a little light-headed."

"You might have low blood sugar. Do you want me to make you something to eat?"

"I'm fine."

"Robert can take Marcus home and I can walk home after. I don't want to leave you alone if you're not feeling well."

Kate's concern would have been touching, if only Frances could believe it.

"I'll eat something. It's okay."

Charles returned then, his backpack slung over his arm. As he stepped into his shoes, Kate spoke to Frances. "Thanks again. I'll pick up Marcus next week and he can come over for a play-date."

"Yes!" Charles exclaimed.

No, Frances thought. But she held her tongue and forced an acquiescent smile.

As she watched Kate escort her son to the waiting vehicle, her heart clenched with emotion. The thought of losing the Randolphs' friendship was almost too much to bear. And maybe she didn't have to? Recidivism rates were much lower for women who committed crimes than for men—she'd gleaned that factoid from TV courtroom dramas. If she could forget what Kate had done in the past, they could still be friends.

But could Frances forget about Courtney Carey, the fifteen-year-old who had been raped and tortured and degraded? Who had suffered such indignities before she was murdered, her body dumped in the mountains like a bag of garbage? What did it say about Frances if she was able to continue this friendship, knowing what she knew?

But if she couldn't, Frances was a hypocrite. Her own sister was dead because of her.

She closed the door and went back to the kitchen.

daisy

NOW

Dylan's party was in full swing when Daisy arrived, flanked by Mia Wilson and Emma Menendez. It had been easy to fall back into the comfortable fold of their friendship, like slipping into a tepid bath she'd left sitting for a few hours. Being a pariah had been tolerable but hardly enjoyable, so Daisy vowed to appreciate the girls' companionship. And she sincerely appreciated the beer that Emma's older brother had bought for them. Daisy had liberated a cannabis cookie from her parents' stash, and the girls had shared it on the way over. Wandering through Dylan's stunning, modern, lakeside home, they were all pleasantly buzzed.

She felt oddly comfortable surrounded by her peers. These kids would turn on her in an instant, she knew that firsthand, but for now, she felt a sense of belonging. Of course, it might be the weed and the beer allowing her to drop her guard, but Daisy knew she was where she should be. She had not heard from David since the disastrous sleepover. She had, however, heard from Frances Metcalfe. The woman's concern, while initially appreciated, was now crossing the line into *nagging*. The texts were frequent:

Have you heard from David?

No

Promise me you won't see him again.

I won't.

You won't promise or you won't see him again?

I won't see him again

God . . . poor Marcus. When he was a teen, his mother would have him on a very short leash. But then again, Marcus Metcalfe would probably grow up to be one of those nerdy kids who spent weekends locked in their rooms playing RPG games and chugging energy drinks. Frances's attentions almost made Daisy appreciate her parents' indifference.

As always, the epicenter of the festivities was the kitchen. Dylan, Liam, and a gaggle of athletic boys occupied the modern, open-plan room, interspersed with Tori and her popular crew. Every kid had a drink: a bottle of beer, a vodka cooler, or a red plastic cup full of smuggled liquor. Daisy sipped the bitter beer Emma's brother had provided, enjoying its numbing effect as they sidled into the jammed space.

Tori noticed her first. "Daisy! You came!" She seemed dis-
proportionately happy to see her. Or maybe she was just drunk.
Liam's eyes found Daisy then. Maggie Waters was attached to his
side, suckered onto him like a pretty, teenage leech, but he offered
Daisy a smile, a slight toast with his red cup. Daisy smiled back
and held up her beer. It was appropriate that they acknowledge
each other. They had had sex, after all: normal, but significant,
full-on intercourse. The popular kids had gone from outraged to
impressed. Suddenly, their host was beside her.

"I'm glad you came," Dylan said, smiling down at her. He
was attractive—blond and square-jawed, with broad shoulders and dark eyelashes. He played football, too. Or maybe he
played baseball. Daisy had never gone in for that all-American
type, but she could feel the covetous eyes of Tori and her crew
on their interaction. She should be flattered by this handsome
boy's attentions.

"Great house," she said.

"Yeah. It's a good party pad."

"Where are your parents?"

"Hong Kong." He tapped her beer with his red cup. "Can I
get you something stronger? Vodka? Tequila?"

"Why not?" She may as well try to enjoy herself. Just because
she felt more mature than these drunk, silly kids didn't pre-
clude her having a little fun.

Dylan hustled toward the makeshift bar set up near the sink
and returned with a red cup half-full of alcohol. Daisy took it

and drank it down, her throat burning, her body shivering with revulsion. It tasted gross, but it was better than a pink vodka cooler. When she finished, she wiped her hand across her lips and looked up at Dylan. He grinned. "I like a girl who knows how to party."

"That's me."

He took her cup again and refilled it (tequila or vodka? she had no idea, but it was disgusting), and led her to the living room. It was dark. Kids were dancing to some EDM she didn't recognize. The air was humid and close, heavy with the scent of sweat and pot and hair product. Dylan's hands on her hips guided her into the thick of the gyrating teens. Daisy swayed a little, sipping her drink. It was crowded; she was stoned, and drunk, and overheated. Dylan was so close to her, his solid, warm body pressing against hers. His breath smelled like the booze she was drinking. Dylan's hands moved to her waist, pulling her toward him. She closed her eyes and went with it.

His lips were soft but insistent, the patchy stubble on his chin rougher than Liam's, more masculine, almost manly, but not quite. Her fingers drifted along his biceps, his muscular chest. He was big and strong; he could take care of her. . . . When he grabbed her hand and practically dragged her toward the stairs, his forcefulness was sexy.

He took her to a bedroom—tidy and spacious, with a king-size bed and a cozy seating area: his parents' room, obviously.

They stumbled inside and resumed their kissing. Dylan didn't push her toward the made bed (apparently, he had some respect for his mother and father's furnishings), but navigated her toward the cream-colored love seat. They didn't sit, but leaned against it, hands and mouths exploring each other.

She heard a *zip* and then Dylan's hands moved to her shoulders. He stopped kissing her and smiled a drunken, lascivious smile as he pressed her down. Daisy held her ground. She tried to squirm from his grip, to kiss him again, to distract from his intention, but the pressure on her shoulders increased. An intense wave of anger and revulsion swept over her. She didn't want this, not with him. She pulled away.

"What's wrong?"

"I don't want to do that."

"Why not?"

"I just don't, okay?" Her stomach churned, disgust and inebriation threatening to manifest in vomit. She had to leave. She stumbled toward the door.

"Seriously?" He scoffed in her wake. "You'll have dirty, crazy sex with Liam but you won't even give me a BJ?"

She turned back to look at him: handsome, popular, arrogant. Daisy could respond, could stand up for herself, but why? This boy's opinion of her was irrelevant. And she was too drunk to mount a proper defense.

"Sorry."

She yanked open the door and scurried down the stairs.

* * *

Outside, it was cold and dark and raining, but it was still a relief from the clammy, sweaty, hormone-filled interior. She huddled into her coat as she trudged up Dylan's winding driveway toward the main road. She wasn't exactly sure where she was, but when she emerged from the forested enclave that concealed the opulent home, she would get her bearings. She fingered the reassuring outline of her phone in her back pocket.

She already knew what she was going to do. In fact, she may have known the moment Dylan unzipped his fly. She had been stupid to entertain the boy's attentions, stupid to have danced with him, kissed him, let him lead her upstairs. . . . There would be social repercussions; a return to teen exile was likely. But Dylan wasn't her biggest mistake. Her biggest mistake was pretending she belonged here, with these children. She didn't. She was done playing their game.

At the road was a mailbox, an ornate brick structure with the address posted prominently above the letter slot. Pulling out her phone, Daisy took a fortifying breath. She typed:

Can you come get me?

The response was almost instant.

Send address

Daisy was a liar. She had made a promise to Frances Met-calfe that she had never intended to keep. If the woman found out, she would be upset, angry, even afraid for Daisy's safety. But Frances would never know. And in that moment, Daisy felt only relief and anticipation.

David was coming for her.

frances

NOW

All weekend, Frances avoided Kate, citing a "bug." She turned off her phone to dodge her pal's concerned texts, her offers of soup or to take Marcus for the day. How could Kate be so caring to a friend with a virus, and so heartless and cruel to Courtney Carey? Frances told the same fib to her husband. Marcus had a soccer game on Sunday. Under normal circumstances, both his parents would have attended. But these were not normal circumstances. Frances had to feign illness to return to her research.

Opinion on the World Wide Web was that Amber Kunik had gotten off easy. Yes, she had been physically, mentally, and emotionally abused by Shane Nelson; there was ample evidence of that. She'd been lured into the relationship at the highly impressionable age of eighteen. Nelson was older, charismatic, already exhibiting signs of sadism and sexual deviancy. Amber would have been considered a victim . . . if not for those tapes.

Consensus by anyone who saw them (or read the transcripts) was that Amber Kunik had been a willing and enthusiastic participant in the atrocities committed against Courtney Carey. Amber's were not the actions of a battered woman, playing along out of fear and self-preservation. She had relished the vile acts, instigated torture, suggested abuse. No one was that good an actress, sources said.

Shane Nelson's claims that Amber had murdered the teenager were more contentious. His lawyer had argued that Nelson left the two girls alone, that it was Amber, not Shane, who had caved Courtney's skull in. The jury didn't buy it. It was too grasping, too desperate. But many in the online community believed the convicted man.

Frances couldn't face the onslaught of information anymore. She needed to talk to someone, to discuss the facts, to verbalize the contentious thoughts swirling through her head. She couldn't confide in her husband, not yet. Jason would jump to conclusions, he'd panic, he'd blow the whistle. And her spouse couldn't offer the clarity she sought. Frances needed to connect with someone who'd been there, someone with firsthand knowledge of the case.

Her initial thought was the prosecutor, Neil Givens, but her research indicated that he had died several years earlier. Stomach cancer. Was it guilt over the deal he'd made with Amber that had caused the tumor in the attorney's gut? Was it regret that turned his body against him, remorse that made his cells malignant? Had Amber Kunik effectively killed him, too?

She could easily speak to Amber's lawyer. He lived a couple of blocks away, she even had his cell phone number. Robert Randolph had negotiated Amber Kunik's plea deal, had kept her name off sex offender registries, had created a new persona for her. Obviously, he knew everything that Amber had done, and he had forgiven her. Perhaps Frances could, too? She knew that good people sometimes got caught up in bad situations. Young, impressionable women were regularly corrupted, manipulated, and led astray. But they could recover, go on to build a life, have a career, friends, a family. . . .

It never left them, though. What Frances had done to her sister haunted her. It disturbed her sleep, damaged her self-esteem, informed her every action. Kate Randolph was so confident, so light, so fun and free. . . . Perhaps she was blameless in Shane Nelson's atrocities. Or, perhaps, she had no conscience.

That left Shane Nelson's lawyer. A Google search indicated that he had moved to Palm Beach, Florida. Frances wondered when Martin Bannerman had relocated to the opposite side of the country and why. Was it simply a great place to retire? Or did he want to distance himself from the life he'd built in Arizona defending murderers?

The retired attorney sat on the board of a public art gallery. It took only a few clicks through the gallery's site to find his contact information. The phone number stared back at her, tempting her, taunting her. Could she talk to this man who had vociferously argued that her friend Kate was a murderer? Could she accept the things he would tell her? But Bannerman's job had been to defend his client. He didn't necessarily believe Kate—Amber—was guilty. She was punching in the numbers when she heard Jason's car pull into the driveway. She saved the digits, dropped the device, and moved to the door.

"How was the game?" It was a rhetorical question. Marcus's glum countenance, his defeated posture, made it clear his team had lost.

"Terrible." The boy stepped out of his muddy cleats. He was soaked. Soccer games went ahead, rain or shine. "I'm going to have a shower," he grumbled, stalking from the room.

Jason hung up his jacket. "Four nothing for them," he said, with a grimace.

"Poor guy. He takes losing so personally."

"I suggested that Charles could come over. That seemed to cheer him up."

"No," Frances said, quickly. "Charles is sick."

"Someone else then?"

They shared a look. Marcus had made significant social strides, but still . . . There was no one else. Charles was their son's only friend; it didn't need to be articulated.

"Let him play a video game," Frances said. "I'm going to the gym."

"I thought you weren't feeling well."

"I feel better now."

Jason gave her a bemused smile. "You never work out on Sundays."

"I'm stepping up my regimen," she said, grabbing her phone and her keys. "I'll be back in an hour."

She drove toward the gym, her heart thudding with anticipation—or dread. When she was a sufficient distance from her house, she pulled into the parking lot of a daycare center. It was vacant—the children were spending the weekend with their working parents. She pulled out her phone and dialed the number she had saved. The ringing was barely audible over the raindrops tapping on the car's metal roof, and her pulse pounding in her ears.

"Hello?"

She forced a professional tone though her voice was tremulous. "Is this Martin Bannerman?"

"Yes?" The response was deep, masculine, wary.

"My name is Frances Metcalfe. I'm calling about Amber Kunik."

"I have no comment."

"I'm not a reporter," she said quickly. "I'm her friend. I mean . . . I'm a friend of Kate Randolph's. That's the name she uses now. Our sons go to the same school. They're best friends. Kate and I—*Amber* and I—are close." She was rambling, but she couldn't stop. "I just found out who Kate really is. I'm confused and afraid and I . . . I need to talk to someone who knew her."

There was a long pause. Then:

"You'd be wise to stay away from that woman."

"Amber's changed, though. She's a wife and a mom now. I've known her for a while. She's kind and funny and caring."

"She plays people. She charms them. That's what socio-paths do."

Sociopath. Frances thought about all the compliments Kate had given her, the support and commiseration. Was it all just a game? Was Frances just a toy? A pet to be dashed against the pavement when Kate grew tired of her?

"Do you . . ." Frances's throat closed, but she forced the words out. "Do you think she's still the same person who did those awful things?"

"Of course she is."

"Is Kate—Amber—still dangerous?"

"Anyone who saw those videotapes knows that Amber Kunik is capable of unspeakable evil." Bannerman's masculine voice had become subdued; he sounded older, almost fragile. "What I saw . . . What she and Shane did to that girl . . . I think about it every goddamn day. Some nights, I can't sleep."

Frances could imagine what kept the man awake; the acts she had read about would be seared into the attorney's brain. "But Amber was just a girl. Shane Nelson abused her. He manip-ulated her."

"Shane Nelson is a piece of shit," the attorney stated. "He'd been assaulting and raping women for years. But it wasn't until he met Amber Kunik that a girl ended up dead."

The words landed on her like snow sliding off a roof, sending a chill to her very bones. She tried to process the lawyer's observation, but her brain refused to take it in. She couldn't accept that Courtney Carey was dead because of Kate. It was too horrible, too surreal. But even as her mind denied the possibility, her body was reacting. She was trembling and sweating. She felt like she might be sick.

"Thanks for your time," she managed.

"Be careful." He hung up the phone.

Frances sat for a few minutes, letting her nervous system settle. She breathed deeply as the rain beat down, painting her windshield like an oily canvas. She should turn the key, drive to Curves, and perform her circuit. The exercise might offer some clarity, the endorphins might dissipate the mental fog that clung to her. But she didn't have the energy. She felt weary, weak, beaten down. Jason would be confused by her prompt return, but she would tell him she'd had a relapse. She was too ill to work out. It wasn't a lie. She was sick to her stomach.

She started the car and headed for home.

daisy

NOW

*D*ear Aunt Marnie . . . The cursor on the laptop screen blinked at her, taunting her to write more. But what could she say?

I'm Daisy, the daughter of the brother you disowned after he reconciled with his philandering wife. . . . Got any Christmas plans?

She took a sip of her second green tea. She was tucked in a back corner of the busy coffee shop at Yarrow Point. If she didn't keep ordering, she'd have to give up her table.

It was 3:30 p.m. now; school would be finished. Daisy had skipped. She wasn't up to facing a spurned Dylan Larabee. But dread wasn't the only thing that had kept her from school today. Her general lack of enthusiasm for her education had now been combined with an extreme lack of focus. She couldn't even compose a simple e-mail without her mind drifting to the events of Saturday night. To David.

He had come when she'd called for him, the growl of that big car sending relief coursing through her as she stood alone, in the dark and the rain. When she'd climbed into the passenger seat, David had looked her over. "Are you okay?"

"Yeah."

"Did someone hurt you? Do I need to go in there?"

The thought of this big strong man defending her honor made her heart feel light and happy. The mental image of him beating the crap out of Dylan made her warm all over. But she pressed her lips together and shook her head. "I just want to get out of here." And then, shyly, "Can we go to your place?"

His apartment was empty, a lamp burning in the living room. She sat on the couch while David went to the tiny kitchen, returning, moments later, with a glass of tap water and a large, yellow pill.

"Take this."

"What is it?"

"Vitamin B complex. It'll help with your hangover tomorrow."

She wondered if he knew how sick she'd been the last time she was here. Hopefully not. She had been sure to clean up after herself. Obediently, she'd swallowed the tablet.

He'd disappeared into his bedroom then, while Daisy waited: stoned, drunk, but vibrating with nervous energy. When he came back, he had a pillow and blankets. "You should sleep," he said, propping the pillow against the arm of the sofa.

"I'm not tired."

"I am." It was late now, close to 2 a.m. She obliged him, lying down, letting him place the blankets over her, appreciating the feeling of his hands on her.

"Good night, Daisy."

"Good night, David."

He left her there, lying in the darkness, eyes open, formulating her plan. Her judgment may have been impaired—by the alcohol and the weed—but she was resolute. Despite her inebriation, she'd experienced a sudden clarity of emotion. She waited, her heart fluttering with anticipation, until David was silent in the adjacent room. Then she waited some more, letting him drift into sleep, his defenses down. When sufficient time had passed, she threw the blanket off her and stood. Removing her jeans and shirt, she tiptoed, in bra and panties, to his room.

The door creaked softly as she entered. "What are you doing?" He was awake, his voice soft in the darkness.

"I don't want to be alone," she said, slipping into bed next to him.

"Daisy . . . ," he admonished her, but he let her in, allowed her to curl up next to his warm body. She pressed herself into him, savoring his scent, the softness of his bare skin. Before she could chicken out, she propped herself up on her elbows, and kissed his mouth.

He didn't push her away, but his lips remained closed, unresponsive. Still, it felt intimate and arousing—a black-and-white movie kiss, not a slobbery make-out sesh like she'd had with Liam or Dylan. She could taste cigarettes, ever so faintly, and something fresh like cucumber or melon. Her hand tentatively crept up to touch David's face, her fingers drifting over the stubble on his strong jawline, finding their way into the hair at the back of his neck. She moved her leg over his, crawling on top of him. But he lay like a stone, lips together, body solid and unyielding. She rolled off him.

"What's wrong?" she asked.

"This is a bad idea."

"No, it isn't." Her inebriation made her brave. "I . . . I love you."

He turned his head to look at her. "No, you don't."

"I do." That had to be what this feeling was: intense, uncomfortable, unfamiliar.

"You're just a kid," he said. "You don't even know me."

Humiliation burned her face, clogged her throat, weighted her chest. A sob shuddered through her. She was so stupid. A stupid fucking child. She had to go.

But as she climbed out of bed, David caught her wrist and pulled her back down. She didn't have the energy to free herself, and of course, she didn't want to. She collapsed on his chest, emotions bubbling out of her. Her tears slicked his skin as he stroked her hair and let her cry on him. Before long, she was exhausted, the pot, the booze, and the night's events taking their toll. She felt warm and safe and not quite loved, but comforted. Soon, she was asleep.

Her green tea was cold now, but she took a sip as a group of women in workout gear eyed her table covetously. She turned her attention back to the missive on her screen.

Dear Aunt Marnie . . .

She accepted the blinking cursor's challenge and typed:

My dad gave me your e-mail address and said that it would be okay to get in touch. I am interested in knowing more about you and your family, and my grandma.

I hope you will write back to me. Maybe we could even meet one day?

Sincerely,

Daisy Randolph

Without rereading, she hit send.

As she pretended to drink her tea, staring at the blank computer screen, her mind drifted back to yesterday morning. She had woken up in David's bed, her mouth dry and fuzzy, a dull ache in her head. She had been curled on her side, facing the window, away from her partner. She had rolled toward him, prepared to make an excuse—*I don't really love you, I was just wasted*—but he was gone.

She'd called an Uber. There was no way she could reach out to Frances this time. The woman would be angry, disappointed, disgusted. Rightly so. Daisy was stupid. She was pathetic. She should have stayed way.

The cold green tea was almost gone when her phone buzzed in her backpack. It would be David again. She didn't need to look, but she did.

We need to talk

They didn't. Because there was no point. Daisy had opened herself up, had let herself become attached, and it had blown up in her face. She had romanticized her connection to David into something more than it was, but now the blinders were off. He didn't care about her. The man had targeted her. She was just another *troubled teen*, a social pariah, the product of a cold and loveless home. David would have drawn her in, made her feel safe and loved and special, and then . . . what? What did he want with her? Her young mind couldn't fathom all the possibilities.

"Excuse me. . . ." It was one of the workout women who had been eyeing her table. "Are you done here?" Her tone was pointed, condescending, like she could intimidate this girl out of her seat. This lady didn't know who she was fucking with.

"Nope." Daisy stood. "I was just about to order more tea."

frances

NOW

It should not have been this easy to talk to a convicted murderer. But here Frances was, seated at her kitchen table, preparing to have a face-to-face with Shane Nelson. She had never heard of video visitation until a few days ago. But in her hunt for online answers, it became apparent that, after filling out a few forms, ensuring her laptop had adequate software, and submitting her credit card number, she could go to the source. She could ask Shane Nelson himself if Amber Kunik had killed Courtney Carey. It had been his claim when he was fighting for his life, but the fight was over now. He had no reason to lie to Frances.

Pay-per-view contact between prisoners and the outside world was controversial. Proponents said it improved security, cut down on contraband, allowed for increased group and long-distance visitation. Detractors said it was the prison industrial complex monetizing the basic right of an inmate to connect with his or her loved ones. They said such visitation lacked intimacy, that it was cost prohibitive to poor families. But Shane Nelson was not Frances's loved one. And she was willing to pay to find answers.

She had created an account, scanned in a piece of picture I.D., and waited. The process was sure to take days, if not weeks. But to her shock, a confirmation e-mail had arrived on Monday afternoon. All she had to do was click a link, and she was taken to a calendar to schedule a video session. She wondered why Nelson had agreed to talk to her. She supposed he was bored, lonely, desperate for any sort of connection. The convict had no family left, no friends, no support system on the outside. Years ago, he had been of interest to reporters and crime writers. There had been books about the attractive young killers, magazine articles, and tabloid-style news programs. Nelson was legally prohibited from profiting from his crimes through any form of media, but that hadn't stopped his participation. Since time had passed and interest had waned, Nelson must be hungry for attention.

Frances sat on a kitchen chair, sweating in her pale blue sweater. On the table, her laptop sat open and ready. At precisely 1:30 p.m., three minutes from now, she would invite a murderer into her home. Her mind flitted to Kate. . . . Perhaps this wouldn't be the first time. But that did nothing to quell her nerves.

She had blown out her hair, donned the flattering blue sweater, and applied a peachy lipstick. Why? It had been automatic—like prepping for a job interview or a meeting with the principal. But now, as she watched the minutes pass in the bottom corner of the laptop screen, she regretted her efforts. There were women who were infatuated with convicts, who fell in love with men behind bars. Handsome killers had no shortage of admirers. She hoped her hair and makeup didn't send Nelson the wrong message.

Suddenly, the screen flickered, and the inmate appeared before her. Frances's jaw clenched as she took in his lined but still loosely handsome face. Shane Nelson was over fifty now, and thinner than he had been on the outside, shriveled like a dried apricot. Usually, prisoners got bigger while incarcerated, but Nelson was in segregation; he was protected. There was less impetus for him to get strong.

He wore the horizontal black-and-white striped uniform of a bygone era. (Maricopa County was one of the few prison systems in the U.S. to reintroduce the outdated garb.) Frances assumed it was a humiliation tactic: prisoners should look like prisoners. The convict's head and shoulders filled the screen perched in front of her. It felt uncomfortably close, like the prisoner was there, in her messy kitchen, with her. She had a sudden urge to wipe off her lipstick.

"Hi." He smiled. "I'm Shane." As if he needed an introduction.

"I'm Frances." She purposely omitted her last name. Chances were infinitesimal that Nelson would ever be paroled, but just in case . . .

"Nice to meet you, Frances." He was grinning, maybe even flirting. He thought she was a fan; he was enjoying the audience.

"I want to talk to you about Amber Kunik."

The sagging face instantly darkened. "What about her?"

"Amber lives near me. In the Pacific Northwest." She was intentionally vague. "Our sons go to school together. They're friends."

"How cute," he sneered. "How old are Amber's kids now?"

It couldn't hurt to tell him. "Eleven and fourteen."

"Poor little bastards," he scoffed. "She still married to her lawyer?"

"Yeah."

"Amber could manipulate anyone," he sniped. "Men, women, the judge, the jury . . . No one had a chance with her."

Frances played along. "It must seem very unfair. You're locked up. She's free, living a normal life."

"Yeah, it's fucking unfair. . . . Especially since Amber killed that girl."

"So, you stand by that claim?" Frances said. "Even now?"

"Of course I stand by it. It's the fucking truth." Nelson leaned back in his chair. "But no one in court would believe me. They were all under Amber's *spell*."

Like she was magic. Like she was a witch.

"It was her word against mine. They chose hers. But my lawyer believed me. He knew I was telling the truth."

Martin Bannerman's words niggled at the back of Frances's mind.

It wasn't until he met Amber Kunik that a girl ended up dead.

"I wasn't even there when it happened," Shane continued, tipping forward. "Amber sent me out for chicken. I came home, and Courtney was dead. Her head all bashed in and shit. Amber said the kid got herself untied and tried to escape. They tussled. Amber grabbed an iron and hit her with it."

Frances could feel beads of sweat on her upper lip. "Amber claimed that you abused her, that she had to do what you wanted, or you'd beat her."

Nelson let out a sardonic chuckle. "We abused each other. She hit me, I hit back. Harder. Maybe too hard. But most of the time, she started it."

"What about the rapes? Do you put that on Amber, too?"

"I take responsibility for what I've done," he snapped. "I was sick then. I was a deviant and a sadist. I deserve to be locked up for it." He leaned forward, his face blurring, spilling off the screen. "But I didn't kill Courtney Carey. I wasn't even there."

He sounded so sincere, so adamant, but Frances couldn't let herself be swayed. Shane Nelson was a psychopath who'd attached himself to a narrative: the wrongly convicted killer, the pawn of an evil, manipulative woman. The call had been a waste of time. It had been a mistake.

But Nelson wasn't finished. "That bitch cost me everything: my freedom, my friends, my family. . . . People think I'm a monster. The only person who stood by me was my mom. She's dead now. Diabetes."

"I—I'm sorry."

"Thanks." There was no sadness, evidence that Frances was not dealing with a normal, sentient being here. The prisoner leaned toward the camera, his face filling the screen, pixelating before her eyes.

"Amber Kunik is an evil, lying bitch. You'd better watch your kid—" His voice cut off.

The screen flickered, and static filled her ears. The image of Nelson was frozen, disintegrating, the prison stripes losing their symmetry. Then the screen went black. Frances closed the laptop.

She felt unnerved, shaky . . . and dirty. Hurrying to the shower, she turned the water to hot, and washed away the filth of her encounter. With a facecloth, she scrubbed away the lipstick and eyeliner, washed the anti-frizz product from her hair. Then she stood, lost in her thoughts, as the hot water beat down on her and steam filled the tiny room.

Nelson had provided no more clarity than his lawyer had before him. Talking to the men involved in the trial was pointless. They still had their agendas, they still clung to their disproven claims. And then, as Frances rinsed the conditioner from her hair, she realized to whom she needed to speak. There was one person who knew Amber better than anyone.

She turned off the water.

dj

When DJ had first observed Shane Nelson's defense attorney, he had compared him to a bulldog. Now, as Martin Bannerman resumed his cross-examination of Amber Kunik for the third day, the boy realized he was more like a terrier: tenacious, scrappy, determined. The attorney was not going to let this slight girl defeat him. He was going to show the judge, the jury, and the gallery, that Amber was a lying, deceitful monster.

"Tell me about your relationship with Courtney Carey," he instructed.

DJ tensed at the sound of his sister's name. His father sat up straighter.

"I liked her," Amber said, sweetly. "I felt like we were friends. We did stuff together, like put makeup on each other, and we painted each other's nails."

"Where was Shane when you were doing your makeup and painting your nails?"

"He was watching TV. Or out getting food or booze or whatever."

"So, he left you and Courtney alone?"

"Sometimes."

"Why didn't you let her go?"

Amber hesitated for just a beat, long enough for DJ's chest to fill with hope. "I was afraid. Of Shane."

"But Shane wasn't there," the attorney said, feigning confusion. "You could have let Courtney go and you could have run away, too. You could have gone to your parents." The lawyer indicated Amber's mother and father, sitting, like stone, across the aisle from DJ and his dad. The Kuniks came every day, unwavering in their support for Amber. Not once did DJ see them glance his way.

"Your parents would have helped you," Bannerman continued. "They would have rescued you."

"Shane said he'd kill my mom and dad if I ever told them."

"You could have gone to a friend. You could have gone to the police."

"I was too scared. And I was too ashamed." She looked down, playing the part. "I didn't think people would understand the things Shane had made me do."

"But you said you liked Courtney. And you knew Shane was going to kill her, eventually."

"I—I didn't know for sure."

"*You didn't know for sure, Ms. Kunik? You testified that Shane said, 'We have to get rid of her.'* "

"*I don't know,*" she said, flustered. "*I wasn't sure what he meant.*"

The lawyer paced for a moment, ramping up the tension. "*Ms. Kunik, was it actually you who decided this game had gone on long enough? Was it you who decided to get rid of Courtney?*"

"*No . . . I never said that.*"

"*Isn't it true that you sent Shane Nelson out to buy fast food on the afternoon of March 5? And, while he was gone, Courtney managed to get herself untied and saw an opportunity to escape. You tried to stop her. The two of you struggled, and, in your panic, you hit Courtney on the head with an iron.*"

For just a moment, Amber looked like she might break. Her eyes fell on DJ, but he couldn't read them. What did she see when she looked at him? A fat kid who spent too much time eating junk and playing video games? A boy whose shaggy brown hair needed cutting? Whose shabby clothes he'd outgrown?

Or did Amber see a brother who had lost his only sister? A son whose mother's heart had been so crushed that she could no longer be a parent? A child whose father's pain had made him mean and violent and drunk?

Amber turned her gray eyes back to Martin Bannerman.

"*It was Shane who bashed Courtney's head in with that iron. Not me.*"

DJ knew then that Amber Kunik had no soul.

frances

It was approximately a three-hour drive from Bellevue to Portland, but Frances was on track to complete it in under two-and-a-half. She'd dropped Marcus off at school a little early this morning and set off from there. Her son must have sensed her impatience, because he'd obediently deposited his iPad in its case, kissed his mom's cheek, and climbed out of the car at the drop-off point. She was now approaching the bridge that housed the Washington/Oregon state line. By her calculations, a five-hour round trip would allow her just under an hour to speak to Amber Kunik's mother and still make school pickup.

Kate had mentioned that her mom lived in a mobile-home park north of Portland. Armed with that information, it had not taken long to find the matriarch. The Kuniks had moved from Arizona to Oregon after the trial, but Marlene hadn't changed her name, despite the continued, and justified, fascination with her only child. What kind of woman raised a daughter who became a killer? Surely, Frances wasn't the first person to wonder.

There were many photos online of Marlene Kunik and her husband, Terry. Frances learned that the patriarch had died years ago, while his only child was still incarcerated. Heart attack. By all accounts, he'd been a smoker and a drinker. The images depicted the couple attending their daughter's trial, escorting Amber to and from court. They held the girl's hands, or linked arms at the elbow: protective, supportive, loyal. Marlene was an attractive woman then, a little hard, a little heavy. Her husband had a stalwart European look to him, but his lifestyle was already taking its toll.

Frances had considered calling, but she couldn't risk Marlene hanging up on her. And she needed to see the woman in person, to connect to her as a mother. Marlene knew her daughter like few others could, and she had stood by her. If Marlene could forgive Amber, perhaps Frances could, too? As her tires crunched along the gravel drive of the "mobile living community," her nerves activated. Mrs. Kunik could refuse to speak to her, could slam the door in her face, could tell her to go to hell. She should have phoned first.

But there was no time for procrastination if she was going to make it back to Forrester in time for the end of her son's school day. She parked the car in front of Marlene Kunik's shabby double-wide trailer. It had a drooping wooden porch extending from its side, a wart on an ugly nose. Exiting the car, Frances marched up the wooden steps, slimy with moss and damp, and rang the bell. The sound was met with a chorus of high-pitched barks from an unknown number of small dogs inside. She could hear Marlene shushing her pets, moving slowly, laboriously, toward her.

The door opened a crack to reveal Kate's mother. The plump but pretty woman from the photographs had disappeared, swallowed by this bloated, flabby version of her. Marlene was eating or drinking her pain; Frances, of all people, understood the psychology. The older woman's puffy eyes narrowed at the stranger on her porch. Frances would not have been the first to stand here.

"Hi, Marlene. My name's Frances Metcalfe. I'm your daughter's friend. Well, I'm Kate Randolph's friend. I just found out who she really is. . . ." Emotion made her voice wobble. "I need to talk to you."

"You're not a reporter? You're not writing a book?"

"No. I'm a mom. My son is friends with your grandson, Charles."

The woman's pudgy features relaxed. "Come in."

Stepping into Marlene Kunik's home was like stepping back in time. The décor looked untouched since the seventies: plaid couches, matted shag carpets, and avocado kitchen appliances. How had Kate developed her sense of style? Perhaps it was born of deprivation. Above the mantel of a faux-brick fireplace was a family portrait: Kate, about thirteen, her dark hair cut into the poufy mullet popular in the late eighties, was flanked by her pretty mom and striking father. As in all family portraits, the subjects looked stiff, awkward . . . normal. Jesus . . . what went wrong in this family?

Three small dogs, curly mutts, swarmed around Frances's feet, yapping and jumping on her. Marlene scolded them and swatted at them as she hobbled to an oval dining table, its plastic tablecloth dusted with crumbs. Amber's mother slowly, painfully, lowered herself onto a chair. Frances sat across from her.

"Do you want some tea?"

"No, thanks." Frances didn't have the heart to make her stand up again. And the smell in the trailer—mildew, fried food, animal urine—was unappetizing. "I won't stay long, but I wanted to ask you a few questions. About Amber."

"You're not writing a book about her? Or one of them murder blogs?"

"No. I'm her friend." Her chest filled with emotion again, but it suddenly seemed indulgent. She looked at the obese woman across from her, the mother whose baby had grown up to commit such a heinous crime, and shook off her self-pity. "I'm trying to understand who she really is. . . ."

"Well, she's innocent. That's for sure."

A swell of hope filled Frances's chest. "You don't think she had anything to do with Courtney Carey's murder?"

"Anything Amber did, it was because Shane made her do it."

"Because he beat her? And abused her?"

"Yes." A dog hopped up on Marlene's lap and licked her face vigorously. "Amber kept it hidden from all of us, but he was horrible to her. She put on a brave face, pretended she was happy, pretended she was in love. But we found out later that she was terrified."

"So . . . you never suspected he was hurting her?"

"He was so handsome and charming. He seemed so loving. Shane fooled us all."

Or had Amber fooled them all?

Marlene seemed to read Frances's doubts. "I took the stand at Shane's trial. His defense attorney asked me why, if Shane was such a monster, I hadn't seen any evidence of the abuse." She stroked the ball of fluff now curled comfortably on her soft, pillowy stomach. "He tried to make it look as if Amber was lying. But she wasn't. She just didn't want to worry us, so she put makeup on her bruises, she wore long sleeves and scarves, and she kept her mouth shut."

"Did she tell anyone? Any of her friends or anyone at work?"

"No . . . But they don't, do they? The battered women . . ." She pushed the dog off her lap. "They think they're in love, so they protect their abusers. It's all a big head game."

Frances nodded, her eyes on the specks on the table before her. They were cookie crumbs, a boxed brand, chocolate chip. She felt a strong urge to sweep them up, brush them into her hand, and dump them in the trash. But she didn't want to offend her host. She looked up.

"What was Amber like? As a little girl? As a teenager?"

"She was sweet. And so smart. All her teachers loved her. She always had the neatest handwriting in the class, always had the top marks. . . . She was a leader, too. A regular little bossy boots." Marlene smiled at the reminiscence, and Frances smiled, too. This sounded like the Kate she knew: the perfectionist, the brave warrior unafraid of the mean moms.

"She changed a little in high school, went through all the normal phases. For a while, she dyed her hair crazy colors and wore goth makeup. She always loved horror movies." Marlene seemed to notice the crumbs for the first time, and brushed them into a little pile with her fat fingers. "She went through a phase where she carved designs into her legs: stars and crosses, mostly."

"*Carved?* Like with a knife?"

"Just a little penknife. It didn't last long."

Frances was puzzled, both by the woman's indifference to her daughter's self-mutilation, and her willingness to talk about it. If Marcus was cutting himself, she would have immediately plunked him into therapy (*more* therapy, in his case). And she would have told no one, would have blamed herself for her son's disturbing actions. But it was a different time then. And clearly, Marlene Kunik was a different type of mother. Frances pressed on.

"Would you say Amber had a happy home life?"

"For the most part, yeah. We were a normal family. Terry and I had a normal marriage, the usual ups and downs. He had a little problem with the hookers, which pissed me off, of course. But otherwise, he was a good husband. And a good dad."

Frances felt her cheeks flush. "Did Amber know about the uh, *hooker problem?*"

Marlene played with the pile of cookie crumbs. "She knew. The police came to the house. Terry went to court. Ended up doing a little time, weekends only." She pressed a chocolate chip onto her finger and popped it into her mouth. "Amber was pretty disgusted with him."

"That must have been hard on her."

"It was hard on *Terry*. Amber was so angry. She called him Pervert after that, not Dad. . . . *Good night, Pervert. Thanks for the ride, Pervert. Love you, Pervert.*"

Frances felt queasy. The smell of dogs and food and unwashed body was almost overwhelming. The Kunik family was toxic, sordid, and dysfunctional. But were they bad enough to turn their daughter into a killer? Marlene read the struggle on her guest's face. She leaned forward, elbows on the table.

"We went through some hard times, but Amber had a lot of happy years. And then she met Shane, and he ruined everything."

"I'm sorry."

"It wasn't all bad. . . ." She clapped a clammy palm on top of Frances's hand. "When Amber was in prison, she got her art history degree. For free."

"I should go." Frances stood. Marlene watched her, seemingly considering the effort it would take to see her guest out. "Don't get up, please. . . ."

With dogs swirling around her feet, Frances rushed to the door.

She drove to a diner she'd passed on the way to the trailer park. She wasn't hungry—quite the opposite—but she was rattled, unnerved, concerned about her ability to drive. The meeting with Marlene Kunik had been shorter than anticipated, so Frances had some time to spare. When the middle-aged waiter approached her, she ordered a gin and tonic. "And a club sandwich with fries," she added, for appearances. It was 11:48. No one would bat an eye.

As she sipped the bitter drink, felt the alcohol take effect, she reflected on the conversation. Her friend had hardly had a Norman Rockwell upbringing, but many—including Frances, herself—had suffered worse, without turning into monsters. If Kate's home life had been relatively normal, did that mean Shane Nelson was to blame? Frances's online research indicated that he'd been raised in a violent home, with rampant drug and alcohol abuse. Or did Kate's stable upbringing mean that she was just plain evil?

"Anything else, ma'am?"

The waiter's presence jarred her from her thoughts. She looked down at the table. She had finished the gin and tonic, the sandwich, and every last fry.

"Just the bill."

She would have been on time, but she hit traffic just past Tacoma. An accident: three mangled cars simmered on the side of the freeway. Of course, Frances hoped no one was killed or seriously injured, but she couldn't help feeling annoyed at the participants. Thanks to their carelessness, she was going to be late to pick up Marcus. Not so late that she needed to call the school—her son was a dawdler and often didn't emerge from the building until three-fifteen at least—but still . . . late. Marcus would occupy himself on the playground for several minutes before he grew concerned about his mother's absence. If she could get there by three-twenty-five, he'd barely notice her tardiness.

The dashboard clock read 3:22 when she finally pulled up to Forrester Academy. She found a spot in the lot, still packed with SUVs, minivans, and the odd station wagon as parents and nannies collected their charges. Hustling toward the playground, Frances assured herself that her son was fine. He would be playing there, alone most likely, or on the periphery of a group of more popular students. Lately, he'd been included in a few group games—soccer and manhunt—and she hoped that would be the case today. His friend, Charles, was always picked up promptly at three o'clock. This meant that Frances would avoid Kate, today at least. At the edge of the play area, she paused, scanning the children for the oversize form of her son.

"Frances . . ." She turned to see Jeanette Dumas, her nemesis, wearing a smart pantsuit and dangly earrings, standing a few feet away. The titans of industry she had been coaching must have let her off early today.

"Hi, Jeanette." She forced a smile, then resumed the visual search for her boy.

Jeanette moved closer. "Allison Moss told me she invited you and Kate to join the community garden committee."

"Uh . . . yeah."

"I've joined and I hope you'll consider it, too." She gave Frances a kind, almost beseeching smile. "I think it's time to put the whole *water bottle* incident behind us. I know Abbey can be a little *domineering*, and some kids react badly to that. And Marcus seems to be fitting in really well now."

Only a few weeks ago, Frances would have been thrilled by Jeanette's forgiveness. But now, with everything she knew, it was irrelevant. "Okay . . ."

The businesswoman continued. "Marcus and Charles are so cute together. Sometimes it just takes one good friend to make everything right."

Unless that one friend turns out to be a murderer. "Have you seen Marcus?" Frances asked. "I'm a little late. I thought he'd be playing out here."

"Kate took the boys home."

"*What?*"

Jeanette was perplexed by Frances's reaction. "She said she was going to text you. She said you gave the office permission for her to collect him."

"Right. I did." *Before* she knew who Kate really was, what she had done, the acts she was capable of . . .

"Kate said she'll join the garden committee if you do. You two would be a great addition to the team."

But Frances was already jogging to her car.

daisy

NOW

Daisy had been loath to return to school, but she couldn't stay home indefinitely. Despite her dread, her return to Centennial had been anticlimactic. If Dylan Larabee was angry or crushed by her refusal to blow him at his party, he didn't show it. When she'd spotted him across the foyer this morning, he'd completely ignored her. Tori, Maggie, and their popular crew also seemed indifferent to the rebuff that had taken place in the Larabee parents' bedroom. They were still chatty, giggly, friendly. It was almost like Dylan hadn't castigated Daisy, like Liam had. Maybe he was too distracted by the upcoming holiday. It was almost Thanksgiving.

The Randolphs had no special plans for the occasion; they never did. Daisy had hoped that, after her dad's trip to see his family, they might receive an invitation to California. Or that her parents might extend one to Bellevue. But of course, her mom would never invite "that judgmental cunt," Marnie, to visit them. Whatever her mother's opinion of her sister-in-law, Daisy had been thrilled, last night, when she received an e-mail from her aunt.

She was in math now, openly scrolling on her phone through the photographs Aunt Marnie had sent her. There was a distinct sibling resemblance between her father and his younger sister. Marnie was tall, like her brother, strong, solid, and athletic. The overbite that gave Robert his resemblance to Goofy was more attractive on a female face, almost sultry. Her aunt had to be in her early fifties; she looked attractive, healthy, kind. . . . She didn't look like the type of woman who disowned her only brother over his wife's affair. But appearances could be deceiving.

Marnie had included pictures of Daisy's grandparents, grainy shots of a glamorous young couple (didn't everyone look glamorous in old photographs?) dressed up for a party or a date. It was hard to feel a connection to these strangers though their blood ran through Daisy's veins. There were some photographs of Marnie and Robert as children, her sophisticated dad a rough-and-tumble boy. Daisy realized this was the first photo she'd seen of her father as a child. Who had he been then? What was he like before all his degrees and his career? Before her mom?

And then there were the cousins. Christina, Marnie's daughter, appeared in her graduation outfit, a pretty girl with dark curly hair and a round face inherited from her father. The boy, Josh, closer to Daisy's age, wore a soccer uniform. There was something Mediterranean in their looks, and Daisy assumed that her uncle Paul must descend from Italy, or Greece maybe. His last name would be a clue, but Aunt Marnie still went by Randolph, and she hadn't mentioned her husband's or her children's surname.

Her aunt had written a warm note, thanking Daisy for reaching out, expressing regret for not being a part of her life, but not addressing the elephant in the room: Kate Randolph. Marnie hoped that they could meet in person sometime. She had often thought about Daisy and Charles, hoped they were happy and well. It had brought tears to Daisy's eyes, knowing that her aunt had wondered and worried from afar. That someone, out in the world, cared about her.

The bell rang, signaling the end of class, the end of the school day, the countdown to the holiday. Daisy didn't relish four days with her parents and brother, but she had no choice. Maybe the Randolphs would have Thanksgiving dinner with their friends the Metcalfes? At least they could pretend to be a happy, normal, well-adjusted family. Daisy gathered her books and headed to her locker.

Pale, vegan Mia was there, waiting. Evidently, their friendship was still intact.

"Wanna get a coffee? Or a smoothie?"

"Sure," Daisy said. "Where's Emma?" Mia and the rosy-cheeked carnivore were usually a package deal.

"She took an extra day off. She's gone snowboarding with her family. At Mammoth."

"Cool." It was a platitude only. Daisy couldn't even imagine a family ski vacation.

The girls took the bus to the Bellevue Collection, chatting, mostly about Mia's restrictive diet. The girl had discovered a new vegan ice cream that she was really excited about. Daisy smiled, but she found it hard to focus on Mia's mundane discourse. Her mind kept drifting away, to the family that didn't know her, to a man who didn't love her, to a life she would never have. The wan girl leaned in, lowered her voice.

"So . . . who has a bigger dick? Liam or Dylan?"

Of course . . . Everyone assumed that Daisy had performed a sex act on Dylan. Why wouldn't she have? Her encounter with Liam had set a precedent. She was officially easy, promiscuous, the school slut. She didn't have the energy to fight for her reputation.

"They were both pretty small."

Mia gasped, thrilled, as the bus hissed to a stop. Daisy stood. "This is us."

As soon as they disembarked on 8th Street, she heard his voice.

"Daisy!"

She turned and saw the big black car parked in front of a garden center, conspicuously close to the bus stop. The driver's-side door was open and David was standing there, leaning his arms on the door and the roof. His stance was casual, but his gaze was intense.

"Oh my god," Mia whispered, her pale face blanching further. "Who *is* that?"

Daisy saw David through Mia's eyes: hot, rugged, menacing, old. . . . "Family friend," she muttered.

David closed the door and moved toward them. "I need to talk to you."

Daisy's heart was thudding in her ears, and she hated that he still had that effect on her, even now, after her humiliation.

"I—I'm with my friend," she stammered.

"I'm leaving town," David stated. "Tonight."

"For good?" Her dread was evident in her voice.

"For good."

"It's okay," Mia said, clearly flustered by the proximity of the dark stranger. "We can hang out tomorrow."

Daisy could have made an excuse, could have simply walked away. But if David was really leaving, she wanted to talk to him, one last time. She turned to Mia and forced a breezy tone. "I'll text you later."

Mia nodded. Daisy could practically see the wheels turning in the girl's head as she walked away. It would be a scandal—another one—but Daisy didn't care. Heart thudding, she headed toward David's car.

frances

NOW

The panic that gripped her as she hurtled toward Kate's house made one thing clear: she no longer trusted her friend. Marcus had been under Kate's supervision numerous times, but everything had changed now that she knew her friend's identity. Frances's tires screeched on the damp pavement as she turned onto 26th Street and raced toward the Randolphs' impressive house. Slamming the car into park on the shoulder, she barreled out of the vehicle, sprinting to Kate's front door. Frances aggressively rang the doorbell several times before trying the door. It was locked. Of course it was.

Moments later, the door swung open. "Hey . . . ," Kate said, her smile fading as she sensed Frances's agitation.

"I'm here for Marcus." She pushed her way inside. "Marcus! Let's go!"

"Frances, what's wrong?"

"I don't appreciate you taking my son home without my permission."

"I texted you. . . . I noticed you were running late, and I didn't want him left alone at the school."

"I was a *couple* minutes late," Frances snapped. "I shouldn't have to hear from Jeanette Dumas that my son has gone home with someone else."

Kate remained calm. "You gave the office permission for me to take him. I thought you'd be fine with it. In fact," she said, an edge to her voice, "I thought you'd appreciate it."

"Well, I don't." Frances moved to the bottom of the staircase. "Marcus!" she yelled, her voice verging on hysterical.

The boy's muffled response came from behind a closed door. "What?"

"Are you angry?" Kate asked. "Have I done something?"

"Let's go, Marcus!"

"Talk to me, Frances. Whatever it is, we can work it out."

Frances whirled on her. "*Talking* is not going to erase what you did."

The words hung in the air for a moment, then their weight settled on Kate. "What do you mean?"

"You know."

Kate's voice was soft, but her features were hard. "Who told you?"

Frances wasn't prepared for this confrontation. Her goal had been to get Marcus and get out, without revealing her hand, without discussing what she knew. She wasn't ready—emotionally or mentally.

"I—I figured it out," she stammered.

"How?" Kate's tone was acerbic.

Should she tell Kate about the photograph she'd found in David's apartment? The apartment where Daisy had spent the night drinking and doing God knew what else? But she wouldn't betray the girl's trust, not now.

"Marcus!" Frances called, but it was quieter this time, less urgent. The boy would ignore her, she knew it.

"Let me guess," Kate said, her voice dispassionate, "You stumbled upon an article about *the girl who got away with murder.*"

"Did you?" Frances asked, her voice a croak. "Get away with murder?"

"It doesn't matter. I've served my time. I'm a free woman. People don't have the right to follow me and harass me and invade my privacy."

Frances said, "It matters to me."

Kate hesitated for a moment, her expression unreadable. Was she considering dodging the question? Concocting a fabrication to appease her friend? Or was she going to tell the truth, even if it crushed Frances's heart? When she spoke, Kate was firm, adamant.

"No. I didn't." She turned then, and marched into the kitchen.

Frances could have yelled again for her son, could have gone upstairs to collect him, dragged him to the car, and driven home. She could have closed the door on all this ugliness, on her friendship with Kate. But something inside her, something desperate and needy, couldn't let it go. Cautiously, she walked into the kitchen. Kate was staring out the picture window, her arms folded.

"What about the tapes?" Frances asked, tentatively. "They show you doing horrible things. . . . They show you enjoying it."

Kate kept her eyes on her bright green lawn, her precisely trimmed hedges, her tidy flower beds. "I was tortured and abused. I was under the control of that monster. I was a screwed-up kid who got sucked into a nightmare, and I paid for it." She turned then, faced her friend. "I *still* pay for it."

Her repressed but evident anger confounded Frances. "What about Courtney Carey?" she gasped. "Isn't she the one who really paid?"

Suddenly, Robert, in his pressed jeans, his blindingly white button-down shirt, was in the kitchen with them. His expression indicated that he had overheard. Or maybe he could just sense his wife's chagrin.

"She knows," Kate stated, flatly.

The lawyer addressed Frances, his tone impersonal. "Who have you told?"

"No one," Frances said, feeling the weight of their eyes on her. "Not even Jason. I've been trying to come to terms with it myself."

The spouses exchanged an unreadable look, and then something clicked. Kate became Kate again: kind, caring, charming. . . . She moved toward Frances, touched her arm tentatively. "This must have been awful for you. I know it's a lot to take in."

"It is."

"You need time and space to process this. I respect that. But I just hope that, eventually, you'll see that I was a victim, too." Kate's eyes filled with emotion; emotion, but not tears. "Our friendship means the world to me. I . . . I don't want to lose you."

Frances couldn't respond. If she spoke, she would cry.

Robert said, "Please don't tell anyone, Frances. The children would be devastated."

She nodded her compliance.

"And Kate has a legal right to privacy. Any invasion of that could constitute harassment."

Was it a threat? Was Robert going to sue her if she confided in someone? Have her arrested for sharing their dark secret? He had moved to his wife now, placed a protective arm around her shoulders. Frances suddenly felt like she had broken into their house.

"I'll get Marcus," she said, hurrying out of the room.

Driving home, Frances fought back tears. Her son, being an appropriately self-absorbed adolescent, hadn't picked up on the tension between Frances and Kate, hadn't noticed his mother's quiet, shaky demeanor. She didn't want to upset him by falling apart. That would be reserved until she was behind a locked bathroom door.

"Can Charles sleep over this weekend?" The boy's voice jarred her from her reverie. Marcus was beside her, in the passenger seat. On his own, without her prompting, he had graduated from the backseat.

"I don't think so, Marcus."

"Why not?"

Because his mother killed a teenage girl.

"It's a busy weekend. You have martial arts and soccer."

"Not at nighttime, though. Why can't Charles come over at nighttime? We'll just be sleeping. And in the morning, I'll go to martial arts and he can go home."

"It's not a good time."

"That's not fair."

"Life's not fair," she muttered, pulling into their driveway.

"Why can't I have a sleepover?" Marcus whined. "Kate would say yes. She always lets us. Why are you so mean?"

Frances slammed the car into park and turned to face her son. "Mean? You think *I'm* mean? You don't know what mean is. You don't have a fucking clue."

The boy's eyes widened with shock and Frances felt sick. She shouldn't have taken her anger out on Marcus. Her son could be difficult and frustrating, but he was innocent and good. And when all this came out, he would be hurt by it, too.

"I'm sorry, honey. I'm just having a bad day."

Marcus nodded slightly and unbuckled his seat belt. He climbed out of the car and headed to the front door. Frances stayed behind the wheel for a moment, eyelids closed. Her friendship with Kate was over—it had to be. The camaraderie she and her son had enjoyed must come to an end. Once Jason knew, when the community found out, there would be no going back.

Joining Marcus on the front steps, she unlocked the door. "Do you want to watch a movie?" She forced a cheerful tone. "Or play a video game?"

"Sure."

Frances's outburst was forgiven.

daisy

NOW

She should have suggested they go for coffee or boba or ice cream. She should have remained in a public place, a safe space. But instead, she had climbed into David's car like some silly little girl lured by a stranger's candy. They were cruising north on the 405, had been for several minutes before Daisy's voice cut through the weighted silence.

"Where are we going?"

"Somewhere we can talk. Somewhere private."

"Why do we need privacy?"

But he didn't answer; he just turned on his indicator and took the next exit. They were in a horsey area now, a bucolic swath of forest riddled with bridle trails. Daisy had enough common sense to be uneasy as she stared out at the naked deciduous trees, creepy and skeletal without their leaves. She had never feared David. In fact, she had felt safe with him, comforted by his presence. But something had changed. The man now seemed cold, aloof, distant. He seemed entirely capable of harming her.

Eventually, the flora thickened, and the traffic thinned. David slowed the powerful car, turning into a parking area surrounded by dense conifers: cedars, firs, and hemlocks. The vehicle grumbled into the lot, empty but for an abandoned pickup truck with a long horse trailer attached. A group of riders were somewhere in the thick woods, but until they returned, David and Daisy were alone. Secluded. He stopped the car and cut the engine.

There was no sound but the thudding of Daisy's heart. She was legitimately afraid now. She glanced over at her driver, silently staring straight ahead, into the dark forest. She couldn't read his thoughts, his intentions; she had never known what he was thinking. But there was only one reason a man would take a teenage girl into the depths of the forest. Then David spoke.

"I came here, to Bellevue, to find you."

She had known their meeting was no coincidence, had been sure it was fateful. But why? He turned toward her, answering her unasked question.

"I came here to hurt you."

The heavy trees seemed to close in on them, choking out the light and the air. Fear pressed down on her, making it hard to breathe, to think, to move. Suddenly, the way David looked

at her, without passion or warmth, with detached, almost clinical interest, all made sense. She was his target. She was his prey.

"Do you know who Courtney Carey is?"

"No," Daisy croaked, her hand slipping to the buckle of her
seat belt.

He shook his head. "Of course you don't."

"Who is she?"

"She's dead. Murdered."

Something terrible was going to happen to Daisy now, she
knew it. And she deserved it. She had been so stupid, so trust-
ing, so gullible. Strangely, her mind flitted to her Aunt Marnie.
If David killed her right now, they would never have a chance
to meet. No . . . not now, not yet. She pressed the button to
release her seat belt and reached for the door handle. But David
was faster. He grabbed her arm in his strong grip, halting her. He
leaned across her, slamming down the manual locking button.

"Don't run." It was a threat.

"Please," she pleaded, tears spilling from her eyes. "Just let
me go. . . ."

"I will . . . but there's something you need to know."

She nodded, but her survival instinct would not let her trust
him. Not again. She pressed her lips together to stifle a sob. Her
life may have sucked, but she didn't want to die.

He kept his eyes on her. "I came here to get you, Daisy. I was
going to take you away, fuck you up, destroy you. . . . It was *her*
I wanted to hurt, not you."

Her?

"But when I got to know you, I couldn't do it. Because it wouldn't hurt her. She wouldn't even care."

Daisy's mind scrambled to make sense of his words. Who was he talking about? She could think of only one possibility.

"You're as damaged as I am. She destroyed us both."

Daisy had to clarify. "Who did?"

His hazel eyes met hers. "Your mom. She's evil."

The epiphany was almost physical, her skin prickling with awareness, understanding, realization. Her family didn't move because of her dad's work: they were on the run. They rarely made friends because they were in hiding. And Aunt Marnie had not disowned them because Daisy's mom had had an affair. Kate Randolph had done something worse . . . so much worse. She had done something unforgivable.

The girl turned in her seat to face David, no longer afraid. Not of him, anyway.

"Who is my mother?" she whispered. "And who are *you?*"

frances

NOW

When Jason arrived home, Frances was seated at the kitchen table nursing a glass of white wine. It was her third, as indicated by the half-empty bottle perched before her. Jason's eyes drifted over the evidence, but he dutifully kissed her cheek. "How was your day?"

"Terrible."

Jason lowered himself onto a neighboring chair. "What happened?"

Frances downed the rest of her wine. "Get a glass," she urged him. "You're going to need it."

"Just tell me." Her partner's handsome face was troubled. "Is Marcus okay?"

"He's fine. For now." She made a grab for the bottle, but he was quicker, moving it out of her reach.

"What's going on, Frances?" He sounded justifiably anxious. "Where's our son?"

"In his room. He's on his iPad." Frances recalled a time, not so long ago, when monitoring her son's screen time had been paramount.

"Tell me."

"Daisy Randolph was seeing this older guy. She went to his apartment, near U-Dub, and she drank too much. She called me to pick her up the next morning. The man, David, wasn't there, but I looked around his apartment for some clue to his identity. And I found a photograph . . . of Kate."

"Why did this guy have a photo of Kate?"

"I don't know." Frances retrieved the picture from under the stack of magazines and mail and slid it toward her partner.

Jason picked it up and stared at the image. "It was taken a long time ago, obviously, but it looks like her."

"Turn it over."

His lips barely moved as he read the words out loud. "Amber Kunik." Frances watched him absorb the information, recollect the name, place it in context. His dark eyes met his wife's. "Jesus Christ."

Frances's eyes welled with tears. "I know."

"I remember this case," Jason said, getting up to retrieve a wineglass. "It was all over the news. Amber and her boyfriend killed that young girl. . . . She was only fourteen."

"Fifteen."

Jason poured himself a glass, topped up Frances's. "Are you sure it's Kate? Could there have been some kind of mistake?"

"She's changed her hair and makeup. She's older, of course. But it's her."

"This is . . ." He drank some wine. "This is unbelievable."

The tears seeped from Frances's eyes. "It is."

"She's been in our home. Marcus slept over there."

"She did some horrible things in the past," Frances said, "but there's no evidence she actually killed that girl."

"She was in on it. Everyone knew that."

"That was Shane Nelson's testimony, but it was never proven. He was trying to save himself."

Jason shook his head. "I remember when those tapes came out after she cut her deal. This pretty, middle-class girl who was capable of such evil . . ."

"She was abused by Shane Nelson. Mentally and physically. She was only twenty."

"She's a psychopath. Why are you defending her?"

"I'm not." But she was. Why? Was it residual loyalty for the friendship Kate had shown her? Was she trying to justify the love she had felt for the woman? Or was it because of what Frances herself had done? She had also stolen a daughter from her parents. From her own parents . . . She looked at the concern etched on her husband's face, and wondered if she could finally tell him the truth. Jason knew her sister had died tragically young: an undiagnosed heart defect was the story. Could she admit her role in her sister's demise? Was it finally time?

But Jason stood then. "I'm going to call the school."

"What for?"

"There's an infamous murderer in the parent community, Frances. People have a right to know."

"Is that necessary?"

"She could volunteer in the classroom. She could invite kids over to her house for playdates. She's dangerous."

"Kate never volunteers. And Marcus is the only kid who goes to Charles's house." Frances stood, too. "I really don't think she'd do anything. The rates of recidivism for women are super-low."

"Stop minimizing what Kate's done!" Jason barked. He picked up his cell phone, nestled among the kitchen counter clutter. "I'm calling the school."

Frances's response was muted in the face of her husband's uncharacteristic anger. "The office will be closed now."

Jason looked at his watch, put the phone down. "Fine. I'll call tomorrow. I'll go in and talk to the principal."

Frances's voice was a whisper. "But Charles . . ."

"Fuck." Her husband ran his hands through his cropped hair.

"He's a sweet boy. He's Marcus's only friend. Marcus needs him."

"Marcus is stronger than you think, Frances. He'll be fine." Jason drained his wineglass. "I'm sorry about the kids, I really am, but you don't seem to realize how dangerous Amber Kunik is. You were removed from the crime, up here in Washington, but I lived in Denver then, one state over. My sister was the same age as the murdered girl. My parents were terrified, everyone was. Amber Kunik is evil, Frances. *Kate* is evil."

"Robert said not to tell anyone. He said Kate has a legal right to privacy."

Her partner emitted a humorless snort of laughter. "Fuck Robert. What kind of sick bastard marries a cold-blooded killer?"

The irony of his remark was lost on him.

"I knew she was coming on to me that night after we got high. They're not our friends. They probably invited us over to have some fucking orgy."

"No . . ."

"They're sick, Frances. They're perverts with no moral compass. How else could Robert forgive what Kate did?"

Tears flowed freely down her cheeks as she took another drink of wine. It was room temperature now and suddenly tasted too sweet, too heady, but she needed to deaden herself to the nightmare unfolding before her. She had cried enough tears for herself, but so many others would be impacted by this revelation. Charles Randolph would be ostracized, bullied, if not expelled. Marcus would be devastated and alone. And Daisy . . . The girl already seemed to be teetering on the brink; what would become of her now? A sob shuddered through Frances's chest.

"I know you don't want to lose your friend, but I'm right about her, Frances. You know I am."

She wanted to explain that she was crying for Kate's kids, for Marcus, not just for herself. She wanted him to come to her, to hold her and comfort her, but he didn't. He headed to the stairs to check on their son. Jason was frightened and angry—he had every right to be. She'd brought a child-killer into their lives. . . . But he would forgive Frances, eventually. What Kate had done could not be forgiven; Frances knew that, but it didn't stop her heart from aching with loss.

She moved to the fridge and retrieved another bottle of wine. Then, digging into the back of a high cupboard, she removed her emergency stash of junk food: chips, boxed cookies, soft licorice.

This was an unequivocal emergency.

SHANE NELSON GETS LIFE IN PRISON

*Courtney Carey's killer avoids death penalty
due to victim's age*

KENNETH WILCOTT

Phoenix

Shane Nelson has been convicted of first degree murder in the death of Tolleson teenager Courtney Carey. Nelson, 29, has also been convicted of kidnapping, forcible confinement, aggravated sexual assault, and committing an indignity to a human body. Today, Justice Noel Calder sentenced Nelson to life in prison with no eligibility for parole. Nelson avoided the death penalty because he has no prior convictions and Courtney Carey was 15 years old at the time of her death. In Arizona, the murder of a person under 15 is considered a capital crime, resulting in a death sentence.

Testimony by Nelson's girlfriend, Amber Kunik, 21, was pivotal to the Phoenix man's conviction. In exchange for her testimony, Kunik cut a deal with the prosecution, pleading guilty to a lesser charge of manslaughter for her role in the murder. While Nelson has maintained that it was Kunik who murdered Carey, the prosecution honored their deal with the witness, though videotaped evidence later showed Kunik's enthusiastic participation in the torture and degradation of the victim. Kunik has already begun serving a 6-year sentence in Perryville's Women's Prison.

frances

Frances sat in her car in the pickup area, waiting for her son to exit the school. Tomorrow was Thanksgiving, and she still hadn't bought a turkey, or bread crumbs, or cranberry sauce. The Metcalfes would spend the holiday alone, their little family of three, as usual. Jason didn't like to fly over the holidays—long lines, delayed flights, lost luggage—so traveling to Denver to be with his family was off the table. They could have easily driven to Spokane to spend it with Frances's parents, but they never did. She blamed traffic. She blamed weather. But the truth was, no one could be grateful when the Downies were all together. The family would only focus on what they had lost.

Still, Frances always tried to make the occasion special. Jason and Marcus both loved her homemade pumpkin pie.

She didn't make her own crust (she wasn't a *pioneer*). She bought a gluten-free crust from a rice bakery, but she added her own blend of spices to the canned pumpkin, and whipped her own cream. This year, store-bought pie would have to suffice . . . if there were any left. She should have been more organized. But since the revelation about Kate, Frances had ceased to function.

That wasn't entirely true. She still made her son's breakfast in the mornings, still drove him to and from school, ensured he did his homework and went to bed on time. But she had not gone to the gym, had not cleaned the house, had not cooked a proper dinner since learning her friend's identity. It had been a week; twenty hours since she'd told her husband. Surely the shock would soon subside and she would emerge from this fog. Eventually, the tension between her and Jason would abate and they could have a conversation beyond their current stilted discourse about chauffeuring Marcus to his activities. It was going to be a tense holiday.

There was a brisk rap at her car window, and Frances jumped in her seat. She turned to see the taut visage of Allison Moss framed in the glass. To Frances's surprise, she felt a swell of relief. It was now Kate's presence she dreaded, not this tiny woman's. Turning the key in the ignition to the right, she lowered the automatic window.

"Hi, Frances." Allison's words were clipped, anxious. "I was wondering if you'd seen this?" She held up her iPhone.

Frances peered at the device: on the small screen was a letter from Forrester Academy.

"I haven't checked my e-mail in a while. . . ." As she spoke, she rummaged in her purse for her phone.

"It's very concerning," Allison said, standing by as Frances checked her messages. The missive was there, in her in-box. She opened it and read.

Dear Parents and Guardians,

It has recently been brought to our attention that a member of our Forrester community has a very serious criminal record.

Jason had done it. He'd spoken to the principal.

This individual does not have a role in the classroom, but has access to school grounds and common areas. While this person has served their sentence, and is free in the eyes of the law, we understand that this knowledge may cause concern among our parents. Please be assured that your child's safety is paramount to the staff and administration at Forrester Academy.

If you would like to discuss this issue with the principal, we ask you to call the office and make an appointment. Please note that the school will not reveal the name of the individual to protect the safety and privacy of the entire Forrester community.

"At first, I thought it was a janitor," Allison said. "Or a gardener."

"Maybe. . . ."

"But why would they protect his privacy? Why wouldn't they just fire him?"

"Maybe he has a contract?"

"Please . . ." Allison rolled her eyes, as though a mere janitor or gardener having an employment contract was the most ludicrous thing she'd ever heard. Frances was reminded why she had once entertained the idea of bludgeoning this woman with a chocolate fountain.

"It can't be a teacher," Allison continued. "I asked about background checks when we applied. It has to be a parent. Maybe of one of the scholarship kids."

"We shouldn't make assumptions."

"The school can't keep this kind of information from us. We have a right to know if our children are at risk."

There would be a witch hunt now, with Allison leading the charge. Kate would be caught, strung up, burned at the stake . . . if she didn't run away first. Emotion shuddered in Frances's chest, but she swallowed, forced it down.

Allison continued. "Kate's husband's a lawyer, isn't he? We must have some legal rights here. Why don't a few of us get together for drinks? To discuss our options?"

"I think Robert does environmental law."

"The law is the law. I'm sure he'd have some insights."

I'm sure he would.

"I'll talk to Jeanette. We'll set something up, after the holiday. We're going to spend a few days at our chalet in Whistler. You?"

At that moment, Frances spotted her son, moping toward the car. "There's Marcus," she said. "I've got to get him to soccer."

"But soccer's canceled for Thanks—" The whirring of the window closing cut Allison off. Marcus climbed in beside his mother. Frances stepped on the gas as her son buckled his seat belt.

"How was your day?" she asked, as they traveled.

"Sucked."

"How come?"

Marcus stared out the side window. "I don't know. . . ."

But Frances did. She didn't want to grill him, didn't want to set him off, so she drove in silence for several minutes. Finally, when they were a few blocks from home, she made her inquiries.

"Was Charles at school today?"

"No."

"Is school hard without Charles?"

"It's okay, I guess." The boy kept his eyes on the familiar scenery. "I like it when he's there, though. I feel more relaxed. I don't get so angry and frustrated."

Frances would not break down in front of her son. Her tears were limited to the shower now, where she let herself weep with abandon.

"Maybe Charles is sick?" Marcus said, turning toward her. "Maybe we could take him some soup or something?"

"I think they went away for Thanksgiving," Frances lied.

The boy's gaze drifted out the window again. "Where did they go?"

"Palm Springs, I think."

"Charles didn't tell me."

"He must have forgotten." She turned onto their street. "Or maybe he didn't mention it because Palm Springs is kind of boring for a kid."

He turned toward her again. "What do you do there?"

"Golf mostly. Sit in the sun and read."

"Yuck."

She chuckled. "Yeah . . ."

"How come Daisy didn't go with them?"

Frances was confused. "She did."

Marcus pointed out the front window. "She's sitting on our front steps."

Frances saw the slender girl, her young face dark and troubled—and her stomach plunged. Something was very wrong in Daisy's world.

"Oh, right . . . ," she said, covering, "Daisy stayed behind to work on a school project."

She parked the car and Marcus climbed out his side, leaving Frances to collect his backpack from the floor in front of the passenger seat. The boy paused at the bottom of the steps, waiting for his mother. He was shy and awkward around pretty, teenage Daisy, which Frances considered a good indication of his normalcy. Daisy was standing now, her expression still dour.

"Hi," Frances said brightly, like she'd been expecting the girl, like her presence was not unusual, not foreboding of terrible news.

"Hey."

Frances unlocked the door and ushered Marcus into the house. "Go get changed and get a snack," she instructed. "There's cut-up fruit in the fridge."

Obediently, her son headed for the staircase to his room. When he was out of sight, Frances closed the door and faced Daisy on the front porch.

"Did you know?" The girl's tone was accusing.

For a moment, Frances considered playing dumb, pleading ignorance. But if this girl knew what Frances knew, she would need someone. That night, almost a month ago, when Frances had volunteered to be there for Kate's daughter, she could never have fathomed this scenario.

"I just found out," Frances said. "How did you—?"

"Is it true?" the girl snapped.

Frances looked down at her small concrete porch, littered with dead leaves and dust that she should have swept up. "Yes," she said, softly. "Your mom is Amber Kunik."

"Oh my god." The pretty gray eyes, so like Kate's, filled with tears. "My mom is a killer."

"There were extenuating circumstances," Frances responded. "She was abused by her boyfriend. She was afraid. She had no choice. . . ."

"Really?" Daisy's voice was cold. "Or was that just what she said to get out of a life sentence? To make Shane Nelson pay for what *she* did?"

Frances pressed her lips together, exhaled through her nose. She could feel the familiar flutter of panic in her chest. She was in way over her head here, scrambling for words, terrified of saying the wrong thing. Marcus was alone in the house, could be getting into all sorts of trouble, could be eating gluten at this very moment.

Daisy continued. "Courtney Carey was a girl just like me. She had a little brother, just like me." Her voice cracked, but she continued. "All these years, I thought there was something wrong with me. And there is. I'm the child of a killer. I was raised by a murderer."

"There's nothing wrong with you, Daisy. You're a good kid."

The girl kept talking, almost to herself. "My mom doesn't love me, she hasn't for years. I thought it was my fault. But maybe she just can't . . . because she's a monster."

Frances felt something defensive well up inside her. "She's not a monster. Just . . . talk to your mom about all this. I'm sure she can explain."

"How can I talk to her?" Daisy's voice was shrill. "Charles and I could be in danger."

"You're not in danger," Frances said, confident for the first time. "Your mom would never, ever hurt you." She saw the girl take this in, accept it as fact. Their relationship may not have been close, but Daisy had never feared Kate.

Frances reached for the girl's hand, continued in a gentle voice. "The person who did those horrible things—Amber Kunik—that's not your mom. She's changed. Your mom is a kind, honest person now. She would never do anything. . . ." But she trailed off. Kate had come on to Jason, had lied to Frances, had killed Charles's gerbil. . . .

Daisy pulled her hand away. "What?"

"Nothing," Frances said, because it was true. In the scheme of things, flirting, lying, putting a rodent out of its misery were nothing. "Your mom is Kate Randolph. And she's a good person."

"Will you still be friends with her?"

The panic fluttered out of Frances's chest, into her throat. "No," she whispered. "I wish I could, but I can't."

Daisy nodded, eyes shining with emotion. "Nice that you have that option. But what am I supposed to do?"

Frances could see the girl's desperation, her loneliness, her fear. She knew what the kid wanted: to be held, comforted, to have someone step in and take care of her. Frances could be that person. She could take Daisy in her arms right now, take her inside, send Jason to collect her belongings when he got home from work. Frances could be Daisy's champion, her protector.

But then she considered Kate. Whatever the woman had done in the past, Frances knew she could not hurt Kate this way. Kate had paid her debt to society. It was not Frances's role to punish her further. She would not usurp Kate's child, make the girl hate and fear her own mother. Frances recalled her own mom and dad, how they had ceased to live after Tricia died. Frances could not take another daughter from her parents.

"Go home, Daisy. Talk to your mom. It'll be okay."

The look on the girl's face was a knife in Frances's heart: disappointment, pain, betrayal. . . . But she gave a slight nod of acceptance and turned away.

Frances watched her descend the steps and walk down the drive. Her departing form was tall and graceful. She even moved like her mom. Suddenly, a thought struck Frances.

"Daisy!" she called. "Who told you? Was it David? Who is he?"

But the girl just kept walking. She never looked back.

dj

*W*ith his sister's killers behind bars, life became a new sort of normal. DJ went back to school. He looked after his father: cooking, cleaning, helping him get to bed when he was too drunk to walk. The boy didn't mind, not really. He just wanted to make his dad's life easier—to keep him happy, to keep him from leaving. DJ missed his mom and his sister, but he had his video games and he had his junk food. When he was playing, when he was snacking, he was numb. He didn't have to think about all that he had lost.

He wondered if his mother knew about the conviction. Perhaps the prosecutor had written to her? He knew that his dad would not have bothered to communicate the news to his mom. And DJ didn't either. His mom's letters continued to come, one every ten or twelve days. She was feeling better, she said. Her family was caring for her and she was getting stronger all the time. She never mentioned the trial or the crime or even his sister. And she never asked him to come. She never said that she was ready to be his mom again. And so, he never wrote back.

DJ and his dad lived in a toxic fugue for nearly six years, the boy eating his feelings, the man drinking his. The liquor made his father sick and yellow. He refused to see a doctor, but it was clear to DJ, to anyone, that his dad would die soon. DJ felt no sorrow at the thought. Not because his father had been cruel and abusive, physically, verbally, and emotionally. But because DJ had become inured to loss. It felt like his destiny.

His eighteenth birthday coincided with the release of one of his sister's killers. He and Amber Kunik would be granted their freedom the same year. DJ had a few months on her, though. He was a man; she was still incarcerated. As a legal adult, he applied for visitation. He didn't know why, but he needed to see Amber in person. He had been a child when he'd sat in the courtroom and watched her play with the lawyers, the judge, and the jury. He wasn't sure his perceptions, his memories, could be trusted. It was doubtful that the inmate would accept DJ's request, but he had to try. Surprisingly, she agreed to his visit.

Amber Kunik was in a women's facility with minimal security. In the eyes of the law, she was not a cold-blooded murderer. They met in a sterile room furnished with utilitarian tables and chairs. Around them, husbands, mothers, and children visited their inmates. Two guards stood sentry: a sleepy-looking male and a young, wiry female. The boy knew that, if he wanted, he could lunge across the table and strangle Amber before they reacted. With his considerable weight, they wouldn't be able to tear him off in time to save her life.

His sister's murderer had not changed much since the trial. She looked healthy and slim. She was wearing makeup, which surprised him.

"Why did you want to see me?" she asked, her tone suspicious, eyes wary.

He felt a strong and undefinable surge of emotion. "I—I don't know. I just had to."

Her face softened. "I'm sorry about your sister," she said, in that sweet voice he'd heard on the stand. "She was a beautiful girl and she didn't deserve what happened to her."

Was this why he had come? To hear her apologize?

"I feel terrible for what Shane and I did to your family," she continued. "I was young and confused and stupid, and I'll never forgive myself."

He accepted this with a nod, his throat clogged with loss.

"How are your parents?"

He broke down then, fat tears rolling down his plump cheeks. He told her everything—about his mother's abandonment, his father's drinking and abuse. He told her how he couldn't stop eating, how it was the only way to make the pain go away. She listened, her pretty face twisted with sympathy. When he had finished, she opened up about her own family. Her father had been arrested for solicitation, humiliating both Amber and her mother. Her mom's blind loyalty *to her husband had felt like a betrayal. Shane Nelson had offered an escape. He was older, handsome, charming. But he was sick, a sadist, a deviant.*

DJ and Amber, an unlikely pair, connected through their pain. Their conversation segued into common interests, shared likes. They were both fans of Friends; *they loved Tom Cruise and chocolate. When their time was up, Amber bestowed on him that infamous smile. "Maybe you could visit me again," she said. "I've still got three more months."*

DJ nodded. His heart felt strange, lighter. Was it forgiveness seeping into the constricted muscle?

"Next time you come, could you bring me a little treat?" she continued, in the same girlish voice. "The food in here is terrible."

He smiled at her. "Chocolate?"

She smiled back. "How about an Oreo Blizzard?"

He looked at her open, innocent face. Was it possible she didn't remember connecting with his sister over the frozen dessert? Had she forgotten using it to lure Courtney to her death? No . . . the bitch had been playing with him. He was a diversion, a distraction, a toy. His childish observations had been accurate. Amber Kunik was a psychopath, just like Shane Nelson. He stood then, his bulk shifting the table. She remained seated, watching him, her pretty face blank and innocent, but for a cruel glimmer in her eyes.

He turned and left. He never went back.

frances

The Thanksgiving holiday brought a thaw in the Metcalfes' marital relations. Over a substandard turkey dinner finished off with a greasy, store-bought pie, Frances and Jason put on a happy façade for their son. But when the meal was over, and Marcus had gone to bed, they cleaned up in tense silence. Finally, as Frances was hand-washing their wineglasses, she tentatively broached the subject they had been avoiding.

"Did you talk to Principal Stewart?"

"Yep," Jason said curtly, dropping a plate into the dishwasher. "I told you I was going to."

"He sent out an e-mail to all the Forrester parents."

"I saw it."

Frances placed a wineglass in the drying rack. "So what's going to happen now?"

"I don't know," Jason said, his tone defensive, "but at least the administration can keep an eye on Kate. They can make sure she's not alone with any kids, that she's not a danger to anyone."

She's not dangerous. Not anymore.

But Frances didn't say this out loud. The way her partner was roughly cramming bowls into the dishwasher told her that he would not be receptive.

"The power-mommies are curious," she said, rinsing a glass. "There'll be a witch hunt. Kate and Charles will be run out of the school."

"It's for the best."

Frances turned off the faucet and faced her husband. "Really? You feel no pity for them? Not even for Charles?"

"Of course I feel sorry for Charles," Jason said. "And Daisy, too. Amber Kunik should never have had kids."

She hadn't wanted children. It made sense now. It was Robert who had pressured her into it.

Jason continued, "But I don't care what happens to Kate—to *Amber*. . . . I care about keeping the kids in this community safe. I care about Marcus, and I care about you. That's it."

His protectiveness warmed her. Frances had been a lesser wife than Jason deserved, but still he loved her. Even after she'd brought a child-killer into their cloistered universe, Jason remained loyal, loving, devoted. If she told her spouse that she had caused her own sister's death, he would stand by her then, too. Probably . . . Now was not the time to test that theory.

"I love you," she said.

His response was gruff but sincere. "I love you, too."

The détente established, she spent the rest of the weekend concentrating on what she *had*, not what she had lost. It was Thanksgiving, a time to be grateful, and she was. For her husband. For her son. For the home they had built. Frances didn't need girl talk over wine, gossipy coffee dates, a friend whose texts made her giggle, or an ally on the school grounds. She had lived her entire life without this kind of camaraderie, and she had been fine, content even. And she would be again . . . when the ache of loss had subsided.

Focusing on gratitude did nothing to quell the apprehension she felt as she drove her son to Forrester on Monday morning. Her hands on the wheel were clammy and her heart fluttered like a moth at a porch light. Her anxiety could be attributed to the fear of encountering her former friend, and fear *for* her. Frances knew how cruel the Forrester mothers could be over a harmless prank (okay, peeing in a water bottle may have been more like an inappropriate act of retribution than a harmless prank), but she could only imagine how they'd react when they found out Kate's identity.

As she approached the school, she saw them: television vans; reporters with cameras, microphones, and recording devices. There were tripods and lights, cables and booms. Over the weekend, someone had identified the killer in their midst and alerted the media to her presence at Forrester Academy.

Was it someone in the office? A teacher? An industrious parent? Now the press was waiting, *salivating*, for a glimpse of Amber Kunik. A security guard had materialized (he must have been hired when the school learned of the notorious murderer in its parent community), and the stocky man kept the press off school grounds. But they hovered on the periphery, milling on the sidewalk, chatting into phones or to one another, blocking a smooth entry for students and their concerned parents.

"What's going on?" Her son craned his neck at the media scrum.

"I'm not sure," Frances fibbed, pulling into the parking lot, "but I'm going to walk you in today."

"I'm fine, Mom."

"I'll just walk you to the front doors," she said, parking the vehicle. "I won't go inside."

Her son acquiesced and unbuckled his seat belt. "Is Charles back from Palm Springs?"

"I don't know." If Frances were in Kate's shoes, she'd never return to Forrester. She'd homeschool her son, buy a cabin in the woods, and go into hiding. But Kate was tougher, braver, stronger. . . . How else could she have gone on living after what she'd done?

They crossed the parking lot and approached the throng. Gripping her son's elbow, she led him through the phalanx of media people toward the school. No one turned in their direction, no one paid them any attention; all eyes were trained on the school's front doors. Kate must be inside. Frances hadn't noticed her SUV in the parking lot, but how else to explain the press's laser-like focus on those front doors? Kate must have escorted Charles into class, and now she was trapped. If she came out, she'd be mobbed by reporters. But if she remained cloistered within the school's walls, she'd be accosted by outraged Forrester parents. Frances would have taken on the media any day.

When they reached the bottom of the staircase that led to the double doors, she paused.

"Bye, Mom." Marcus moved to ascend the stairs, but she held on to his backpack. Amber Kunik, notorious child-killer, was inside the building at this very moment. How could she send her only child into her lair?

"What are you doing?" her son grumbled, but she held fast to his bag. The boy needed to go to school, needed his routine. The letter from the Forrester administration had assured parents that their children would be safe, protected and cared for by teachers and support staff. And Frances knew, logically, that Kate wasn't going to go on some child-killing rampage at her son's private school, but still . . . she couldn't let go.

At the top of the staircase, the school doors opened. Both Frances and Marcus looked up; the latter with mild curiosity, the former with abject terror. She couldn't face Kate right now. Not in this public setting, with her son as witness, with cameras trained on them. Frances didn't know how she'd respond to a face-off with her friend; she was torn between pity and loathing, compassion and fear. A confrontation would be messy.

But it was Jeanette Dumas and her mini-me, Abbey, who exited the doors first. They were trailed by Allison Moss and her daughter, Lila. Jeanette, always sharp in her business attire, met Frances's anxious gaze as she descended the stairs.

"Have you heard?" she asked.

Frances nodded her response.

"We're pulling the kids from school until Charles Randolph is expelled," Jeanette informed her, as Allison and her charge joined them.

"What?" Marcus asked. "Why?"

Allison ignored the boy and addressed Frances. "Forrester was negligent when they allowed Charles to attend this school. They can't take our money and place our children in this kind of danger. Will you take a stand with us?"

"What kind of danger?" Marcus queried.

Abbey Dumas looked at him, a glint in her eye. "Charles's mom is a *murderer*."

"No, she's not!" the boy snapped.

"Yes, she is," Lila Moss piped in. "Charles's mom killed a fifteen-year-old girl."

"Stop lying!" Marcus shrieked. Her son's face was red, sweaty. He was going to lose it, Frances could sense it.

"We're not lying," Abbey sniped, and Frances had a sudden urge to pee in the kid's water bottle herself. Instead, she turned to her son.

"It's complicated, honey. I'll explain later."

"*Complicated?*" Allison said, eyes wide with shock. "You can't make excuses for what Amber Kunik did to that girl."

"O-of course not," Frances stammered, "I just meant that Kate isn't—"

Jeanette gasped. "Have you known who Kate really was all along?"

"Oh. My. God," Allison said. "You knew, didn't you?"

"No . . . I just found out." But it sounded disingenuous.

"When?" Allison snapped. "Before the letter from the school?"

"A few days before."

Jeanette shook her head. "We knew you were desperate for a friend, Frances, but not *that* desperate."

Allison snorted. "You risked your son's safety so you could have a BFF?"

"Marcus was never in danger!"

"You're in denial," Jeanette said, so righteous, so superior. "Kate's a child-killer."

"Mom"—Marcus was on the verge of tears now—"what's going on?"

Jeanette reached out and patted Marcus's shoulder. "You poor thing."

Frances felt rage well up inside her, and the homicidal caprices she thought she'd suppressed made an appearance. In her mind, she slashed at the women with a machete, delivered a roundhouse karate kick to their jaws, bludgeoned them with a baseball bat. These imaginings, though twisted, were harmless.

She had no weapons, she didn't know karate (even if she had, her plump leg would never have reached towering Jeanette's jaw), and she knew she would never, *ever* act on these impulses. What was truly dangerous was how much, in this moment, she wanted to defend her friend.

Kate may have done something terrible in the past, but she's a kinder person than you are!

Amber Kunik was just a girl! She was under the spell of Shane Nelson! She's served her time!

Kate's changed! She's not Amber Kunik, the child-killer, anymore! She's my best friend!

But she couldn't say any of it. It would be social suicide. For her and for her son. And she didn't know if she truly believed the statements running through her mind or if they were just a product of her anger. She grabbed Marcus's sleeve.

"Let's go home."

When they were locked in the car, Frances put the key in the ignition. She was vibrating with repressed emotions: rage, fear, sadness. . . . She wasn't sure she was safe to drive, but she had to get out of there, had to remove her son from the chaos and strife.

"Mom . . . ?" She turned toward the quivering voice beside her, took in her child's concerned face. "What were they talking about?"

Frances couldn't hide the truth from him any longer. She

took a deep, calming breath and reached for the boy's hand. "I'm going to tell you everything, Marcus," she said, clutching his clammy palm in both of hers. "It's not going to be easy to hear, but you're mature enough to handle it now. I'd like to wait until we get home, okay?"

Her son nodded his agreement and allowed her to peck his forehead. She was about to put the car into gear when she heard the mob of reporters erupt. Frances and Marcus peered through the windshield at Forrester Academy's front doors, and saw Kate and Robert emerge.

As the pair descended the steps, the media pounced. The security guard hired to keep the horde off school grounds was no match for them, rats scurrying to feed off a carcass. Cameras flashed. Crews jostled for access. Reporters called out one name, over and over again.

"Amber!"

"Amber!"

"Amber!"

Robert's arm was wrapped protectively around his wife's shoulders, his other arm outstretched, pushing reporters away. Kate held her expensive purse up to her face, trying to shield it from the cameras, from the gawking, prying eyes of the press. The reporters were hungry for her, more like sharks than rats, a feeding frenzy. The security guard attempted to escort the couple (had the school hired him? Or had Robert?), his elbows up, hands shoving, blocking, body-checking.

The scrum was moving toward the parking lot now, toward the silver Audi that Robert drove. Frances hadn't noticed it before, but she saw their destination now. The sleek car was parked in the row in front of her Subaru and to the left—closer to the school, for quick, easy access. Kate and Robert wouldn't notice Frances and Marcus sitting in their car, watching them.

The group was nearing the vehicle. Robert released his wife so she could move to the passenger door. The security guard splayed his arms, an attempt to hold back the throng and allow his charge access. Kate scurried for the refuge of the Audi, her pricey bag obscuring her face as photographers and cameramen lunged for her. Frances's tall, confident friend suddenly looked small and vulnerable, a victim. As Kate opened the car door she lowered her purse, and Frances saw her.

The flawless features were set in stone: hard, cold, brittle. Kate was outraged by this intrusion into her life, furious at the violation of her freedom. Was she shielding her face to protect her privacy, or to hide her unsympathetic fury? Frances knew how her friend's annoyance would look to the general population: callous and self-centered. But Frances understood Kate like few others could. The hard line of her friend's jaw, the flinty look in her gray eyes. . . . It was a mask, a protective scrim to keep her true feelings shielded. The pretty woman may have looked pissed, but Frances knew her better.

Kate Randolph was terrified.

daisy

NOW

Daisy had spent most of the holiday weekend locked in her room, on her computer, researching her mother. Each click brought a fresh horror; the internet did not care to protect her feelings. She read courtroom transcripts, old newspaper articles, Reddit debates on Amber Kunik's culpability. . . . Daisy's dad had defended the beautiful young killer. Her father knew every vile act, every gory detail, and yet he had fallen madly in love with her mother. She and Charles were the product of this sick union.

On Monday, she stayed in her quarters while her parents took her brother to school. Normally, her mom played chauffeur alone, but today, her dad was accompanying them. Moral support? Protection? If Frances Metcalfe knew the truth about her mom, it was only a matter of time before the entire school community knew. And it was only a matter of time before the Randolphs would be run out of town. Again.

When she heard her parents return, their voices tense and strained, she gathered her courage. But it wasn't until she saw her father's Audi backing out of the driveway that she emerged. Her heart rattled in her chest as she descended the staircase to the main floor. This conversation needed to take place between Daisy and her mother without distractions. But now that she knew what the woman was capable of, she was slightly afraid to be alone with her.

She was still on the staircase when she heard "Why aren't you at school?"

Her mom's voice, in the darkened living room, startled her. The blinds were drawn and the lights were off, leaving the room dim and gloomy. Kate Randolph sat stiffly on the sofa, her hands knotted in her lap.

Daisy reached the main floor and moved tentatively toward her. "I need to talk to you."

"This isn't a good time."

Daisy stopped in the middle of the room. "I know who you are. And I know what you did."

Kate's features hardened slightly, but she remained mute. Daisy waited for her mother to deny it, to assure her daughter that it was all an ugly lie, a terrible mistake. She waited for the inquisition: *How did you find out? Who told you?* But the woman just sat there, in the faint light, her eyes veiled and hollow. Daisy filled the silence in a trembling voice.

"I know that you're Amber Kunik. That you and Shane Nelson murdered that girl. That you tortured her and raped her, and then you killed her." Tears slipped from Daisy's eyes, and sobs made it difficult to get the words out, but she persisted. "I've been reading about you online. Courtney Carey was only fifteen. She was just a kid, like me. And you . . . you murdered her."

Kate sat silent and stoic. She didn't defend herself, didn't deny it, didn't explain.

"Say something," Daisy cried. "Tell me it's not true! Tell me Shane Nelson made you do it!" She wanted nothing more than to absolve her mother of blame, to grant her forgiveness. If only Kate would ask . . .

But she didn't. She just watched her daughter, cold and impassive. Finally, her mom spoke in a calm, level voice.

"You've already made up your mind that I'm a monster. There's nothing I can say now." The woman stood then. "The community knows, so we have to move. Charles is going to be kicked out of school. You'll be next."

"I—I'm not going with you."

"Suit yourself." She walked past her daughter toward the kitchen. "But you can still help us pack."

The words sent a shiver through Daisy. She had felt her mother's indifference for years, but it had never been so blatantly articulated.

"D-did you ever love me?"

Kate stopped, whirled on her. "Of course I did. You were my baby. But then, you grew up. And you changed."

"Do I remind you of her?" Daisy said, her voice hoarse. "The girl you murdered?"

"No," Kate said, with the slightest hint of a smile. "You remind me of *me*."

The words were an insult, an accusation. "I—I'm nothing like you."

"Yes, you are. You're superior and distant and bored with everyone around you. If the wrong guy came along, offered you thrills and excitement, you'd make the same mistakes I did."

"I wouldn't," Daisy said, but her voice was weak. David had come for her, and she had gone with him, willingly, not knowing who he was or what he wanted. If he had pushed her to do cruel, horrible things, would she have complied?

No . . . Daisy was not her mother.

Kate moved into the kitchen, Daisy trailing after her. Her mom was taking glasses out of the cupboard, setting them on the counter.

"Why did you have kids? You must have known this was no life for us, all this running and hiding."

"Your dad wanted children and I wanted to make him happy." She plunked a glass onto the countertop. "He thought we'd be able to live a normal life once I'd served my time. He thought he could protect me, that people would eventually forget. But they don't."

Daisy absorbed this, watching her mother busy herself with the glassware. "If I hadn't found out, would you ever have told me?"

Her mom paused, a wineglass in hand. "I don't know. . . . That was up to your father."

"Charles has to know."

Kate's beautiful face contorted, an ugly mix of anger and fear. "Don't you breathe a word of this to your brother." She stabbed a finger at Daisy. "Do you understand me?"

It was a threat. A frisson of fear ran through Daisy. If pushed, her mother would still be capable of ruthless acts.

Her dad entered then, his arms wrapped around a flat of packing boxes.

"What's going on?"

Kate set the wineglass on the counter. "Your daughter needs to talk to you."

She took the packing boxes and left the kitchen.

dj

THEN

DJ sat on the sofa with a bag of Doritos and a container of sour cream dip to watch Amber Kunik's television interview. Now a free woman, she had agreed to one interview only. She looked demure and pretty, her face slightly fuller than the last time he'd seen her. (He would later learn that she was already pregnant with her lawyer's child, but she didn't admit this to the interviewer.)

The reporter, an attractive South Asian woman with a British accent, addressed her subject. "After six years behind bars, you're a free woman. Why have you chosen to do this interview today?"

Amber's voice was soft and melancholy. "I want people to know that I'm not a danger to anyone. I was involved in a terrible, horrible crime, but I'm not the same person now as I was then."

"How have you changed?"

"Well . . . while I was in jail, I worked really hard on my rehabilitation. I did a lot of cognitive therapy, and I was a peer counselor to other inmates. I also read a lot of books about abused women," she continued. "It's given me a better understanding of the mental and emotional manipulation that I endured."

The interviewer pounced on the comment. "So . . . you see yourself as a victim of Shane Nelson?"

"No . . ." She cast her eyes down. "Courtney Carey is the real victim. I just meant . . . I understand the mistakes I made more clearly now."

She was so convincing, so lovable and charming and full of remorse.

"Do you think the media and the public will ever be able to forget what you did to that innocent young girl?"

"Probably not—not for a very long time, anyway. But I hope that, one day, I'll be allowed to live a normal life."

"What will a normal life look like for you?"

"I want to contribute to society, to make up for what I've done in some small way."

"How would you do that?" The journalist leaned forward, intrigued.

"Well, I know that, with my past, I won't be able to work directly with people. So, I'd like to work with animals. . . ." She smiled a gentle, beatific smile. "I'd like to help sick and injured animals."

The interviewer smiled, too, impressed with the contrived answer. She resumed her questioning.

"*Courtney Carey's family may be watching this interview. Is there anything you'd like to say to them?*"

Amber looked into the camera then, her eyes welling with tears. "*I'm sorry for the pain I caused you. I wish I could go back in time and stop Shane from hurting Courtney. I wish I had been stronger. And braver.*" She looked down then, weeping gently. "*I'll have to live with what I did for the rest of my life.*"

The interviewer was moved, her dark eyes full of emotion. She reached out and squeezed Amber's hand.

DJ turned off the TV, went to the bathroom, and puked. The thought of Amber Kunik free, leading a normal life, rescuing kittens, made his stomach revolt. Would she continue to charm everyone she encountered like she'd charmed the interviewer? The detectives and lawyers? Even him, that day at the prison?

He stopped eating after that. The thought of Amber's evil released on the world had killed his appetite. The processed foods that had given him such comfort now stuck in his throat, turned his stomach. The weight fell off him. He got stronger and healthier. In a weird way, Amber Kunik had saved his life.

His father died eight months later. It was an accident at the meatpacking plant, not the alcohol, that killed him. Booze had contributed, though. His father had been hungover, or possibly still drunk, when he got himself caught in the hide-fleshing machine. DJ didn't dwell on his dad's gruesome death. He buried him, sold their small bungalow, and left Tolleson.

DJ went north, went to college, and studied psychology. He

made friends, he dated, but he kept his past to himself. He'd had his sister's name inked beneath his heart, and then he stopped talking about her, about all of it. Amber Kunik, Shane Nelson, and the evil they had perpetrated on his family were relegated to the dark recesses of his brain. Even after he reunited with his mother, they never talked about his sister's murder. It was too painful, too traumatic for them both to acknowledge.

After grad school, he worked as a drug counselor, eventually returning to university to obtain a doctorate in psychology. Helping people who were sick, broken, and damaged was therapeutic. Focusing on their grief and loss and anguish distracted him from his own. The trauma he'd experienced, though repressed, made him an empathetic, compassionate healer.

Eventually, DJ came out. He fell in love twice before he met his soul mate. They married in a small ceremony attended by a few friends and his mom. For the first time, DJ felt safe enough, loved enough, to share what he had been through. He told his husband everything, sparing no detail. The words, dammed for so long, poured out of him, every tragedy, every loss, every heartbreak. It was a relief to unburden himself and share his story, to finally have a caring, supportive confidant. He could finally put the tragedy behind him.

Until one day, years later, he got a phone call. And the soft, sweet voice on the line brought the nightmare rushing back.

frances

NOW

Frances kept her son home from school on Tuesday. The child had been shaken by the chaos at yesterday's drop-off, traumatized by the information he'd learned about his best friend's mother. Despite Frances's attempts at a gentle explanation, Marcus was grappling with the revelation that someone he'd liked, trusted, possibly even admired, had done something so criminal. It cemented Frances's conviction that Marcus could never learn her own truth.

Staying away from Forrester allowed Frances a reprieve from the judgments and criticisms of the other parents. On the surface, it appeared she was supporting the movement to ensure Charles Randolph's expulsion, but she was still wrestling with her own ambiguity. She knew the horrible things Amber Kunik had done—she didn't deny the cruelty of her actions. But Frances also knew that Amber had been a girl: young, naïve, easily influenced. Some said Amber was the instigator, that it was she, not Shane Nelson, who murdered that poor girl. But these were opinions, not facts. And they didn't quell the stirrings of pity she felt for her friend Kate.

Marcus was on his Xbox, anesthetized to the ugliness and drama nipping at the edges of his innocent world. He'd been on there for more than an hour, but Frances didn't have the heart to tear him away, to make him face reality. He had soccer practice later. The physical activity and socialization would be some compensation for the excess screen time. If only Frances had an activity so all-encompassing that it would distract from her desire to reach out to Kate.

In contacting the pariah she would betray her husband, confuse her son, and devastate her social standing. But she couldn't ignore the sharp pangs of sympathy she felt for Kate Randolph. Perhaps it was the devastating act in Frances's own past that fostered her compassion. Maybe it was gratitude for the verisimilitude of friendship the woman had shown her. Kate had befriended her, defended her, made her feel confident, worthy, even loved. Whatever the reason, Frances felt an almost visceral urge to reach out to Kate, to say something to let her know she still cared.

I'm sorry this is happening to you.

You were a good friend to me.

I forgive you.

She tried to distract herself by tidying her house (effectively spreading the piles of clutter between rooms). Her domestic puttering took her to the front porch, to the dust, leaves, and debris she'd been neglecting to sweep up. As she pulled the broom through the mess, she spotted a car. It was a generic blue sedan moving slowly down the street. Something about the vehicle's pace held her attention. The driver was scanning the street, reading house numbers, looking for someone. An ominous chill ran through her. When the vehicle stopped, Frances knew. . . . The driver was looking for her.

A man got out of the car—mid-thirties, about five-foot-nine, with thinning brown hair and softly handsome features. Instinctively, she gripped the broom handle tighter. It would be an ineffective weapon, but it was all she had. But the man's demeanor, as he approached, was tentative, nervous. He walked down her drive, then stopped, several feet away.

"Hi," he said. "Are you Frances Metcalfe?"

"Yes."

"I'm sorry to show up like this, but Daisy Randolph contacted me. She asked me to come see you."

A tightness gripped Frances's chest. "Is Daisy okay?"

"She's fine. She's in a safe place, now. But she's worried about you."

"About *me*?"

"Kate Randolph is not your friend, Frances." He took a few slow steps toward her. "Kate Randolph doesn't exist. She can change her name, her look, her location . . . but she's still Amber Kunik. And she's still dangerous."

Frances swallowed. "Who are you?"

"My name is Declan Carey Junior. My friends call me DJ."

Carey?

He answered the unasked. "Courtney Carey was my sister."

Emotion welled up inside her—sympathy, gratitude, guilt. DJ Carey, the little boy who had lost his sister in the cruelest way imaginable, had come here to warn her. The selfishness of her grief threatened to undo her. She'd been mourning the loss of her friendship with Kate; Marcus's friendship with Charles; Daisy's relationship with her mother. . . . But compared to what DJ and his family had endured, they were nothing.

Her voice trembled. "Would you like to come in?"

She made tea and they sat at her cluttered kitchen table. Discovering her best friend's repugnant past had put her on her guard, but Frances trusted this man. And only he could provide the answers she so desperately sought. DJ was a psychologist, a field he'd chosen out of a desire to help others, and out of a quest for understanding. What kind of woman murdered a teenage girl? How had she manipulated psychiatrists, law enforcement, and legal teams? Why did she feel no remorse for what she'd done? With Marcus transfixed by video games in the next room, DJ told Frances his story.

He told her about the night his sister didn't come home; his mother's scream when the police told them they'd found

Courtney's lifeless body; and the day they arrested Shane Nelson. DJ recounted the trial, Amber's self-serving testimony, the videotapes that showed her delight in his sister's torture. He told Frances how his mother had fled, how he had gorged himself with food, how his father drank himself sick—all of them trying to escape their pain.

And he described his visit to the prison, just before Amber was released. DJ had wanted to forgive her, to believe she was a young girl led astray, not a monster. Amber had made him believe that—feigning contrition, fabricating a connection, only to cut him again. She had enjoyed playing with him. He had been Amber's toy, like his sister before him.

As Frances listened, her heart breaking for all this man had suffered, she had an epiphany. Frances may have caused her younger sister's death, but she was not a murderer. She had made a terrible, tragic, lethal mistake that had haunted her ever since. But it had been an accident. Sitting here with DJ, a man whose sister had been taken by pure evil, Frances was finally able to forgive herself.

When his story was finished, Frances spoke. "I appreciate you coming here." She picked up her mug. The tea was cold now, so she set it back down. "Where do you live?"

"San Francisco. But I thought I should talk to you in person."

"How did Daisy find you?"

"Online. She called my office and left a message. When I heard her name, I knew she must have found out the truth."

"I've been worried about her," Frances said. "I've tried to call and text, but she's not responding."

"She needs time to process things," the psychologist explained. "She's lived her whole life with a lot of questions. What she's learned has been devastating, but it's also given her answers."

"Where is she now?"

"I don't know." He sipped his tea, despite its tepid temperature. "But she assured me she has someone who will get her away from her mother and keep her safe."

Frances's stomach dropped. "Did she mention the name *David*?"

"No. Who's David?"

That's what Frances had to find out.

Marcus entered the room then, his face flushed, eyes still slightly glazed from the video game trance. "Don't I have soccer practice?"

"Yes. Get your gear on." With a curious glance at their visitor, Marcus hurried away.

DJ stood. "I'll go." As Frances walked him to the door, he said, "I trust you understand how dangerous Amber still is."

"I do."

"And you'll stay away from her?"

She hesitated, for only a second, before smiling. "Of course. Thank you for warning me."

* * *

She had hated lying to DJ Carey, but as she drove to the playing field, Frances knew what she had to do. It was ill-advised
and risky, but her mission could not be subverted. Frances
had turned her back on Daisy once; she wouldn't do it again.
She had to find the girl, to make sure she wasn't being hurt or
exploited. She had to find out who David was. When she pulled
into the lot next to the field, she left the engine running.

Marcus undid his seat belt. "You're not going to watch me
practice?"

Like many modern parents, Frances observed her son's every
activity: soccer drills, tae kwon do training, swimming lessons.
Her own parents had regularly attended their daughters' games,
but they'd never watched their children *practice*. Even her sister
Mary Anne, the volleyball star, had managed to excel without
constant parental cheerleading.

"I have some errands to run," she said, brightly, "but I'll be
back to watch the last few minutes."

Her son seemed almost pleased with this taste of independence. He nodded and jogged off to join his team. She drove
away without looking back.

As soon as she turned onto 26th, she saw that the press
had found Kate's home. They milled about on the street, at
the edge of the manicured lawn, standing sentry in front of the
pricey home. There were fewer than had been at Forrester yesterday. Perhaps some had given up, defeated by the impervious house. The Randolph abode was sealed like a drum: blinds

drawn, curtains closed, doors locked. But the stalwarts would wait . . . for Kate, for Robert, for Charles to emerge, and then they would swarm, snapping photos, recording their progress, shouting questions:

Did you kill that girl?

How could you marry a murderer?

Did you know your mom was a killer?

The Randolphs were effectively on house arrest. Except for Daisy. She was gone.

Drawing nearer, Frances saw that a flimsy structure had been erected on the front lawn. It was built with framing lumber, slim pieces of wood nailed together to create a rickety scaffold. It was about six feet high, four feet across, dominating the velvet expanse of grass. Hanging from the crossbar: a noose.

Her breath caught in her throat. Who had built the make-shift gallows? When had they erected it? Why didn't Robert remove it? Frances pulled over on the shoulder, several yards away, her foot pressing the brake. Part of her wanted to drive off, to head back to the soccer field to watch her son do drills, to distance herself from Kate, from Amber Kunik and her horrible crimes. But she couldn't.

The reporters whirled on her as she approached. She considered shielding her face, as she'd seen Kate do as she left the school, but that read as guilt. Frances had nothing to hide. With her jaw set, she pushed through the group, relegated to the property lines, and approached the house. Their questions trailed in her wake: "Are you a friend of Amber Kunik?" "How can you stand by her when you know what she's done?" But Frances kept mum. She could hear the click of cameras, too, her journey preserved for posterity. This visit would haunt her, but it was too late to turn back.

She rapped loudly on the door. Not surprisingly, there was no response. While the press was legally prohibited from entering the property, the Randolphs weren't about to roll out the welcome mat to visitors right now. France kneeled on the porch and pressed open the mail slot. She positioned her mouth in front of it.

"Kate! It's me! It's Frances! Let me in! . . . Please!"

She waited, heart pounding from the exertion and from humiliation. What if Kate refused to open the door? She'd be a laughingstock, if she wasn't already. What caption would accompany the photo of a plump woman, in her forties, on all fours, yelling into a convicted murderer's mail slot?

BEGGING FOR A CHILD-KILLER'S FRIENDSHIP

Oh, god.

She struggled to her feet. She could hover for a few more seconds before she'd have to scurry away, tail between her legs, her documented voyage for naught. The friend walk of shame. And then she heard the lock click. The door opened no more than an inch.

"What do you want, Frances?" It was Robert, ever protective, always supportive, even knowing what he knew.

"I want to talk to Kate." She pressed herself closer to the crack. "Please, Robert. It's important."

His deliberation took only seconds, but it felt like minutes as Frances stood, raw and exposed, on the front steps. He must have been conferring with his wife, letting his partner decide on Frances's entry. Finally, the door opened. Robert stepped back and let her slip inside.

The room was dim, the shades drawn against the afternoon light and the prying eyes and lenses on the property's edge. A standing lamp in the corner cast a faint glow on the normally pristine living room. Today, it was full of packing boxes, some empty, some half-filled, some packed and sealed. The Randolphs were leaving.

As her eyes became accustomed to the light, Frances looked at Robert. The suave attorney was rumpled, exhausted, tense. Behind him stood his wife. Kate wore jeans, a faded sweatshirt, and no makeup. In her hand, she held a vase wrapped in a protective layer of newspaper. She was paler than usual, her hair slightly disheveled, her expression grim. But still . . . she was so pretty. Backlit by the lamplight, she was almost ethereal.

Robert and Kate exchanged a loaded glance. "I'll go check on Charles," he said, heading for the staircase.

The two women faced each other in fraught silence. The look in Kate's eyes—cool, wary, detached—made Frances uneasy. DJ's warnings rang in her ears, but she wasn't afraid, not really. And she had to know that Daisy was safe, that she hadn't absconded with a predatory older man. Finally, she spoke.

"I heard Daisy's gone."

"Who told you?"

"DJ Carey came to see me."

Kate gave a derisive snort. "What did that fat ass want?"

Jesus.

"He came to warn me. About you."

Kate didn't respond, but she set the wrapped vase on an end table.

"Where is your daughter, Kate? Where is Daisy?"

"She went to Robert's sister. In Berkeley."

Frances's shoulders sagged with relief. "How did she find out about you? About your past?"

"David Reider found her."

"Who *is* he?"

"He's Shane Nelson's son. With that bitch, Louise Reider."

Frances had read about the boy, only six years old when his father was sent away. The boy's mother—a tall, attractive brunette, not unlike Amber Kunik—had kept herself and her child away from the press. But there had been glimpses of the pair. And after the sentencing, Louise had sold a tabloid-y story: MY LIFE WITH A KILLER . . . something along those lines.

Nelson's only child had come for Daisy. Why? Did he want to hurt her? Warn her? Or did he just want to commiserate?

They were both the spawn of murderers. David Reider had been wise to take his mother's name.

Kate elaborated. "David told Daisy everything . . . at least his father's version of everything. So, of course, she panicked and left."

Frances cursed her weakness, but sympathy welled up inside of her. Kate had lost her daughter. She could imagine the pain. "I'm sorry, Kate."

"She'll be better off." Her tone was indifferent. "Did you see the noose on the front lawn?"

"Yes."

Kate gave an acidic laugh. "The Clyde Hill community is pretty creative. Usually, when they find us, they set up Courtney Carey's gravestone on our lawn."

"Some things are hard to forgive."

The perfect, patrician features twisted with anger. "I spent six fucking years behind bars, Frances. I served my time. I'm free." She motioned toward the shuttered window. "But those bastards want to ruin my life."

"What about Courtney Carey's life?" Frances asked. "What about her parents? Her friends? DJ?"

"I'm sorry she's dead." Kate's voice was flat, her eyes blank, unreadable. "But Courtney Carey was never going to amount to anything. She was trash. If she had been raised properly, she never would have come with me that day. If she had been a good girl, she wouldn't have gotten herself murdered."

A chill ran through Frances, and she felt the blood drain from her face. "Courtney Carey didn't *get herself murdered*." Her voice was barely more than a whisper. "Shane Nelson murdered her. Shane Nelson . . . and *you*."

It happened so quickly. Kate grabbed the newspaper-wrapped vase off the end table and held it over her head. She lunged at Frances, poised to bring the porcelain vessel smashing onto her cranium, cracking her skull, sending blood pouring into her face. Frances scuttled backward like a panicked crab, pressing herself against the wall, trembling with fear.

And then, Kate lowered the vase, and laughed. Cruel, mirthless laughter.

"You're not my friend. You're afraid of me."

She was.

Kate's pretty face was ugly with disdain. "I knew you were weak when I saw you standing there, all alone on the edge of the playground. You were such a *victim*. But Charles liked Marcus, so I befriended you. I should have known you'd be like all the rest of them," she sneered. "You're pathetic, Frances."

DJ Carey was right. Kate was still Amber Kunik: narcissistic, remorseless, evil. She was still the sociopathic bitch who'd taken part in the murder of a young girl and accepted no responsibility for it. Frances had to get away. She moved to the door then paused, her hand on the knob.

"Maybe I am . . . weak and pathetic. But you're a fucking psycho, *Amber*."

Kate flinched, ever so slightly, at the verbal attack. At least the woman could feel *something*. Frances yanked open the door and left the Randolph home.

Outside, the media scrambled toward her, yelling their inquiries, shoving their cameras and microphones at her. "No comment," she snapped, marching past them. She didn't hide, she didn't scurry. She held her head high.

But when she was driving away, tears began to pour from her eyes, obscuring her vision. She pulled over; it wasn't safe to continue. Collapsing onto the steering wheel, she let herself weep. The tears were pure shame. She'd been played. She'd been a fool. Kate had lured her in, just like she'd lured Courtney Carey in. But unlike that poor girl, Frances had survived.

The sobs began to subside, and she blew her nose. As she dabbed at her tears, relief slowly seeped into her. She had invited a cold-blooded killer into her life, into her son's life, her husband's, and they had emerged, largely unscathed. Frances had stood up to the notorious murderer Amber Kunik, and she had come out of it stronger, braver, and with a newfound clarity on her own past. She was going to be okay.

Frances pulled back onto the road and drove to the soccer field.

daisy

Daisy strolled down Solano Avenue, savoring the spring sun-
shine on her face. She had been living in Berkeley for nearly
eighteen months. Her aunt's Spanish-style house at the foot of
the Berkeley Hills was starting to feel like home. It was not a
spacious residence, but Aunt Marnie and Uncle Paul had wel-
comed her. Her cousin, Christina, attended UCLA, so Daisy
had been given her room. When the older girl came home to
visit, she slept on the pull-out sofa in her dad's study. Daisy had
offered to vacate, but Christina always insisted she stay. Her
cousin was kind and warm—like her parents, like her brother
even, in his aloof, teenage way. But Daisy secretly wondered
if Christina pitied her. Or perhaps was slightly afraid of her.
Daisy's mother was a psycho killer, after all. How could Daisy
be normal?

The shopping district was bustling with Saturday afternoon patrons going to lunch, coffee, spin class, the nail salon. Daisy pushed her way through the stream of shoppers, her pace quickening. She was running late. He wouldn't mind, but she knew how busy he was. Daisy always looked forward to these monthly coffee dates. Initially, they had been emotional, the two of them connecting over shared heartbreak, tragedy, and betrayal. But as time went on, the tone of their meetings lightened, somewhat. And as always, Daisy had questions.

Dr. Carey was sitting against the back wall of the homey coffee shop, sipping a cappuccino and reading a free newspaper. Daisy didn't call him doctor—he was not her therapist—she called him DJ. DJ wanted her to talk to someone, a *professional*, and one day, she would. But for now, she had him. Their conversations, while not intentionally therapeutic, were always clarifying.

He smiled and stood as she approached. "Hi, Daisy." They shared a quick hug before he asked, "The usual?"

"Yes, please." She settled into her seat as DJ went to the counter to fetch her chai latte and raspberry scone. Daisy could have bought her own. She had money thanks to a part-time job at a falafel joint. But DJ had more money, obviously—he was a psychologist. And he enjoyed treating her, she could tell.

When he returned, they sipped their hot beverages and covered the basics. Tenth grade was going well. Her aunt, uncle, and cousins were all fine. Yes, she still e-mailed with her father once a week. No, she hadn't heard from her grandma Kunik lately, but her paternal grandmother visited frequently. Daisy asked after Glen, DJ's husband, and their two French bulldogs, Slash and Axl. Slash had recently climbed onto the kitchen counter and eaten an entire pie, resulting in a disastrous case of diarrhea. Daisy laughed at the anecdote, but her tone soon turned serious.

"I've been thinking a lot about my little brother."

"Are you worried about him?"

"Yeah . . . Charles is twelve now. That's when my mom turned against me."

"Sociopaths are incapable of feeling love like you or I would. But they can care for a child, as long as it serves them."

"That's why I'm worried," Daisy said, fingers warm on her mug of tea. "Charles won't be as cute as he was. He won't be as obedient. My mom will stop caring about him, just like she stopped caring about me."

"Has your dad mentioned this in his e-mails?"

"No." She sipped her tea. "But he never says anything about my mom."

"Charles might not fall out of your mom's good graces like you did."

The comment stung. Daisy's mother was a sociopath, she understood that. But could Kate Randolph turn her personality disorder on and off like a light switch? Select one child to bear the brunt of her inability to love, feel, and connect?

DJ sensed her pain. "Sociopaths can make relationships work when they need them to. Like with your parents."

Daisy's look begged elaboration.

"Your mom needs your dad. She relies on him financially. She needs him to ensure her safety and security. That relationship is important to her, so your mom puts a lot of effort into it. She acts like the perfect wife to make sure your dad stays with her."

It made sense. Daisy had often wondered how her parents' relationship managed to thrive.

"If your mom loses Charles, she won't be a mother anymore. That label might be important to her."

"So, she'll keep playing the loving mom and Charles will be okay?"

DJ gave a slight nod as he sipped his frothy coffee. "There's another possibility. . . ." He trailed off.

"What?" When they first connected, DJ had promised to be honest with her, to answer all her questions, no matter how much they might hurt.

The psychologist set his cup down. "Sociopathy is a complicated mix of nature and nurture."

Daisy's mind was quick and she did the math. "Are you saying Charles could turn out to be a psycho like my mom?"

"No." He gave her hand a reassuring pat. "That's extremely unlikely. I'm just saying that Charles might understand your mother in a way that you can't."

Could her brother's sweet nature be an act? Could his cheerful compliance be a coping mechanism? Was he an empty shell of a person, just like their mother was? Daisy broke off a piece of scone and put it in her mouth. It tasted liked sawdust.

"Ask your dad how your brother's doing . . . or write to Charles directly. That connection would be good for both of you."

Daisy swallowed the dry pastry and nodded. She would try to save her brother . . . *if* he needed saving.

DJ had to go. He had a long drive back to Noe Valley, and Glen wanted him to pick up wine for the dinner party they were hosting that evening. They hugged goodbye on the sidewalk.

"You call me if you need anything," DJ said. "Or if you just want to talk."

"'Kay. . . . Say hi to Glen and the pups."

"I will." He gave her a paternal smile. "I'm proud of you, Daisy. You've come through a lot, and you're thriving. And the fact that you're worrying about your little brother shows me what a kind, caring person you are."

She wanted to respond. She wanted to thank him for being in her life, for understanding that she was not her mother, for teaching her that she deserved to be loved. But the lump in her throat blocked her words and tears pricked her eyes. She pressed her lips together and nodded.

Walking home, her feet felt heavy, weighted down. Talking to DJ often summoned complex emotions that left her feeling exhausted. Still, she was grateful for the sounding board. She could talk to DJ about her thoughts and feelings, she could ask him difficult and sensitive questions. There was only one subject DJ Carey refused to touch.

David Reider.

Daisy still thought about him. A lot. She didn't pine for his attentions, like she once had. Now that she lived in a stable home where she felt loved and cared for, she no longer craved the man's attentions. But still, David stayed with her, floating through her mind, appearing in her dreams.

She had mentioned David to the psychologist only once, and he'd told her, in no uncertain terms, that she could not have a friendship with him.

"David Reider is a man. You're a teenager. It's inappropriate."

"You're a man," she'd sniped. "I have a friendship with *you*."

"That's different," DJ said. "Reider crossed a lot of lines. He stalked you. He invited you to his apartment. He gave you alcohol and drugs when you were fourteen years old."

It was all true. But it could have been so much worse.

DJ, Frances Metcalfe, Daisy's aunt and grandmother all viewed David as a villain. They didn't know how he had rescued Daisy after Dylan's party; how he had rejected her advances when she crawled into his bed; how he had held her and let her cry on his chest. They didn't trust him. But Daisy did. Because David had done for Daisy what Shane Nelson had not done for Courtney Carey. He had saved her life.

And she and David shared a connection few could understand. Only the child of a killer could appreciate the issues with which he grappled, the endless questions, the relentless self-doubt. David would wonder if evil could be inherited, if he could ever atone for his father's sins, if he deserved to be happy. David would hope that, one day, he'd find someone who understood him. But he already had. That person was Daisy.

She had looked for him online, but the man had no social media accounts. He wasn't mentioned in any articles, wasn't listed as an employee or a member of a club. Years ago, his mother had taught him to hide, and he was good at it. But Daisy knew they would reconnect. In two years, she would be eighteen, legally an adult. Then she could be friends with whomever she wanted.

David had found her once. He would find her again. She knew it.

frances

NOW

"How much longer?" Marcus asked from the backseat. He wasn't whining or complaining; simply curious. This was a road trip they had not taken before.

Jason answered from behind the wheel. "About half an hour."

"'Kay."

Frances looked over her shoulder and watched her son insert his earbuds again. He would be thirteen soon. He was five-foot-nine, skinny and gangly, with solid, pronounced joints that foreshadowed the big man he would become.

"What are you listening to?" she asked.

"A podcast about World War One."

"It's not violent, is it?" Frances's brow furrowed with concern.

"War is violent, Mom. But it's important to learn about it."

Jason glanced over at her. "Our twelve-year-old is listening to a history podcast, Frances. That's a good thing."

She faced forward, a small smile on her face. Marcus had recently taken an interest in world history, reading books, watching movies, and listening to podcasts about ancient Rome, the Vikings, and now, the great wars. He was almost finished with seventh grade; his curiosity would serve him well as he entered his final year of middle school.

They would endure one more year at Forrester Academy; Marcus had already chosen a public high school with a project-based learning model that would suit his passionate interests. While privately Frances was relieved, she had let her son choose this path himself. If he had wanted to stay at Forrester, she would have supported him. And it would have been okay. In fact, the past year at the private school had been surprisingly tolerable.

Marcus had two friends now, both acquired during his Viking phase. The boys had bonded over their shared fascination with the ancient Scandinavian warriors, creating elaborate games of strategy using pine cones, painted rocks, and plastic figurines. While Marcus had not forgotten his old pal, Charles was mentioned less often now. Her son's questions, his requests to contact the Randolph boy, had slowed to a trickle. He was moving on. He was going to be fine.

Frances was moving on, too. After several months as a Forrester pariah, she'd made a new friend. Andrea was a dentist whose daughter was a year younger than Marcus. The women had met volunteering at a fund-raising car wash (the school needed extra money to install a state-of-the-art photo lab, or heated toilet seats, or some other luxury). Andrea was warm and funny. She worked three days a week, so Frances didn't see her often. Theirs was a normal, pleasant friendship. It wasn't intense or overly close, but it was enough.

After Kate—Amber—left, Frances had looked for her online daily. These Google searches were partly out of curiosity, partly out of fear. They had dwindled now, to once every few months. The Randolphs' new locale was still unknown, and Frances hoped it would stay that way. Despite her friend's past deeds, despite her personal betrayal, she wanted Kate to live a life of anonymity. For Charles's sake. And for Daisy, creating a new life in Berkeley.

Kate still haunted her thoughts, popped up in her dreams: some terrifying, some disturbingly intimate, some perfectly benign. It wasn't easy to let go . . . especially since the text.

I miss you

It was from an unknown number, but it had to be her. Who else? Frances had looked up the area code: Louisiana. Kate had waited until Frances had almost put her out of her mind, and then she had reached out. She wanted to draw her back in, to play with her, toy with her like the sick sociopath she was. Unless . . . she was sincere? Maybe she really did miss Frances? Maybe their friendship had been real? Frances would never know, because she would never respond. She couldn't.

She shifted in her seat and gazed out the passenger window. The scenery was becoming familiar now, a sense of nostalgia seeping into her being. She had been content here, once, before everything turned dark and ugly. Her return was bittersweet; both happy and sad. But she had needed to come. She was strong enough, healed enough. It was time.

Her husband's voice cut into her reverie. "How are you doing?"

"I'm okay," she said, smiling at his concern. "A little nervous, but excited."

"It's been a long time."

"Almost five years."

"I guess Marcus has changed a bit then."

Frances laughed. Her parents' last trip to Bellevue had been filled with tension and secrets, but this visit would be different. Jason knew everything now. How Tricia had died, the role Frances had played in her death, how she had blamed and hated herself for years.

"Why didn't you tell me?" he'd asked, when she finally confessed. "You didn't have to carry this burden alone."

She would have carried it forever, if not for Kate.

With her husband's support, she wrote to her family. In a long, heartfelt e-mail, she told them all about her friendship with Amber Kunik. It had been frightening, disturbing, and confounding, but, ultimately, it had allowed Frances to forgive herself for Tricia's death. She hoped her family would be able to forgive her, too.

Her mother had responded almost instantly:

Of course, we forgive you. Tricia would want us to be a family.

So, the reunion had been planned. Mary Anne and her partner were flying in from Texas. Frances had not been to Spokane in years, and she knew her return would be emotional. The family would visit Tricia's grave together. They would cry and grieve and heal, and then, they would work on rebuilding their family. Marcus was excited to get to know his aunt and uncle and his grandparents. They would all have to get to know one another again.

Frances's phone, deep inside her purse, vibrated at her feet, announcing a text. She had been communicating with a creative-writing professor, inquiring about a workshop he was holding. She was eager to hear back from him. Frances had long been interested in writing as an outlet, and she had some stories to tell. Extracting her phone, she looked at the display.

Please forgive me. I can't stop thinking about you.

The area code was 504. Louisiana.

Frances should have responded: *Leave me alone, Kate. I don't miss you. I don't think about you.* She should have blocked the number. But for some unexplained reason, she didn't. Perhaps she was enjoying leading Kate on, just a little bit?

Her husband glanced over at her. "Anything important?"

"Nope." She smiled at him as she deleted the text. "It's nothing."

The exit for Spokane loomed ahead of them. Jason said, "You ready?"

"I'm ready."

Frances was going home.

acknowledgments

There are so many people involved in birthing a book and shepherding it through its life. I owe them all a heartfelt thank-you, starting with my genius editor, Jackie Cantor. She was instrumental in shaping this story into the book it has become. Thanks to my formidable (in a good way) publisher Jennifer Bergstrom, publicist extraordinaire Meagan Harris, and everyone at Gallery Books/Scout Press: Sara Quaranta, Jennifer Long, Liz Psaltis, Diana Velasquez, all the salespeople, designers, and everyone behind the scenes.

A huge thank-you to Simon and Schuster Canada: Nita Pronovost, Felicia Quon, Adria Iwasutiak, Rita Silva, Sarah St. Pierre, Catherine Whiteside, Rebecca Snodden, and the rest of the team . . . Your expertise and support are hugely appreciated. (And you are all so fun to hang out with!) And thank you to Simon and Schuster Australia (Kirsty Noffke and Co.) and Simon and Schuster UK.

To my incredible agent, Joseph Veltre, and the invaluable Hannah Vaughn. My film team, Matt Bass and Bob Hohman. Thanks for sticking with me and cheering me on.

Thanks to Crystal Patriarche and the BookSparks team. Your passion, expertise, and enthusiasm are so appreciated.

To my early readers, the brilliant Eileen Cook and Cindy Bokma: thanks for your insight and encouragement.

To all the librarians, booksellers, bloggers, bookstagrammers, and Facebook groups who devote so much time and energy to spreading the word about books: as a writer and as a reader, I thank you!

To my community: friends, relatives (Aussies and Canadians), neighbors, former colleagues and classmates, my kids' friends' parents . . . Your ongoing support means so much to me.

Thanks to my very first (and always most positive) reader, my husband, John; my biggest fan, my mom; and my kids, who keep everything in perspective. Love and gratitude.